PETER CURTIS

The Witches

First published by Macdonald & Co Ltd as *The Devil's Own* in 1960
This edition published byArrow Books in association with Hammer 2011

2 4 6 8 10 9 7 5 3 1

Published in Great Britain in 2011 by
Arrow Books in association with Hammer
Random House, 20 Vauxhall Bridge Road,
London SW1V 2SA

www.rbooks.co.uk

Addresses for companies within The Random House Group Limited can be
found at: www.randomhouse.co.uk/offices.htm

The Random House Group Limited Reg. No. 954009

A CIP catalogue record for this book
is available from the British Library

ISBN 978-0-099-55384-7

The Random House Group Limited supports The Forest Stewardship
Council (FSC), the leading international forest certification organisation.
All our titles that are printed on Greenpeace approved FSC certified paper
carry the FSC logo. Our paper procurement policy can be found at
www.rbooks.co.uk/environment

Mixed Sources
Product group from well-managed
forests and other controlled sources
www.fsc.org Cert no. TT-COC-2139
© 1996 Forest Stewardship Council
FSC

Typeset by SX Composing DTP, Rayleigh, Essex
Printed and bound in Great Britain by
CPI Cox & Wyman, Reading, RG1 8EX

Foreword by Cyril Frankel

I entered the film industry soon after retiring as a major from the Reconnaissance Armoured Car Division. One of my earliest films, made in 1953, was *Man of Africa*, which was filmed in the hilly district of Kigezi in Uganda. It was the first film made with an entirely African cast. It was whilst I was in Africa that I saw firsthand the influence of witchcraft on the tribes I worked with during filming. I talked to village elders and learnt that they practised witchcraft in the event of domestic upheaval and conflict. As such it was part of their everyday life.

When I returned to England my agent Dennis Van Thal told me that the world famous actress Joan Fontaine had arrived in London with a script and was seeking a director, and that he had recommended we meet. Having been a passionate film goer since childhood, I had of course seen Joan Fontaine's Oscar winning role in *Rebecca*, so I was honoured to have been considered. I cannot recall exactly what we talked about, but whatever it was we must have seen eye-to-eye because after the meeting Joan told Van Thal that she would be happy for me to direct *The Witches*. It was an incredible moment for me, especially as, until then, the one star I had worked with was Googie Withers, who was a delightful, relaxed actress.

At the time my only experience of English witchcraft had been in a pantomime, and the three witches in *Macbeth*, so *The Witches* was a very interesting challenge for me. Together with the writer, Nigel Kneale, I first worked on improving the script before turning my mind to who would play the male role opposite Joan. In the end, it was not a difficult choice; I had been deeply impressed with the subtle acting ability of Alec McCowen in *Waiting for Godot* and I was certain he would be ideal to play opposite Joan. They worked well together, though Joan later joked to me: 'You should have cast a tall handsome man!'

So with the cast in place, and the beautiful village of Hambleden in Buckinghamshire found as the setting, shooting began in April 1966. During this time, I was fortunate enough to meet with Maharishi; he introduced me to a mantra and I began to meditate regularly. This discipline helped me enormously when tensions erupted on set and I needed to calm people down. In this way, I like to think I was practicing witchcraft myself during the filming.

The whole experience of directing *The Witches* was remarkable. Starting with my production of *Man of Africa* and firsthand experience of witchcraft amongst the natives, leading to meeting Joan, studying with Maharishi, and filming in the English countryside, it was a once in a lifetime experience.

Seeing the film again after so many years I am surprised how compelling it is but it is Joan's performance that holds the whole thing together. She floats onto the set and expresses the emotions of each scene almost entirely through the movement of her eyes. It is enchanting to watch.

An interviewer once asked Joan which were the best reviews she had received. She answered without hesitation: 'The best reviews were for *The Witches* and later a stage performance in Austria, also directed by Cyril Frankel.' I like to think we brought out the best in each other.

Man of Africa has yet to be shown in England though it has been featured in several film festivals around the world. I understand that a release of the film is planned to coincide with the publication of my memoir, *Eye to Eye*, later this year.

London, January 2011

vi

THE INTERVIEW HAD BEEN ARRANGED TO TAKE place in London at half-past three on a Saturday afternoon. This was a time so extremely convenient to Miss Mayfield that she was disposed to regard it as providential. It had saved her from the embarrassment of having to ask for time off to attend an interview in which she might not be successful, and from which she might be obliged to return to face her present Head's resentment. In her diffident attempt to maintain secrecy she had left Alchester without the precaution of obtaining a testimonial. This she recognized as the action of a fool, but she had taught in the ugly Midland town for a bare two years, and she carried in her shabby handbag a coolly eulogistic report of her twenty years' work in Africa. If that did not suffice, and if the interview showed any sign of leading to a new appointment, *then* would be time enough to approach Miss Stevens and break the news that she was contemplating a move.

Canon Thorby had written, 'Claridge's Hotel would be

convenient for me, since I have another appointment there earlier in the day. I shall be waiting for you and if you ask at the desk, someone will point me out to you.'

He wrote on thick smooth paper which justified the term 'cream-laid'. His writing was small, elegant, meticulously legible. It called up an imaginary vision of the writer, plump, rubicund, with a fringe of silvery hair and tranquil blue eyes. Kindly, perhaps a trifle pompous.

To Miss Mayfield, whose experience of such places was negligible, the hotel seemed very large, very impressive and full of women whose clothes in no way resembled her own. As she entered, the thought came and remained with her for half a minute, that a new hat might have been a wise investment. She countered this with the certainty that it would also have been a waste, and self-indulgent into the bargain; a hat was a hat, and the one she wore was adequate. Being, though shy, almost entirely without self-consciousness, she asked for Canon Thorby and followed the lordly young man who set out to glide her, with an outward composure that belied her inner trepidation.

Canon Thorby had secured a corner table, half masked by a huge bowl of long-stemmed roses, freesias and white lilacs in unseasonable proximity. From behind this floral screen he was watchful, and was on his feet, regarding her speculatively and then with a welcoming smile before she was within speaking distance. He was quite unlike her mental picture of him, being tall and spare, with a reddish-brown, weathered complexion and a full head of rust-coloured hair, just touched with grey at the temples. His eyes, however, were blue and tranquil.

They shook hands and Miss Mayfield sat down and replied to his questions regarding her journey, his comment on the coldness of the November weather.

'After so long in Africa, I imagine you feel it keenly,' he said. 'I should warn you here and now that Walwyk is much colder than London.'

Perhaps, she thought, his other appointment had been with some more suitable candidate, and he was trying to hint, kindly, that Walwyk was not the place for her. A sense of disappointment, of failure, made itself felt. It had sounded such an ideal post, so quiet, so entirely different from her present one.

Unobtrusively tea had been placed on the table, and from the position of the cups and the teapot she saw that she was expected to pour. She removed her shabby gloves, and hoping that no tremor would betray her nervousness, lifted the pot.

'I take milk, and I like it put in first. No sugar,' the Canon said.

She managed his cup neatly, but in pouring her own she felt her hand waver. Some tea slopped into the saucer.

'I believe you are nervous,' he said with a smile. 'There is no need to be. *I* should be on tenterhooks, for I am still to be put to the test. I had a surprising number of applications, but there was something about your letter . . .' He moved one hand sightly. 'I'm seldom wrong about such things, though I may seem rash and hasty. And now that I have *seen* you, I have, no doubt at all.'

'You mean . . .' she began, and had no breath left with which to complete the question.

'I mean that you are exactly what I am looking for. The question is, can you be persuaded that we are what you are looking for?'

It seemed too easy. It could, of course, be an answer to prayer, but Miss Mayfield, though her faith was strong and humble, had had considerable experience with prayers and knew that the answers were very seldom as direct and simple as this.

She said, 'I haven't asked my present Head for a testimonial. The Walwyk post sounded so attractive I feared there would be great competition. And to go back, having made plain that I wished to get away from Alchester, would have, been . . . Well, I shouldn't have liked it much.'

'The Miss Tilbury with whom you worked for an extremely long time, in what must have been testing circumstances, seems to have thought highly of you.'

'I brought the original of that. And perhaps I should, in honesty, point out that Rose – Miss Tilbury – was my friend.'

'That is itself a credential; twenty years together at the back of nowhere . . . I had great difficulty in finding Entuba, even on a large-scale map. What Mission was it, Miss Mayfield? CMS?'

'Strictly speaking, I suppose it wasn't a Mission at all, not in the usually accepted sense. It was Rose's private and personal venture. She's a . . . very exceptional person; almost a saint, I think.'

She realized that she had not come here to give an account of Rose Tilbury.

'Go on,' Canon Thorby said. 'This is extremely interesting.'

'Rose Tilbury's father was the Squire in the village where my father was the doctor. I was an only child, and she the one girl in a family of boys, so we spent a good deal of time together. When I went to college, Rose had a season in London and made quite a sensation, she was so beautiful. But she didn't get married, and afterwards she went out to visit one of her brothers who had settled in Kenya. She said that as soon as she got there she knew what her life work was meant to be – work for and with the natives. She had some money of her own, and several well-to-do relatives from whom she would beg quite shamelessly. She came home – just after I'd graduated – to tell her people and to collect stores and funds, and she talked to me about . . . about what she planned. And by that time my father was dead, so I said I'd like to go back with her. And I did.' In her enthusiasm she forgot to be cautious. 'It was all very amateur, I suppose. The school seemed to grow up of its own accord, and then another friend of Rose's, who'd had some medical experience, came and joined us, and we had a kind of hospital, too. We were all young, full of ideals and plans, and then – it seemed quite sudden, too – old and tough with experience, but still convinced that we weren't wasting time. Three of the children who came to us knowing nothing, literally nothing, passed on to Fort Hare and did well. There were others who were promising. . . . It did almost break my heart to be obliged to leave.'

She stopped abruptly, feeling the tightening of her

throat, the threat of a quiver in her voice.

'On account of your health, I think you said.'

'Yes. I had recurrent bouts of fever. In the end I was far more nuisance than help. I . . . I was told that the only cure was to come home.'

She was ashamed of her failure to be completely honest and mention that the fever, in the end, had led to a breakdown. But she had learned that people – particularly prospective employers – were very odd in their reaction to that word; they seemed to think that once having suffered a nervous breakdown you might at any minute run berserk with a hatchet.

'And has Miss Tilbury, all this time, supported her venture entirely from her private funds?'

She imagined that he had slipped in the practical, mundane question as a counter to her emotionalism and shot him a grateful glance.

'Practically. There were grants we were eligible for – towards the end of my time there, that was – but Rose always said there were so many strings attached that it was hardly worth it. And then her godmother died and left her quite a lot of money. Our personal needs were very small, of course; books and the children's food and the hospital were the expensive items.'

Canon Thorby leaned back in his chair with an immensely satisfied expression.

'It's quite remarkable – the curious way things occasionally work out. You see, you have precisely the kind of experience to fit you for my post, which is also a private, or – if you prefer the term – independent school.'

Ah, it had seemed too good to be true. Here was the snag. The pay in private schools was notoriously poor; and although Miss Mayfield's personal needs were still small, she had been in the habit, these last two years, of sending to Rose every shilling she could save. It seemed very little to do after having failed her and deserted her.

As though from a long way off, she heard Canon Thorby explaining about his school, which had been started by his great-great-grandfather years before universal education was thought of.

'It began almost by accident. The family had a tutor, much beloved, and eventually it became the question of what was to happen to Mr Seeley. So the school began. When, in 1870, it became law for every child to attend school, that for the whole area – Renham, Catermarsh and Walwyk – was, very wisely, I think, situated at Renham. Children in those days were still deemed capable of walking three miles morning and afternoon, and our school could have closed, but by that time it had become a family hobby. And so it has remained.'

'It must be a very expensive hobby.'

'Oh, it is. Especially nowadays, with all the trimmings, free milk and dinners, which I feel bound to supply. I couldn't bear it if any Walwyk child had cause to think it would be better off in a State school! My Junior mistress is Froebel-trained, my Senior a graduate. My gardener – an ex-Sergeant Major – takes the boys for physical training, gardening and woodwork; I myself teach Scripture to everyone and Latin and mathematics to any ambitious scholar. We have one at the moment, Juliet Reeve, my

7

butler's daughter. We hope to get her into Cambridge. My forebears, you see, were quite disgustingly rich.' He made the statement neither boastfully nor deprecatingly; he might have been saying that they were all bald. 'My grandfather, a far-sighted man who seemed to have considered the possible devaluation of money, endowed the school lavishly. It has never yet cost me a penny of my private money; and if it did . . . Well, though hit by taxes, like everyone else, I am still quite disgustingly rich.'

But even so . . . would he pay the Burnham Scale?

'In your advertisement, Canon Thorby, you made no mention of salary.'

'That was deliberate. You see, I don't hold with this newfangled notion that in order to obtain good people you must offer high salaries. That merely attracts the time-servers. People – more particularly those in occupations which might be called vocational – work best when they work for the love of the job. Isn't that so?'

Exactly what she had feared!

'That is partly true, like most generalizations. But I must be frank with you. I have a commitment. At Alchester I am paid the Burnham Scale for graduates, at a low level; my years in Africa didn't count. In Walwyk, I suppose, my living expenses would be lower, and I should not have fares. I could manage with . . . perhaps fifty pounds less than I now earn. If I went lower than that, I should be acting selfishly.'

'You sound as though you would like to come to us.'

'I should indeed. From the moment when I read your advertisement. To live in the country . . . To be Head . . .

Oh, I know,' she said earnestly, 'that towns like Alchester are necessary, economically, and someone has to live in them and teach in their schools, and I know most teachers have to be assistants and take orders. The truth is, I suppose that I am too old to adjust.'

A silly thing to say; but then, if he couldn't pay what she needed, it didn't matter. She must go back to Alchester, to Miss Stevens with her whims and experiments, which were never successful, to the noisy, overcrowded, often hostile classes.

'I don't think,' Canon Thorby said, 'that we shall fall out about money. I'm prepared to pay Burnham Scale salary for graduates, with the extra emolument for Headmistresses in country schools. I will take into consideration your twenty years in Africa. I also provide, free, a *rather* delightful little house, furnished. It once belonged to an aunt of mine, who left it to me, and I thought the best use to which I could put it would be to provide a comfortable, dignified home for anyone who was prepared to share our way of life and devote herself to teaching our children. You see, I am aware of the drawbacks. We're very isolated. We have been cut off from the outer world for as long as fifteen days after a heavy snowfall or an exceptionally rainy season. At the best of times the nearest cinema is fourteen miles away, the nearest theatre twenty-eight. Our social life is limited and you will not find Intellectual company within a wide radius. It is – we might as well face it – a lonely, dedicated life. You've had a taste of that; you may desire a complete change.'

'I have had that, in Alchester.'

'I'm trying to give a fair picture. You see, I intensely dislike changes. I don't wish you, in six months' time, when you have been in Walwyk for six weeks, to come and tell me that you are lonely, unhappy, buried alive, stagnating in a backwater.' He brought out each expression as though it were set in quotation marks. 'I have a long memory. Some twenty-four or -five years ago we had three changes in as many years, bad for everybody. Then we settled down and that was delightful. Our present Headmistress has been with us for twenty-two years and is leaving for the happiest of reasons. I should like to feel settled again, after Easter. So . . . would you like some time to think it over before deciding?'

Once or twice during the course of her lifetime Miss Mayfield had been aware of a voice in her mind which had issued a criticism or a warning which had little or nothing to do with her conscious thought. As though another, more cautious and sophisticated person had made a comment. It happened now. The voice said quite clearly, *You should see the place.*

But this, she argued back, is the last week in November. If I am to leave Alchester at the end of the Easter term, I must give in my notice by the end of December, to take effect at the end of April. I have no other free weekend before Christmas. And then there are the fares. She thought of Miss Stevens; she thought of the 'flatlet' which she shared; of the fog; the clatter.

She said, 'I think I have decided. If you consider me suitable, I should like, very much, to come to Walwyk.'

'Splendid. I will confirm, in writing, my offer of salary

and accommodation. And I hope, from my heart, that you will spend long happy years with us. Now, what are your immediate plans? Are you staying in London overnight?'

'Oh no. I must get back. I looked up the trains. There is one at five-fifteen. I might even catch that.'

He glanced at his watch.

'If you wish to, you shall,' he said. They rose and walked towards the entrance. Nobody came running, complaining that the tea had not been paid for. He was known and trusted here, obviously.

Outside the door the man in uniform flicked a finger and a taxi slowed and swerved. As it did so, suddenly from nowhere a little wizened old woman popped up, holding on her arm a flat basket in which lay small bunches of desiccated white heather. She said, in a mechanical, whining voice:

'Buy a bitta white hevva for luck for the lydy, sir?'

The commissionaire made a wide, scornful gesture of dismissal. Canon Thorby cried:

'Wait! We've had our luck, haven't we, Miss Mayfield, but we may as well have the symbol of it.'

There were times during the ensuing weeks when Miss Mayfield would look at that little bunch of crumbling herbage to assure herself that the whole thing had not been a dream.

2

'You want a taxi?' asked the Selbury porter, eyeing Miss Mayfield's battered trunk, suitcase and corded crate. ''Cos if you do, you'd best run and grab one. I'll foller.'

'I'm being met, thank you.' She had the Canon's latest letter in her handbag; her fingers brushed against it as she took out her ticket and the two-shilling piece she had placed in readiness.

The Selbury station stairs smelled strongly of fish, of years of engine smoke; but outside in the yard the air was fresh and clean. It was one of those warm mid-April days that held the whole promise of summer.

Two taxis were just driving away. The woman with the baby who had shared Miss Mayfield's compartment was being greeted and packed into a small car, bright with new green paint. The only other objects in the whole wide space were a third taxi, without a driver, and two dogs, ill-matched in size, happily engaged in canine miscegenation.

The porter clanged open the gate of the luggage lift and

dragged Miss Mayfield's possessions out, one by one. He gave her a look which said, very clearly, 'Being met, eh?'

'You need not wait,' Miss Mayfield said, meaning it kindly. Although she had lived in England for two years, she was still geared to the timeless pace of Entuba, where a porter, unless told to do otherwise, would wait for ever. The Selbury man gave a little snort which said, 'Wait – I should think not.' Then he stumped away, somewhat mollified by the florin; he had expected sixpence.

The station yard was bordered by a high hawthorn hedge; dazzlingly green; there was a gap in the hedge, and through the gap came a man, short, bow-legged. At the sight of Miss Mayfield and her luggage he quickened his pace.

'Sorry to keep you waiting,' he said.

'I'm not waiting for you. Someone is supposed to meet me.'

He nodded and went and leaned against the bonnet of his cab, rolled himself a cigarette and stood there smoking. She knew that he was watching her. Presently he called:

'Care to go in and sit down? Take the weight off your feet. I shall be here till twelve-ten.'

'That is very kind of you,' Miss Mayfield said. She sat down thankfully on the worn leather seat and took out Canon Thorby's letter. She had made no mistake. She was to be met at Selbury on Friday, the seventeenth of April, at eleven-thirty. She looked at her watch; it was a quarter to twelve.

A man on a bicycle rode into the yard, threw his machine, against the wall and said:

'Hallo, Ed. Broke down?'

'Just waiting,' Ed said.

'You all right for tomorrow night?'

'Reckon so. Not afore half-past seven. Pick you up then. All right?'

'Lovely,' the man said, and went into the station. Ed made and slowly smoked another cigarette. The whole procedure occupied twelve minutes. Throwing away the stub, he opened the door of the driver's seat, thrust his head in and said:

'D'you think something's gone wrong? Where was you making for?'

'Walwyk.'

Interest and amusement sparked in his face.

'Canon Thorby's owd Rolls? Punctual as Big Ben as a rule. Must hev broke down at last. Twenty-five years owd, but cared for like a baby. Still . . . Eh?' he said. 'You the lady thass taking Mrs Westleton's place?'

She smiled. This was the first evidence of the intimate, friendly life in country districts of which she had read, for which she had longed.

'Yes. I'm the new mistress at Walwyk.'

'Fancy that. Well, look, s'pose I take you out there. There's only the one road, and if we meet the Rolls, you can change over. And if I take you the whole way – fourteen miles, that is – I 'on't hurt you. I'd do it for fifteen bob.'

'But why should you?'

'I'd like to see the owd place again. Got like they say about lost things, sentimental value for me, Walwyk hev. Thass gone twelve now,' he said persuasively. 'Something musta gone wrong for Baxter to be that much out. And do somebody get off the twelve-fifteen and want me, then I'd hev to dump you, see?'

'Very well, then. Please drive me to Walwyk.'

The man with the bicycle made a timely reappearance and responded willingly to a request to 'lend us a hand with this'. The luggage was loaded and the car moved out of the yard.

Selbury was a small town, little more than a single main street, bulging out in one place into a market square. The street changed almost imperceptibly into a suburban road, lined with newish-looking houses and bungalows, all set among flowering cherry trees and pink almonds.

'If you look out on your left, just coming up now, white, with the blue shutters, see it? Thass Mrs Westleton's new house. Lovely, they say it is, even the washing-up done by pressing the switch. Still, she deserved a bit of luck, she did.'

'Why?'

'Had a ailing man on her hands to keep and look after for the best part of twenty years. He had a good job, and she was all set to leave school when she married, and then he got ill. There weren't so much talk about polio in them days as there is now, but I reckon that was what got him. Never walked again. He could just feed hisself and he could just do his Pools, and bless my soul if back in last November he didn't go and win sixty thousand pounds. They say thass sweetened his temper, too, which ain't to be wondered at. Can't be much of a joke seeing your wife go out and keep you, can it?'

Miss Mayfield remembered Canon Thorby saying that Mrs Westleton was leaving 'for the happiest of reasons'.

The road ran on, perfectly flat, between wide green fields. It was good agricultural land; where the soil showed, it was black and rich-looking, but it was not pretty; there were few trees and no hedges. Ditches, shining with water, or fences of posts and wire divided field from field.

'One time,' Ed said, as though answering her thought, 'this was all fen. That grow good crops – beet and celery and potatoes – and thass good pasture, too. But it ain't pretty. Not like Walwyk. Walwyk is as different as can be. Prettiest little place you ever saw.'

'What is your connection with Walwyk?'

'Well, nothing you could call a *connection*, rightly. Only once, when I was a nipper, we had a outing, Sunday-school outing, there. They don't hev that sort any more, more's the pity. Day at Southend on the Dodgems is more their mark. But in the owd days we used to go out in wagonettes and the ride itself was a treat. And one time we went to Walwyk. We had games and tea in a medder. That was in the owd Rector's time, but Mr Harold – him thass Canon now – was home, in a lovely blue blazer. Funny how a thing like that'll stick in your mind while what happened last week is all of a jumble. Strawberries and cream we had for tea that time, and I don't care what anybody say, they tasted better than they do today – like a lot of other things.'

'They say that the change is in us; that our palates grow dull as we grow older.'

'So they may. I'd bet the Walwyk strawberries and

cream'd taste the same. Look, I said I reckoned it was the prettiest place I ever saw. All right, I was a nipper, I'd never been anywhere. Nineteen twelve I joined the Army; I did fifteen years, went all over the place. Kashmir now, thass in India and thought highly of, I been there. Seen the Taj Mahal, I hev – by moonlight, too. Table Mountain, Malta, the lot. And I still hold Walwyk is the prettiest.'

'How lately were you there?'

'Oh! Coming up to where it ain't so clear. Two year ago, three maybe. Don't get calls to Walwyk. The Rectory Rolls is at everybody's beck and call. But two, three year ago Mrs Westleton's car let her down and I drove her home. And I still felt the same way.'

'I'm looking forward to seeing it.'

'We come to a bridge presently and then you'll see the change. That time I towd you, in the wagonettes, our own parson rode with us, and he towd us that Walwyk was cut off till the marshes was drained, and they had wolves in the woods there years after they'd all been killed off in other places. Put the wind up us a bit in case there might still be one or two left. When you see them woods maybe you'll understand.' His voice changed a little. 'You may find the people a bit unfriendly to start with; they're still kind of cut off – in their minds, I mean. They'll call anybody from Renham a foreigner. Thass true! But if you don't mind my saying so, if you go slow and don't try too hard, they'll come round. Like dogs; thass best to let the dog come to *you*, and sniff and make friends.'

'I know exactly what you mean. I spent many years in Africa, where I was truly a foreigner.'

'Ah, then you'll know. Here's the bridge now.'

It spanned a slow-moving stream, and rose, hump-backed, so abruptly out of the flat road that the taxi-man had to change gear.

'Whoever built that was daft, I reckon. Both ends lay so low they're under water in a wet spell, so where was the point making the bridge so high?'

'Could it have been so that boats, and barges perhaps, could go under?'

'Never thought of that. Now, round this corner . . .'

It seemed almost as sudden as a transformation scene. The road now ran between sloping banks thickly dotted with clumps of primroses. At the top of the banks the woods began, stretching away on either hand in ever-darkening avenues and arcades of green. At the edge thousands of white windflowers shimmered and trembled, and among them were the dark purplish-blue spears of bluebells in bud.

Slowing down, Ed asked:

'Now, ain't that a sight for sore eyes?'

'It's beautiful,' Miss Mayfield said in an awed voice.

Sometimes in Entuba, at the end of a burning, dust-tormented day, she and Rose had talked of the time when, very old, past all usefulness, they would retire and live in a small cottage in a green English lane. It was an impossible dream, and they knew it. Rose had once – only once – admitted that. It was just after she had spent her godmother's legacy on the hospital.

'We'll never have our cottage now, Deb. We'll die in

the damned hospital, either of bed-sores or an injection from an unsterilized hypodermic, being too feeble to see that things are properly done.' That was the remarkable thing about Rose; she saw things clearly and unsentimentally. She had given her life and her money to Africa's service, but she was entirely disillusioned about all but a very few of the people themselves. On that occasion, having made that gloomy forecast, she had immediately recanted and said:

'I don't mean that. I needed the hospital and God gave it to me. When I need and have qualified for a cottage, I shall have that, too, no doubt.'

Now, moving between the freshly leafed flowering woods on the outskirts of Walwyk, Miss Mayfield indulged in another little daydream. Out of her much-increased salary, perhaps she could save something; perhaps here, in the very heart of the country, she could find a tiny cottage and have it ready to welcome Rose in, say, twelve or eighteen years' time; perhaps even, freed from the outrageous demands of Miss Stevens's careerist experiments, she might find time and energy to do some extra work – a little coaching, an evening class. Under the heady excitement of her first glimpse of this beautiful place, she thought of addressing envelopes at so much a thousand, or baby-sitting.

The woods gave way at last to cultivated land along the highway, though they still loomed, green and mysterious on the skyline. A house, a large one, a good example of Tudor half-timbering, came into view.

'One or two right substantial people live hereabouts,'

Ed said. 'Thass Mr Frisby's place. He breed them black-and-white cattle called Frisbians.'

Miss Mayfield tucked away this piece of information as a titbit to tell Rose.

'He do very well in all the shows, and last year he sold a bull to somewhere abroad for three thousand guineas. Then this here next place is Mr Tharkell's; he train race horses and he do well, too. I allust look out for his; he's lucky for me. I bought this cab out of what I made backing Viking, and two years later, when Sibling run, I even borrowed a bit to put on, and that paid off my house. The only thing is, with him thass more a hobby like. He've got other interests, and he'll take off and go abroad any time the fancy take him.'

Mr Tharkell's house was Georgian and stood high on a terrace.

A little farther along, on the opposite side of the road, was a farmhouse, whitewashed and neatly thatched, flanked by a dazzling white cloud of pear or cherry trees in full bloom. And then the cottages began, each one as pretty as a postcard, or an embroidered tea-cosy. Most-were whitewashed, though some were pale pink or greenish blue; all were thatched. The long gardens blazed with wallflowers and polyanthus, daffodils and tulips. They stood along the left-hand side of the road. To the right, the grass verge had widened out and become a village green, roughly triangular in shape. Directly ahead, occupying the whole of the shortest side of the triangle, was a high red wall, with a pair of iron gates set between ornamental pillars.

'The Rectory's in there, with the church beyond,' Ed said. He turned right and drove between the Rectory wall and the Green, then right again, where the road ended in a cul-de-sac.

'Here we are,' he said, beginning to slow down. This piece of road served only two houses. One was a sprawling, new-looking bungalow with a deep veranda, which brought to mind the houses built by prosperous people in Africa; the other was a Georgian dolls' house, prim and symmetrical behind a clipped box hedge, solid as a wall, upon whose top two topiary peacocks stood, one on each side of an elegant wrought-iron gate. A paved path ran from the gate to the porticoed doorway; on either side of the path was an oblong of smooth grass, which, near the house, gave way to a rose bed.

'You mean that this is the *school* house?'

'Thass right. The school is two minutes' walk away, down that little lane alongside the Rectory.'

'But it's so . . . elegant. I wasn't expecting anything like this. You are sure?'

'I towd you, I brought Mrs Westleton, time her car broke down. She was grousing about it not heving a garage. She kept her car at the Rectory. You aiming to keep a car?'

'I can't drive; and I certainly wouldn't dare begin now.'

Their arrival had been expected. The door of the dolls' house opened, and a young woman came hurrying down the path. She smiled, showing a beautiful set of teeth, and said:

'Welcome to Walwyk, Miss Mayfield. Canon said I was to say it the *very* first thing. I'm Berta Creek.'

Miss Mayfield knew a moment of embarrassment. In the old days, before she went to Africa, one would simply have said, 'Good morning, Berta.' But since then egalitarian manners had come in and familiarity might be resented. So she stretched out her hand and said, 'Good morning, Miss Creek,' and so made her first wrong step in Walwyk. Far from being pleased, the young woman was resentful.

'Miss Creek indeed,' she said, recounting the incident later. 'I ask you! And me in my apron. Made me feel a real fool. I s'pose I should just hev said me name was Berta and left it at that; but how was I to know?'

At the time, however, the *gaffe* was overlooked. The taxi-driver, perhaps feeling that introductions were in the air, said:

'I'm Ed Higgins. Now, if you'd just lend me a hand.'

While they lifted the trunk between them. Miss Mayfield snatched the suitcase and hurried towards the house. She wanted to be alone at this wonderful moment when, for the first time in her whole life, she entered a place which was really her own. Her father's house, where she had spent the first eighteen years of her life, had been a sentimental shrine to the mother who had died when she was ten. Even so small a variation as the substitution of one flower vase for another would evoke a comment, all the more forceful for being made in a sad and gentle manner: 'Your dear mother always used the green bowl for daffodils.' At college, one's room was, in theory, one's own, and girls with money to spare had added to or altered the basic furnishings; Deborah Mayfield, with no money to spare and assigned a room of such odd shape and proportions, had been obliged to accept hers as it was and be content. In Entuba, as in a medieval monastery, nobody owned anything; on more than one occasion Miss Mayfield's very bed had been commandeered; always, she admitted, after Rose's own. 'Darling, I knew you wouldn't mind. It's the dressings, you see, so difficult for Joyce to do when the patient is on the floor.' And then there had been Alchester. There, in that overcrowded ant heap, Miss Mayfield had been, she realized, extremely lucky. Janet Lovelace, the Domestic Science mistress, had invited her to share her 'flatlet'. This was a large attic at the top of a vast decaying house; it had a gas-ring in a corner; the bathroom was thirty steep stairs and two passages away. Janet's manner of life was a violent and perhaps understandable rebound from all that she taught; she was slovenly and untidy, extravagant as far as her means allowed, and she lived entirely upon pre-prepared or tinned food. Miss Mayfield had made a few determined attempts to cook upon the gas-ring, but had, in the end, been persuaded that Janet was right. When you boiled anything, the steam made the wallpaper blister and bulge; when you fried, the odour got into your books, on to your pillow. To tidy up after Janet was a mere waste of time. Miss Mayfield had contented herself by buying a wastepaper basket made of metal, into which incompletely extinguished cigarette ends could, with safety, be dumped, and by getting her own supply of Vim, with which she scoured the communal bath. Janet, not easily provoked, had once thrown at her the epithet 'old-maidish'. Miss Mayfield had replied equably, 'That may be so; an instinct run to seed. I suppose I should be cleaning up the bathroom after three or four boys who had been playing football. Then you'd call it motherly.'

Now, here at last, miraculously, almost unbelievably, she was walking into what was to be, so long as she stayed in Walwyk, her very own house.

And what a house! Inside the door was a square hall, paved with black and white tiles upon which lay, casually strewn, several richly coloured, silky-surfaced Persian rugs. Under the window, to the left of the door, stood a carved dower chest; in the centre, a black gate-legged table bearing a blue-and-white bowl full of spring flowers. The stairs, covered with dark-blue carpet, curved upwards from the wall opposite the door. Beyond the point where the stairs began, there was an archway, the entrance to a short passage with two doors in it, facing one another. That to the left was closed; the other was open, and Miss Mayfield could see a white sink, some shining taps, a red tiled floor.

She saw so much before Berta and Ed, carrying the trunk, entered the house.

'Might as well take it straight up,' Berta said.

When they had gone by, Miss Mayfield turned to her right and opened the door which was on that side of the hall. The sitting-room! For a moment she was afraid that she might cry. White panelled walls, a rose-scattered chintz on sofa and chairs, an antique writing table, white-painted shelves for books on each side of the fireplace, more flowers.

Wrong perhaps, weak – to take such pleasure in nice surroundings, to set such value on what was, after all, mere material. One must remember, always, how little such things really mattered. . . . But even that Puritanical thought could not diminish her pleasure. God had put beauty into this world – even a snowdrop was meticulously designed – and He had given to men the skill to make beautiful things, so, if by chance, one were fortunate enough to encounter lovely surroundings, one should be appreciative and grateful.

Miss Mayfield turned back into the hall just as Berta and Ed set down the crate of books.

'Leave it there,' she said. 'I can open it and carry the books to the shelves a few at a time.'

As she spoke a large black cat came stalking out of the kitchen, walked straight to her and began to rub against her ankles, purring heartily. The last, the perfect, touch of welcome, she thought, bending to stroke the glossy fur.

'*S'posed* to be a sign of good luck,' Ed said, 'but I can't say I take to them myself. Terrible thieves, too.'

'Does this one belong here?' Miss Mayfield asked.

'Well, you know how cats are,' Berta replied. 'Here one minute and gone the next. I will say, all the time I've been getting the house ready, he've hung about as though he was waiting for you.'

Something about the last seven words of that speech went direct to Miss Mayfield's sentimental heart. She could not remember any time when anyone or anything had awaited her coming, for in Entuba she and Rose on their extremely rare outings always went together. Still bending over the ecstatically purring cat, she thought, My cup is full. She added a humble and heartfelt, Thank you, God.

3

BY EIGHT O'CLOCK THAT EVENING MISS MAYFIELD had only one job left to do before her moving in was complete, and that was to arrange her books.

She had opened the crate when the cat made one of his dramatic appearances, and she remembered that it was some time since she had last seen him; it was time that he went out. She straightened herself and set the front door open, saying, 'Come along, puss.' The cat took three steps in the desired direction and then jumped sideways, taking refuge under the gate-legged table. She bent down, resting one hand on the crate, which stood between the table and the door, and extended the other towards him enticingly.

'Come along,' she said. 'If you are going to live with me, you must get into good habits.'

'Quite right, Miss Mayfield,' said a voice from the doorway.

She straightened herself and turned in a quick, nervous movement, and then was ashamed because it was only Canon Thorby.

'I do hope I didn't startle you,' he said. 'I could see you; I didn't realize that you couldn't see me.'

'I wasn't startled, just surprised. Please come in.'

He walked to the table and smacked it sharply with the flat of his hand.

'Out!' he said, and the cat shot across the hall and out at the doorway, as though propelled from behind.

Canon Thorby laughed.

'I seem to have influence with cats! I never knew. Well, I thought I'd just look in and say hullo, and welcome, and apologize for the breakdown in the transport arrangement this morning. You had my message?'

'No. No message. But it was quite all right. I found a taxi – or, rather, a taxi found me.'

'Really,' he said, with a hint of petulance in his voice, 'they are careless these days. I telephoned the Station Master and explained, and asked him to apologize and have a cab standing by. How aggravating! You see, we've had an old woman in Wandford Hospital, making good progress, too, but at eight o'clock this morning I had a message to say she was sinking, so the car had to take her two daughters there. Both highly hysterical types, so I went with them. And a very horrible day I have had. All the way there, noisy unrestrained grief, and all the way back, an acrimonious squabble about which should inherit the grandfather clock.'

She could see that he looked exhausted; the uniform high colour of his face had given way to a mottled crimson and grey, and all the lines around his eyes and mouth had deepened.

'You shouldn't have bothered about me at the end of such a day,' she said earnestly. 'I'm used to making my own way about. Do sit down. Would you . . . may I make you a cup of tea?'

'The universal panacea! We seem to have been sustaining ourselves all day on cups of tea – some so strong you could stand on them. No, if you really wish to offer me a reviving drink, Miss Mayfield, offer me a brandy and soda.'

She gave him a look of dismay.

'But, Canon Thorby, I haven't such a thing in the house.'

He had sat back in the low comfortable chair, but now straightened himself abruptly.

'I gave orders. Don't tell me something else has gone amiss! Not knowing your tastes, but going on Mrs Westleton's, I ordered sweet sherry and Madeira, and for myself, anticipating an occasional evening call, brandy and soda. In the cellarette of your sideboard.'

'Oh,' she said. 'I'm afraid I haven't looked. I will now.'

She hurried into the little dining room and opened one of the cupboards in the serpentine-fronted sideboard. He was right. Some bottles and syphons stood at the bottom, and on a shelf above was a bewildering array of glasses. In the faraway past, she had seen her father, after a specially heavy day, drink whisky from a tumbler. Was brandy the same? Oh dear, Rose would have known! Anyway, soda fizzed and splashed about – even she knew that – so a tumbler seemed to be the thing.

'Am I to drink alone?' Canon Thorby asked as she set the tray down.

'I . . . I never take alcohol. It isn't prejudice or anything like that. I just don't.'

He said mildly, 'It's never too late to acquire a pleasant habit, you know. It used to give me pleasure to see that Mrs Westleton was provided with just a little more than bare necessities.'

'You've already provided so much. This beautiful home. And the larder stocked. Even my lunch was prepared. You've been far, far too generous.'

'Nonsense. Did you imagine that we should allow you to arrive at lunchtime and begin to scramble eggs? That is a thing about which you must be very careful; ladies living alone, I understand, tend to have makeshift meals. Mrs Westleton, of course, had her husband to think of and, poor fellow, he *did* enjoy his food. I told Berta that every Saturday and Sunday she was to see that you had a good substantial lunch; and on other days she is to leave you something that can be heated – or otherwise prepared with the very minimum of bother.'

'I wanted to speak to you about Berta. She seemed to think that I would employ her permanently.'

'Well, why not? Don't you like her?'

'Very much. But I can't – I mean I ought not to afford her. I know I'm earning a great deal more than I did in Alchester; but I must meet the responsibility I spoke of; and I have thought of another plan, which will mean that I must be *very* economical indeed.'

'Berta won't burden your budget. She is employed by

the school. She attends to the needs of the Headmistress, and every afternoon she cleans the school premises.'

'I see. Really, Canon Thorby, it's all too much. I can't help feeling that it is a dream from which I shall wake up.'

'Tell me that sometime around next March, when you've wintered with us.' He took a little sip from his glass and looked about the room. 'You do fully understand, don't you, that this is *your* home and you are free to make any changes that you wish? The furniture stands now as it did in my aunt's time. Mrs Westleton had a passion for triangular chairs with tubular legs, and until this week all this was stored in one of our attics. It can go back to make room for anything you wish to install.'

'I wouldn't change a single thing. It is exactly the home that I never even dared *dream* of having.'

His look of warm approval indicated that she had pleased him.

'It is pleasant for me to see the old familiar things in their proper places again. Oh, and I must not forget my other errand, which was to ask you to lunch with us tomorrow. My sister would have written, but she has had a terrible migraine for the last three days. The advantage of migraine – she told me to tell you – is that its course is calculable, and she is sure that she will be quite restored tomorrow.'

'If you are sure of that, of course, I shall be delighted to lunch with you.'

'Good.' He turned his glass about, looking at it with a small frown. 'Miss Mayfield, I think I may as well warn you that you may find my sister rather . . . strange. Oh no, nothing mental; nothing, in fact, to which one could give a name. But you might think, quite wrongly, that she was unfriendly. Her manner, at times, gives that impression. She has very poor health, and her whole life has been somewhat disappointing. She is brilliantly clever; she should have had a successful career as an archaeologist. However . . . Anyway, I can assure you of this, no woman ever had a kinder heart or a more generous disposition, and if at any time when you are in Walwyk you should need to take a woman into your confidence, you couldn't do better than to go to her. You may think this sounds like a doting brother speaking; you would be wrong. Isabel and I are fond of one another and live in tolerable accord – but you will find that the village people share my opinion.'

For lack of anything else to say – and, for some reason, with the mention of the Canon's sister an odd kind of tension had come into the room, so that something *must* be said – Miss Mayfield asked:

'Was it the ill-health which ruined her career?'

After a little pause, he said:

'Frankly, no. That came later. On one of her expeditions something went wrong – I tell you this in confidence; we suspected an unhappy love affair. She returned home completely changed and has lived in virtual retirement ever since. She reads a great deal and, I think, writes a little: About that she is very secretive. She may very well "take to" you; she and Mrs Westleton had nothing in common, which was a pity for them both.' He lifted his glass and drained it and set it down.

'Oh, and before I go, I must explain to you our curious

transport arrangements. Saturday is Selbury market day. My car, which, with the driver, holds eight in moderate comfort, goes in, without fail, starting at nine o'clock. Two accommodating gentlemen, Mr Frisby and Mr Tharkell, leave a little later and run up to the Rectory gates, with a view to picking up anyone who has missed Baxter. Baxter will undertake to fulfil any commission – he has been known to buy a hair net for somebody who wanted one but did not wish to spend the morning in Selbury. Once upon a time we had a bus, a real red Eastern Counties bus, but it had so few patrons that now it comes no nearer than Renham. So the procedure is very simple. If you wish to go to Selbury, or to give Baxter an errand, be at the Rectory gate at nine o'clock. If you do not wish to leave so early, or in the unlikely event of seven people being ahead of you, you wait for Mr Frisby or Mr Tharkell. In Walwyk, I must say, we really practise that sadly discredited thing, communism.'

He rose, and smiling down on her, added:

'It remains for me to say what I should have done when I entered. I hope you'll be very happy with us, and stay in Walwyk for many, many years.'

'I hope you'll be satisfied with my work, Canon Thorby.' She glanced around. 'It doesn't seem to me that anyone could possibly deserve so much.'

She saw him out and then stood at the door for several minutes, calling, 'Puss, puss,' at intervals. The cat did not return, and finally she closed the door and locked it, went through to the kitchen and locked the door that gave upon the little walled yard.

Now, at last, she thought, I am alone in my own house. Quite alone, in my very own house. She returned happily to the unpacking of her books.

Later, when she was undressed and ready for bed in her voluminous old-fashioned nightdress, the work of the most advanced sewing class at Entuba, she knelt down, as was her custom, to say her prayers. After a moment she felt something pressing against her knees. Startled again, she opened her eyes, looked down and saw the cat, arching its back and beginning to purr as it rubbed against her. It must have run in, unobserved, as Canon Thorby left.

'And where do you sleep, I wonder,' she said aloud. The cat leaped lightly and gracefully up on to the bed and began to knead the blue eiderdown with its paws.

'Well, I don't know that I shall allow you to make a habit of *that*,' Miss Mayfield said: 'But just this once . . .'

4

'Now, my dear,' Canon Thorby said, 'you go and have your rest, and I will show Miss Mayfield the church. Then, as you know, I have to go to Wandford. I may be late.'

Miss Thorby rose and extended a limp, graceful hand.

'I hope that you're going to be very happy in Walwyk, Miss Mayfield, and that we shall see a great deal of one another.'

Like everything else that Isabel Thorby had said during the visit, it was friendly, well intentioned, but quite meaningless. Canon Thorby had, Miss Mayfield reflected, shown great perspicacity to have seen the effect his sister might have on people; her manner was gracious, her words well chosen, her smile sweet and frequent, but it all added up to nothing. *She* was not there, and she somehow reduced you to nothing, too. But – and this was what Miss Mayfield found so disconcerting – three or four times she had caught Miss Thorby in the act of staring at her in a manner both searching and speculative. Each time, the stare had changed immediately to a smile and some comment had been made, some question asked, as though the stare had been a mere waiting for attention. But that was not true. It was as though you stood facing a house whose windows were all closely curtained; nobody at home here! Then you looked away for a second and looked back and caught just a glimpse of a curtain twitched aside, of an avidly observant eye watching. And then nothing again.

Perhaps behind this lifeless façade there lived a real woman, with hopes, and fears. Perhaps Isabel Thorby looked thus at any female with whom her brother was brought into contact. Danger here? Well, in that case, she could be reassured; the new schoolmistress was forty-four, not well preserved, not well dressed, and, more important still, long, long ago resigned to spinsterhood. Quite harmless.

'We go through the garden,' Canon Thorby said. In the afternoon sunshine the wide, newly mown lawns lay like green plush, stroked this way and that. In two oblong beds immediately outside the drawing-room windows, pink tulips swam in a blue haze of forget-me-nots. Some stone steps led up to another lawn, and here, on each side of the path, was a wide herbaceous border, which in a week or two would blaze with colour. After that the path branched, and they took the way that led through a shrubbery and ended at a gate in a wall. Beyond lay the church, a small grey building, which at its western end incorporated a circular stone tower in such a way that one half of the tower was within the main building and the other half formed a rounded bulge in the wall.

'Yes,' Canon Thorby said, although Miss Mayfield had not spoken, 'it is very unusual. The tower is very much older than the church and was built for purposes of defence. Thor's Tower. The church is late Norman, and there are no signs of any earlier building, which suggests that Christianity reached us rather late. These two large yews are *said* to have been here before the Norman Conquest. We have no proof, of course, but they look old enough, don't they?'

They were two enormous dark trees, with their lower, sagging branches supported by iron props.

The porch of the church was on the north side, and as they stepped into its cool shadow Canon Thorby said:

'You mustn't expect anything very grand, you know. The finest churches in this area are in the villages which profited from the wool trade. The difficulties of transport forbade Walwyk to do that. Conversely, my forefathers had at least the good sense to avoid Victorian additions. You see it, more or less, in the original state. And here it is.'

He threw open the door.

It was plain that he was very proud of his church, and she did her best to make her comments sound enthusiastic and intelligent; the truth was that she had, upon entering, been immediately conscious of a feeling of oppression. The small round-headed windows admitted little light; the immensely thick pillars were too heavy for the size of the building they upheld. It was, like everything else she had seen in Walwyk, meticulously well kept.

Of the east window, over the altar where tall white

tulips stood stiffly, she could say, truly: 'I don't think I have ever seen such beautiful colours in stained glass.'

The window, like the others, was small, and whoever had planned to fill the aperture with coloured glass had wisely refrained from the attempt to compress even one human figure into the limited space; instead, he had represented Noah's dove, carrying the olive branch above the waste of blue waters. The dove's plumage shaded from a delicate silver grey to a dusky purple; its bill was a soft yellow, its feet, pressed backwards, close to its breast, rose pink. The sky about it was a pure azure blue, and below it the waves, in even symmetrical curves like those in a child's drawing of the sea, varied from greenish turquoise to indigo.

'You know why?' asked Canon Thorby, in reply to her comment. 'That is one of the few medieval windows which Cromwell's men did not knock out with their pikes. And it must be at least six hundred years old. We know that by the ruby glass in the border. That was always in short supply and finally gave out altogether in the last quarter of the thirteenth century.'

'So much beauty,' Miss Mayfield said sadly, looking at the dove, 'all set up, by some men, to the glory of God, and destroyed by others – for the very same reason.'

'Well, we saved that small piece; but that is our secret. We don't want sightseers coming in coaches to see our window, or our two statues, or our font, in which, by the way, Cromwell's men did not water their horses, for the simple reason that they had to come on foot across the marshes.'

'Oh, they came? I thought perhaps – seeing the window and all the other things – that Walwyk escaped a visitation.'

'They came. Twelve of them, under a Sergeant with one of those Biblical phrases for a name, not quite "Obadiah bind-their-kings-with-chains", but something very much akin. The Thorby who was at that time Rector had fallen victim to the seventeenth-century passion for journal keeping, and he left a vivid account of their visit and its sorry end. He wrote with some humour. I must show you his book.'

'How did he save the window, and the other things?'

'He? Oh, he did nothing. The men had been in the district some little time, and being strangers, without inbred immunity, they had fallen sick of what was called marsh fever in those days. It sounds like a particularly unpleasant combination of dysentery and influenza. They arrived in a very poor state. Ten died. Sergeant Love-thy-neighbour Smith and the other survivor left somewhat precipitately as soon as they could walk, having lost all interest in Walwyk's Popish relics and practices. Those who died were buried by my journal-keeping forefather, with a pomp and ceremony that must have made them lie uneasy in their graves. In fact, their corner of the church-yard is popularly believed to be haunted. I'll show you their stone presently.'

They walked back to the west end of the church, where the inner half of the circular tower bulged out into the nave, just as the outer half bulged out into the churchyard. An immensely thick narrow door in its base stood ajar.

Canon Thorby pushed against it strongly, and it opened a little more. Inside, it was almost dark and even colder than the church. Miss Mayfield gave a little shiver.

There was a stone stairway clinging to the tower wall, curving around it as it rose; the steps were worn hollow. They ended in a square hole cut in the solid wood which was the ceiling. Through another, much smaller hole a bell-rope dangled, ending in a great tassel of purple silk. Taking this in his hand, Canon Thorby said:

'I don't know how many church bells are still used as a general alarm – which was one of their old functions – but this old boy certainly is. One tweak,' he said, with a mischievous gleam in his eye, 'and every able-bodied adult in Walwyk would come running to deal with the fire or the flood. It was last used – now, let me see – six years ago, when the cottages in Curlew Lane had to be evacuated at a moment's notice. They lie very low, close to the river, which had to deal not only with an exceptional rainfall but with a phenomenally high tide as well. You are quite safe,' he hastened to add. 'Your house and the one next door are the highest-standing in all Walwyk.'

She was so cold by this time that the mere thought of chilly flood-water rising made her shiver again.

'You're cold,' he said, instantly solicitous. 'Let's get out into the sunshine.'

It was a mental, as well as a physical, relief to step out into the mild, bright afternoon. From the corner of the churchyard to which Canon Thorby led her, she looked back at the solid building with its dark guardian yews and for the first time in her life suspected that things could be *too* old for comfort; she remembered Rose's account of her visit to the Catacombs and of the physical and spiritual malaise which had attacked her there.

'Here we are,' said Canon Thorby.

The stone lay flat in the centre of a close-clipped mound roughly the size of a double bed. The inscription had weathered into illegibility, but the deeply carven cross above it was still quite clear.

'It says: "Under this stone lie the bodies of ten men who, though they came uninvited, were well tended in their dire sickness and buried according to the rites of the Established Church." It then lists their names and requests prayers for their souls. The date is 1653.'

'He was a bold man, that ancestor of yours. Puritanism was in full flood then; how did he know that another contingent of Puritans might not arrive and accuse him of Popery?'

'Maybe he had faith in the marsh fever. Or maybe he waited until after the Restoration before setting up the stone. Either way, I'm sure he thoroughly enjoyed his verbal ambivalence. Well, you have now seen our little church, and I'm afraid I must tear myself away and get ready to go to Wandford. Oh, one thing more. On no account do I wish you to feel that teaching in our school puts you under an obligation to attend church unless you wish to. I know places where that is the unwritten rule, and I think it highly reprehensible.'

'I rather enjoy attending church.'

'You'll find my sermons tiresomely simple. I fit my discourse to the capacity of my audience, and – and here's a strange thing – despite all these years of better-than-average education, our villagers are *still* simple. You'll find them bilingual, too. Inside the classroom, all but the very dullest will speak and write with some regard for grammar; outside, all but the very exceptional revert to the vernacular. You mustn't let that depress you. It's just a fact that must be faced: hotly as the faddists would deny it, at least three-quarters of all compulsory education leads to nothing at all.'

'I've always tried to bear in mind the Parable of the Sower.'

'Precisely. Mind you, I have always thought he was either very careless, inexperienced or purblind.'

It was exactly the kind of remark which Rose Tilbury sometimes made, and Miss Mayfield laughed.

'I'll step into school on Monday, at about nine, just to introduce you. Until then, goodbye.' He opened the gate which led into a short lane which served both school and church, skirted the Rectory and debouched into the road which led to Miss Mayfield's house.

Once on her way home, she found her feet moving faster and more lightly than they had done since her illness. She had been away from her little house for less than three hours, and she was longing to get back to it, already imagining how the hall would look when she opened the door, how she would go into the neat kitchen and put on the kettle and take one of the rose-spattered cups from the hooks on the dresser.

Very faintly and far away, the admonitory voice in her mind issued a little warning: *You mustn't become too much*

*attached to this house, you know, because one day you must
leave it.*

Yes, she answered it, I do know that, but perhaps when
I leave, it will be to go and share a cottage with Rose, and
that, of course, would make up for everything.

5

'Lord, behold us with Thy blessing
Once again assembled here . . .'

THE TWENTY-FIVE PUPILS, RANGING FROM A TEAR-
ful five-year-old recently separated for the first time from
its mother to a rather elegant young lady with a ponytail,
faced their new teacher as the words of the traditional
hymn for the opening of term was sung by those who
knew them.

Miss Mayfield was reminded of her first sight of a
group of Africans; they all looked alike, she had thought
then, and the same thought occurred to her now. I shall
have difficulty in telling one from the other. With a
single exception, they bore an almost family resemblance
to one another; flaxen hair, blue eyes, clear, fresh
complexions, and features slightly rugged, lacking the
blurred, boneless look associated with the faces of the
very young. Even the weeping infant had a nose, not a
smudge of putty. The one exception, a boy of about

twelve, stood out like a member of another race; his round head was covered with dark-brown hair, his round face looked almost sallow.

Probably, until very recently, there had been a good deal of inbreeding; and she remembered having read that the modern theory was that, given good healthy stock to start with, inbreeding was not so harmful as it had been held to be. These children all looked healthy enough, very healthy; at least . . . Miss Mayfield's eye found and lingered on one other face which varied slightly. Towards the back, among the taller children, one rather pale face, pretty or was it that prettiness was simply a matter of being a little different from the general run?

I must notice every little difference, for there is nothing that children dislike more than to be called out of their names. There's a head of hair that could have belonged to the child who was the model for 'Bubbles', and next to it two wonderful thick plaits; there's a boy with noticeably prominent ears, and then, of course, the one with glasses. I shall distinguish them in time, and wonder that I ever found them confusing, just as I did in Entuba. And there are so few of them. Eight, at least, look as though they will come under Miss Benson's care; that leaves me seventeen. I can give them absolutely individual attention. And I shall be in charge; if I'm in the middle of something interesting, there'll be no bell ringing to make me stop and go running down a mile of corridor to another class. It's going to be wonderful.

It was still wonderful when, on a Tuesday morning a fortnight all but a day later, the girl with the wonderful flaxen plaits, whose name Miss Mayfield now knew, halted by the tall desk and said:

'Ethel Rigby's gran towd me to tell you Ethel got a cowd.'

'Ethel has a cold,' Miss Mayfield said in the distinct voice which she used for such corrections.

'Thass what I said,' Audrey Head remarked, and went on.

Ethel Rigby was the girl who was paler and prettier than the others; she had a drooping kind of grace, a meek, rather repressed manner. She was backward for her age and at fourteen was roughly the equal of – though being daily outpaced by – the dark-haired boy, Sydney Baines, who was almost twelve. Because they were working at the same sums and were friendlily disposed to one another, their desks stood side by side, and as Audrey Head passed on her way to her own desk. Miss Mayfield's gaze rested for a second on Ethel's. The thought that went through her head was that now Sydney would master Simple Interest and leave Ethel entirely behind. But that thought dwindled. Sydney was looking at Miss Mayfield with a peculiar expression, as though he were trying to suppress a hiccup or a belch. His face seemed to swell and darken; then, aware that he was under observation, he took out a handkerchief of such dazzling whiteness that it might have been part of an advertisement for a washing powder, held it to his face and coughed. And you, thought Miss Mayfield, will be the next to have 'a cowd', sitting next Ethel.

At twelve o'clock, as usual, everybody except the one

girl and one boy whose turn it was to act as waitress and waiter in the canteen went out to play in the yard. The school dinner which Canon Thorby provided – somewhat unnecessarily, Miss Mayfield thought, since most of the pupils were within, ten minutes' walk of their homes – was cooked in one of the big redundant kitchens at the Rectory by a woman specially engaged for the purpose, and brought through a connecting doorway on a trolley. Miss Mayfield, who had taken the school dinner in Alchester, had often wondered during her fortnight in Walwyk whether the children realized how lucky they were; the food was superb, everything of the very best and carefully prepared. The waiter and the waitress set the tables; Miss Mayfield and Miss Benson dished up; two girls then washed the dishes, and a boy rolled back the trolley. Dinnertime was twelve-thirty, so there was a half-hour which could be spent in marking or preparation for the afternoon lessons.

On this morning Miss Mayfield was marking; and lifting the next book from the pile, she found herself looking down upon a piece of paper, lined paper, obviously torn from an exercise book. On it, written in a squarish, back-sloping hand, were the words 'Ethel Rigby's granny treat her something crool.'

Miss Mayfield stared down at the sentence. She had a sharply photographic memory and knew immediately that the writing was not the natural handwriting of any one of her seventeen pupils. A disguised hand. And it was difficult to reconcile the correct placing of the apostrophe with the misspelling of a simple word like 'cruel'.

Let's not bother about who wrote it, she said to herself. *Is it true?* On three occasions during her two years in Alchester, there had been cases of children so ill-used that the NSPCC had been forced to take action; With those wretched little victims, Ethel Rigby appeared to have nothing in common; she was well, if somewhat old-fashionedly, dressed; she was neither bruised nor emaciated.

But someone in this room this morning, had been prompted to write those words and bring them to the teacher's attention.

After a moment's thought Miss Mayfield lifted the paper rather gingerly, using only a finger and thumb, as though it were in someway contaminated, and carried it into the Junior room, where Miss Benson held sway. A little – and this she herself admitted – deterred at first by the Froebel teacher's brisk, airy, cynical manner, Miss Mayfield had, in the last week, realized that she was as fortunate in her assistant as the children were in their canteen arrangements. Sally Benson would say, 'He's a damned little thug, and I'll break his bloody neck for him,' and then sit down by the thug and say, 'Look here, Willy, how would you like it, if I, just because I'm bigger than you, . . .' and reason the aggressive Willy into an apologetic state of mind. That she was a sound good teacher, Miss Mayfield knew from the grounding given to all those who had passed through her hands. Privately, in fact, she had decided much of Miss Benson's good work had been wasted by Mrs Westleton.

Also, apart from her own merits, Miss Benson was a useful person to consult, for she knew Walwyk thoroughly. She was niece to Mr Frisby, the cattle breeder, and being an orphan, had been brought up in his house.

'I've just found this, sandwiched between two books. What do you make of it?'

Miss Benson took the paper, read it scowling and then smiled.

'That's an easy one. Somebody's trying to pull your leg, Miss Mayfield. If ever there was a daft doting old grand-mother, Phoebe Rigby is it. This,' she waved the paper, 'is as though I said *you* gave yourself three helpings of food every day and made Bobby Fakes go short. See?'

Bobby Fakes was the newcomer, who had very quickly decided that school was nothing to cry about.

'But why should anybody play such a joke on me, Miss Benson?'

'Well, you'll remember St Augustine – "Not Angles but angels." It works the other way, too – "Not angels but Angles." You mustn't be misled by all this flaxen hair and blue eyes.' As she said this, Sally Benson made a movement of her head, which set her own golden curls astir, and narrowed her blue eyes with a kind of knowing mirth, ranging herself, most endearingly, alongside the Angles who were not angels. Almost immediately she was grave again:

'Look, I do know. Old Rigby was my uncle Eric's head stockman, and a bull they trusted absolutely went savage suddenly and killed him. The old girl had adequate compensation, but apart from that all she's had these last years has been Ethel. And she *does* dote on her. You really can take my word for that.'

'Why does Ethel live with her grandmother?'

'She's illegitimate. Her mother just ran away and went to the bad in Wandford, sometime during the war. When she had the baby, they notified Granny Rigby, and she went and fetched it right away. And I'm sure no child ever had a better home.'

'You don't think, then, that I should do anything about this?'

'Just ignore it, and then next week put "cruel" on the spelling list, and whichever little brute wrote it will know you've seen the joke.'

Helping to dish up, and then eating her own lunch, Miss Mayfield turned this over in her mind. As soon as the meal was finished she went back to her classroom, took a new exercise book from the cupboard and counted its pages. When the class was assembled again, she said something vague about ordering stock and asked for all exercise books to be handed in so that she might judge how near they were to completion. That gave her an opportunity to leaf through all the books quickly. Only one had fewer pages than an unused book, and that was Sydney Baines's geography book.

On the previous week there had been some dispute about whose turn it was to sharpen the pencils, which, in well-provided Walwyk, was done by a rather fascinating little machine. At the end of this afternoon Miss Mayfield said:

'I've decided that in future the pencil sharpening is to be done in turns, alphabetically. So you will do it today, Sydney.'

'Yes, Miss.'

'I have a name, Sydney,' said Miss Mayfield.

'Yes, Miss Mayfield.'

She let him work away for a while, thinking over what she knew of him already. Most of her information had come from Miss Benson, and Sydney, because of his different colouring, had been the subject of one of her earliest inquiries. So now Miss Mayfield knew that Sydney's father, Wesley Baines, was the village handyman; he could do anything, carpentry, thatching, shoe repairing, even watch mending; he was an unorthodox Walwykian, in that he was a staunch Methodist and walked to Renham every Sunday to attend chapel there; he had gone to the war, reached sergeant's rank, and won a Military Medal; and he had married a 'foreigner', a Bedford woman who was a nurse. Miss Mayfield knew from observation that Sydney was intelligent and good-natured; watching him now as he performed his task, she saw that he was neat-handed and thorough.

Presently she said:

'Sydney, come here a moment.'

When he stood by her tall desk she held out the paper and asked:

'Did you write this?'

Across his nose and the top of his round cheeks he had an endearing spatter of freckles which leaped into sudden prominence as his face paled.

'This isn't my writing, Miss . . . Mayfield.'

'Not your natural hand, I'm glad to say. But did you write it?'

'I don't spell "cruel" with a double *o*.'

Methodist, she thought; he had probably been reared to believe that little boys who told lies went straight to Hell. He was making a gallant, rather pathetic attempt to avoid both lie and truth.

'I know. You spell very well. Whoever wrote this wished me not to recognize the writing or the spelling. And whoever wrote this – if it is true – did absolutely right. If it is true, I shall, of course, do something about it; but I can't take action until I know who wrote it and whether it is true . . . or a bad joke.'

'It's true enough.'

'How do you know, Sydney? Has Ethel told you so?'

'I've seen Ethel's granny be cruel to her.'

'So you wrote this to draw my attention to it. Is that right?'

'Miss, why did you pick on me?'

'Because this is written on school paper, and the only book that is short of pages is yours.'

He made no reply to that.

'I'm afraid, then, I must just tear it up and forget it.'

She saw the tears come into his rather lovely hazel eyes, his lower lip begin to quiver.

Oh dear, she thought, I'm a bully – the worst kind, a mental bully. She put her arm around his shoulders and pulled him towards her.

'It isn't a joke, is it, Sydney? You wanted me to know.'

Leaning against her, he groped for his handkerchief and snuffled into it.

'I hoped there was something you could do, Miss. I'd

hev told you straight out, I ain't afraid, but there's my mum to think of. Once I did tell my mum something Ethel's granny did to Ethel and my mum went straight round and *spoke*, and then Ethel's granny give my mum the shingles terrible bad, and my mum said best thing to do was not to hev no more doings with Ethel. But last night . . .'

'What happened last night?'

Under the stress of emotion, grammar went by the board. 'I seen her do it. She put Ethel's fingers in the mangle.'

Miss Mayfield's stomach turned a somersault.

'You say you saw her do it? Did she do it in front of you?'

'No. You see Ethel hev rabbits, and afore the row I allust used to help her get their cow parsley; and I still do, though I ain't supposed to. While we was plucking the parsley, Ethel say to me she's going to hev another accident, she know; there's something her granny want her to do and she 'on't, and whenever she 'on't do what her granny want, then she hev a accident. Poured a kettle of water over her foot last time — that was when I told my mum. So last night Ethel and me, we took the rabbit food round their yard, and her granny was in the wash-house. She say to me, "You run along, Sydney Baines, don't you'll get your breeches warmed. And you come here, Ethel, and give us a hand with this mangling." I didn't go straight away, I looked in the wash-house winder and I seen Ethel's granny take her hand and hold it in the rollers time she give the handle a twist.' He shuddered and gulped, and Miss Mayfield held him more firmly.

'You're *sure* that it wasn't an accident, Sydney?'

'Sure as sure. It was done deliberate. Besides, Ethel knew something was going to happen to her.'

'What happened then?'

'Ethel give a terrible screech and fell down. I give a shout and went round to the door, and as soon as she see me, Granny Rigby say as sweet as pie, "Sydney," she say, "what a good thing you're here. Run for your mum and tell her to bring her first-aid things." So I did, and my mum come and did Ethel up as good as any doctor. And then, on the way home, she kept saying it was just a accident and anyway I shouldn't hev been there and tonight I got to write "Honour thy father and thy mother" coupla hundred times. Though my dad never said nothing about going near Ethel any more. Only my mum.'

There was something entirely convincing about the boy's account, strange and horrible as the central incident sounded.

'You hoped that I should take this matter up?'

He nodded.

'We don't hev a Sunday paper, my dad don't hold with them, but once I see one that somebody had brought wrapped round their shoes. It had a bit in it about some children treated like Ethel, and it said the schoolteacher told the Cruelty people and got it stopped.'

'I see. Well, I shall certainly investigate. I shall go round and see Ethel this evening. Meanwhile you and I will keep this between ourselves, shall we? I think you acted rightly, and bravely, Sydney.'

'You ain't afraid of getting shingles?'

'Not from Ethel's granny, certainly. That would be quite impossible.'

'Thass what my dad said. He laughed at my mum, and she was mad. She don't often get mad, but that time, she was.'

Miss Mayfield looked at him. He always appeared to be an unusually clean little boy, but the one or two tears which had brimmed over his lids had left muddy smudges about his eyes.

'You'd better have a little wash before you go home,' she said. 'And look, Sydney, don't worry about this any more. Try not to think about it. You've done what you thought right, and now you can leave it to me.'

He took two steps backwards and there stood looking at her with a curiously adult air, as though he were measuring her up.

'She'll tell you a packet of lies, Miss. You should get the Cruelty man. Even if she did tell him lies, just seeing him might make her lay off Ethel.'

It was a very shrewd remark.

'I think I should find out a little more first. The NSPCC inspectors are very busy people, unfortunately. I think I must have a little more to go on before I bother the Society.'

'She'll pitch you a yarn,' he said, in that same adult way. 'But I ain't a liar. My dad walloped me out of telling lies a long time ago.'

'I'm quite sure of that, Sydney.'

Not lying, mistaken. Please, God, let it be a mistake. Not here, in lovely Walwyk, should this ugly, thing rear its head.

Berta Creek had set the tea-tray, and beside it, under an upturned basin, was a freshly made cherry cake. Miss Mayfield drank two cups of tea but left the cake untouched, and when, at about half-past five, she set out to visit Ethel, she carried it with her, neatly wrapped.

She was not yet familiar enough with the village to know in which cottage the Rigbys lived, so she stopped at the little general shop-*cum*-Post Office and asked her way. The Postmistress, a friendly plump woman, came out and pointed.

'There, look, between the pink house and the allotments, thass Curlew Lane; that run right down to the river. Rigbys' is the first you come to, stand all alone with a holly bush in front. You can't miss it.'

It was another of the picture-postcard cottages, with a long front garden in which flowers and vegetables grew side by side. She might almost have been expected, for she had hardly tapped on the door before it opened to reveal a little old woman who exactly matched the cottage; neat in her old-fashioned black alpaca dress, her shining white hair parted in the centre and drawn into a bun at the back, pink-cheeked, blue-eyed, Mrs Rigby stood there smiling.

'Miss Mayfield,' she said, 'do please step in.'

It could have been a model of a Victorian parlour. A round rosewood table stood in the centre, bearing a group

of wax fruit under a glass dome. There were four rosewood chairs with seats of horsehair, and a sofa to match
stood under the window. On the sofa lay Ethel, with a
patchwork cushion behind her shoulders and a rug of
knitted wool squares covering her legs. Her left arm was
supported by a sling made of one of those vividly
patterned red-and-yellow handkerchiefs which were once
the working neckwear of the countryman. Her face was a
trifle paler than usual, but her expression was cheerful and
composed, and she smiled as she said:

'Good afternoon, Miss.'

Miss Mayfield said, 'Hullo, Ethel. Audrey said you had
a cold, so I came to see how you were and bring you
something that I hope will tempt your appetite.'

Mrs Rigby, closing the door, said:

'I told you, my girl! I said it wouldn't work.'

Ethel gave a shamefaced grin.

'I asked Gran to say I had a cold. They're always on at
me about being so cack-handed.'

'Clumsy, she means, Miss.'

'Clumsy, then. They're always on at me for being
clumsy, and if they knew I'd gone and got my fingers in
the mangle, they'd never let me hear the last of it.'

'Please sit down, Miss.' The old woman turned to Ethel
and said, 'This time it wasn't your fault for once. I take all
the blame.' She looked at Miss Mayfield and went on.
'Mangling's the one job about the house I really hate, so I
go at it savage-like. And there, before you could say knife,
Ethel's poor fingers were in. But no bones broke. Sydney
Baines was here and he fetched his mother and she came

and said no bones broke and did Ethel up as nice as could be. And I made her a herb brew and she had a good night, didn't you, dearie?'

'Slept straight through,' Ethel said. She looked at Miss Mayfield and smiled. 'Gran's a wonderful one with herbs – better than doctor's stuff, she says.'

'I never said better. I said as good. After all, people who lived in out-of-the-way places in the old days they couldn't get a doctor, could they? They sickened and they got better with the help of what was to hand. The old ways are mocked at now, but take this penny-sillin they make so much fuss of; nothing but a mould, they say, and everybody that knew anything knew that a good bread poultice should be made of bread gone blue with mould. My mother always had a piece, in a special crock, blue and green, in case of accidents. But get me talking about the old ways,' she said with a smile, 'and I could talk the leg off an iron pot. I expect what you really want to know is when is Ethel getting back to school. The truth is, she could come tomorrow if she wasn't so silly. It's her left hand that's out of use and her legs and ears are all right. Juliet Reeve is the trouble.'

Miss Mayfield, looking at Ethel, saw a bright flush of colour run over her pallor.

'She's so sarky, always showing off and using long words. Not so long ago she said I was accident-prone. I said, what do you mean by that, and she told me. It meant you couldn't thread a needle without it pricked you, or cut a slice of bread without you slashed your finger or hammer in a nail without banging your own thumb. So I ain't – I *am*

58

not coming to school wearing this.' She twitched at the sling and slumped lower on the sofa, her face set in a mutinous, sulky expression.

Miss Mayfield's mind went back to the ill-treated children in Alchester; she remembered their obvious dread of their parents, the parents' truculence, the squalor of the surroundings. Nothing here was in any way akin. Ethel's manner indeed bore out Miss Benson's opinion; she was behaving like a spoilt child.

'Well,' she said, 'in that case I suppose school must wait. Actually, I didn't come to ask about that. I brought you a cake – cherry. I hope you'll like that kind.'

'It's my favourite,' Ethel said. 'Could we have a piece now? And I tell you what, Gran; a glass of your cowslip'd go with it nicely.'

'It'd take Ethel to think of that,' Mrs Rigby said with fatuous pride. 'Ethel's the one to think of things, I must say.'

She rose and went to a corner cupboard, which would have been worth a considerable sum in the right market, and took out three glasses, shaped like tulips, on long stems.

'You'll take a glass, Miss. It's sound and wholesome.'

'Won the Women's Institute prize,' said Ethel, raising herself again. 'Not just Walwyk, the whole county. Anything Gran put in for, she win every time.'

'Except chutney, love. Don't forget the chutney,' said Mrs Rigby, going towards a door at the back of the room.

'Don't you forget we want a plate and a knife for the

cake.' No, not thus did ill-treated children address their tormentors.

More mystified than ever, Miss Mayfield saw the door close behind Mrs Rigby. Now was the moment to ask some quick, searching questions. Is your granny kind to you? How did the accident happen? Silly as it seemed, in the circumstances such words would sound impolite, slightly crazy. On the other hand, Sydney had made a serious accusation, and it would be wrong to let self-consciousness and embarrassment stand in the way of investigation.

Before she could speak, however, Ethel said, in an eager but carefully quiet voice:

'Is Sydney all right?'

'Sydney? Why yes, of course. Are *you*, Ethel? Sydney seemed very worried about you.'

'He tell you about this?' She touched her sling.

'He . . . mentioned it.'

'Tell him to shut up. I'm worried about *him*. His mum's very strict and don't like him being friends with me. Last night I went all faint for a bit, or I'd hev stopped my gran sending for Mrs Baines. I knew Sydney'd catch it. But he'd gone before I came around.'

She said the last words in such a dreary tone and looked so worried that Miss Mayfield made haste to say:

'He only has to write a few lines for disobedience. . . .'

'Is that Sydney Baines?' asked Mrs Rigby, entering with a nice old black papier-mâché tray upon which stood a black bottle, a cake dish on a stem and some plates and knives. 'I'll be frank with you, Miss, and say that I've no patience with Emily Baines and her airs and graces. We'll grant she's better educated and had a profession, not a job, but if she wanted to look down on her neighbours, she shouldn't have married the village cobbler. I was in *good* service before I married – head parlourmaid – and one thing I did learn was that women take their standing according to their husbands. For her to make out that a cobbler's boy is too good to play with Ethel, whose grandfather was a *head* stockman, is just plain daft to me.'

She drew the cork out of the bottle with a sharp, explosive pop and began to pour a pale-yellow crystal-clear wine into the glasses.

'I haven't yet met Mrs Baines. Sydney seems a very nice boy.' That was all Miss Mayfield could think of to say. She realized that she was now catching a glimpse of the other, less pleasant side of village life – the little squabbles, the petty snobberies. She was almost sorry that she had put herself into a position where she must be even slightly involved; and she was as much in the dark as ever as to the truth of the situation. One thing was clear: Sydney was concerned about Ethel, and Ethel about Sydney, and they, at least, seemed sincere.

Mrs Rigby, cutting the cherry cake, said with the exquisite tact often found in simple people:

'But, there, Miss, you don't want to hear about our silly little differences. All you should bear in mind is that anything Emily Baines says about me – and anything I say about her, for that matter – is spite talking. We never hit it off; but that don't stop Ethel and Sydney being very fond of each other.'

Ethel said with startling vehemence:

'I am not *fond* of Sydney, Gran. I've told you that a thousand times. He's a help to me getting the rabbit grub – food – and thass all. Anybody else that'd come and pull cow parsley and drag it home for me I'd be just as thankful to.'

'So you say. I know better.'

'Then you know wrong.'

Now, this, thought Miss Mayfield, is surely very curious. She had a feeling that it might also be significant – if only she had a clue as to the meaning of Ethel's denial of interest in Sydney.

Mrs Rigby's years in good service had not only improved her grammar, and modified her accent, it had given her some social grace. Now, in her capacity as hostess, she asked all the correct little questions. How did Miss Mayfield like Walwyk? Did she find country children slow compared with those in towns? Did she mind living alone?

Ethel placidly ate her cake, picking out all the cherries and laying them aside to eat at the last – a simple, childish action somehow Miss Mayfield found very reassuring. When at last, having learned nothing, she rose and began to take her leave, Ethel said:

'Please, Miss . . . don't go and tell on me, being so clumsy. Juliet Reeve'd go and call me a self-operating mangle or something.'

'Oh, I'm only supposed to know what Audrey Head told me,' Miss Mayfield said.

Mrs Rigby laughed.

'You don't know Walwyk, Miss. Everybody in the

village'll know by this time that you came to see Ethel; and very nice they'll think it too – as I do. Thank you for the cake, too.'

She opened the door and stood aside; Miss Mayfield stepped out, and as she set foot on the path, from the dark shadow of the holly tree a shadow moved and began to circle around her feet.

'Well, how extraordinary! My cat. He must have followed me and waited, like a dog.'

'Now, Miss,' said Mrs Rigby in a light, rallying voice, 'we can't have you laying claim to *my* cat. Five years I've had him. Look, I'll show you something. Hi, Vesper! Up, boy, up!'

The cat in one little movement jumped up and landed on her shoulder and stood there balancing, his four paws bunched together. Miss Mayfield looked straight into his greenish-amber eyes.

'Well,' she said slowly, 'perhaps I was wrong to say "my" cat, but that is certainly the cat which spends a good deal of time with me.'

'I suppose that is possible,' Mrs Rigby said, in a voice which said the opposite. 'But it's a good long way, and right across the road, too.' The cat nuzzled his head against her ear. 'He's my Vesper, though, my lovely boy, aren't you, love?'

Something drew Miss Mayfield's eye to the interior of the room. Ethel was sitting bolt upright on the sofa, her face, a paper-white mask of horror and repulsion.

Informed by the expression on Miss Mayfield's face, Mrs Rigby then turned and said:

'Oh dear, I'm sorry, Ethel. Wasn't thinking.' She lifted the cat down and set him on the path. 'Ethel just can't abide cats, but she loves rabbits. Funny, don't you think? But I have to humour her.'

They said good evening to one another, and Mrs Rigby, having watched Miss Mayfield to the gate, closed the door.

'Smut,' said Miss Mayfield, addressing the cat by the unimaginative name which she had given him when Berta Creek said that so far as she knew he had no other. 'Smut, come along home.'

It was her cat. He fell in beside and slightly behind her, his tail held high; and together they walked home through the level golden light.

6

'Well?' Miss Benson's voice had a teasing friendliness. 'Did you discover the rack and thumbscrews?'

It was five minutes to nine on the following morning, and Miss Benson, carrying the big hymn-book, paused on her way to the piano to ask her question.

'You tell me something first. How do you know I went to look for them?'

'Elementary, my dear Watson. At five thirty-five, or so near as makes no matter, you were seen inquiring the direction of the Rigby cottage of one Gertrude Flack, Postmistress in this village. The said Gertrude Flack has a sister Ella, who is number one in Aunt Edith's chain-gang of daily helps. She laid information about your movements – together with the kippers – on the breakfast table this morning.'

'The information was correct.' Miss Mayfield tried to match the girl's manner. 'Following instructions, I proceeded along Curlew Lane and reached the Rigby cottage at approximately five fifty-five. All the evidence of my eyes and ears convinced me that your estimate of the relationship between Mrs Rigby and her granddaughter was right.'

'Well, I told you it was a joke. Your rushing off there must have given the joker great pleasure. Humour is a bit crude in these parts.'

'So long as somebody is pleased,' Miss Mayfield said a trifle sourly. She had had a bad night, going over and over again every word, every change of expression, seeking for some explanation, and finding none. She'd have another little talk with Sydney presently, she promised herself.

'Oh, you mustn't *mind*,' Miss Benson said quickly and kindly. 'They're all simply *staggered* that you took so much trouble. Mrs Westleton wouldn't have done it. That's what they're saying, and, by Jove, for once they're right. She damn well wouldn't!'

'Did you . . . tell anyone *why* I went?'

'No fear. I never tell tales out of school. And I don't approve of jokes on teachers. *Esprit de corps*. By the way, did you find out who wrote it?'

She was saved from being obliged to answer that by the hurried, self-important arrival of a boy named David Fletcher, who held out to her a white envelope, marked with several of his thumbprints.

'Miss, from Mrs Baines. Sydney ain't well.'

'Sydney *isn't* . . .' Miss Mayfield began in her correcting voice. Then she heard again Ethel's quiet urgent question 'Is Sydney all right?' Nonsense!

She broke the envelope with a roughness alien to her and pulled out a sheet of paper covered with small neat handwriting, completely without character, just the hand in which to fill in charts.

Dear Miss Mayfield,

Sydney will be unable to attend school today. He has a slight temperature and complains of headache and lassitude. I should be greatly obliged if you could spare me a few minutes after school this afternoon; there is a matter upon which I should like your advice. It is a school matter.

Yours faithfully,
Emily Baines

She could only have been a nurse, Miss Mayfield thought, brought face to face with Sydney's mother at four o'clock that afternoon; you'd have guessed her profession if you had met her in the desert. She had the look, crisp, sensible, reliable, slightly antiseptic; and her clothes had the restrained gaudiness which is the natural reaction to uniform.

'How is Sydney?' Miss Mayfield asked.

'He's worse. I stopped at the Post Office and telephoned to Dr Macdonald. He said he'd be here by five, and since my husband was home and I'd said I would come, I did. But I think I ought to get back.' She looked at her wrist watch, a large clear-faced one with a second hand, by which, Miss Mayfield knew, many a pulse had been checked. 'But I did want to talk to you,' she added. And then Miss Mayfield noticed her eyes. They were at odds with the rest of her. They were large and rather beautiful, like Sydney's, and the same colour, but their expression was – Miss Mayfield sought for the right word – wild, distraught? No, those were temporary states, easily attributable to concern for Sydney's health; it went deeper – unstable, that was the word. Across a wilderness of thirty-five years' remembering, Miss Mayfield heard her father's voice, speaking of a horse he had been offered. 'It's got an unreliable eye.'

She then heard her own voice saying soothingly:

'Well, if you want to go straight back, Mrs Baines, please do. Don't bother about me. Or if you have something on your mind, sit down and tell me about it. You say your husband is with Sydney and the doctor is coming at five . . . That leaves quite a bit of time.'

To her surprise, Mrs Baines, ignoring these reasonable remarks, said violently:

'Oh, if only you'd let things *be*. If only you hadn't gone and stirred it all up again.' She dragged out a dazzling white handkerchief that reminded Miss Mayfield of Sydney's and dabbed angrily at her eyes. 'Wesley thinks I'm crazy. You'll think I'm crazy. But twice couldn't be accident. Saying things are crazy is the *easy* way out. I believe in looking things in the face. Sydney came home with some tale about Ethel Rigby's granny scalding her – away back last October that was. I went round to *see*. Who wouldn't? And I'm struck with the shingles. Then, there we are, day before yesterday, Ethel's fingers in the mangle. You go round to see. And now Sydney's struck with something I couldn't name, no matter what depended on it. There's something *wrong*. It may be crazy, but it's wrong as well, and I wish to God I could get away from it all.'

In some obscure way something of what the woman was saying accorded with Miss Mayfield's private thoughts. Something wrong. She had felt that since the moment she found the sheet of paper between the two books.

'But by your reasoning, Mrs Baines, I am the one who should now be afflicted. You inquired and had shingles; I inquired . . . Nothing has happened to me.'

'Sydney's taken the punishment this time. At least . . . that's what I'm afraid of.' She linked her strong clean-looking fingers together and moved them violently up and down. 'The thing is, I *know* it all sounds mad, five hundred years behind the times, but I did beg Sydney not to say a word; and he must have for you to go round there so fast. And this is the result!' Her eyes flooded with tears. 'I punished him for going near Ethel again. A fine thing it'd be if the last thing I ever did to my own poor little boy was to punish him!'

'Mrs Baines, you mustn't even think such things. Sydney may have a simple chill, or be preparing to go down with one of those childish complaints – mumps, measles.'

'It could be something like that, I suppose. Or just shock and worry, leading to acidosis; that can take peculiar forms. But I have a feeling inside myself that . . .' She broke off and once more angrily applied her handkerchief, and again looked at her watch.

'You'll be easier in your mind if you get back,' Miss Mayfield said. 'I'll walk with you, and then if you feel like discussing the other matter, we can talk as we go: If not, we can leave it till another time.'

'I'm afraid it's too late already,' Mrs Baines said, going to the door. 'It's about the eleven-plus that Sydney should by rights have taken in February.'

'Why didn't he?'

'They none of them ever do. And if you look at it from one way, why should they? They're safe here, being taught well, in the best of circumstances, till they're old enough – like Juliet Reeve – to go on to college. If they stay in Walwyk, there's the point. And there again, who'd want to move? Pretty cottages, all up to date, septic tanks and everything, ten shillings a week at the most. Mr Frisby and Mr Tharkell, *and* Tom Maverick if you come to that, are as good employers as you'd find anywhere. Nobody ever wanted to move, so why should their children be bothered with the eleven-plus? Now I do want to move, and what I want to know is, is there any way of getting Sydney into a grammar school now? When he's better, of course, I mean.'

'I can't answer that at the moment; but I can find out for you.'

'I'd be everlastingly obliged if you would. You see, they've tied things up so nowadays you can't buy your boy an education unless you're rolling in money. I could go private nursing and knock up quite a bit; I could *pay* for Sydney to go to grammar school, but it just can't be done, not without this eleven-plus.'

Miss Mayfield made some noncommittal sound of agreement, and Mrs Baines went on, as though this chance to open her heart was welcome:

'My husband won't *like* it. He's Walwyk born and bred, never went further afield than Selbury till he went to the war. We were married as soon as he was demobbed, and nothing would suit him but to come back here for our honeymoon. Still . . .' She paused for a moment; and Miss Mayfield, glancing upwards and sideways, saw her profile as set and hard as stone. 'Let me once get Sydney out of this and *we're* off. Wesley can please himself. As I said before, I can always make a living.'

Miss Mayfield, who, like most unmarried women, was sentimental about the sanctity of marriage, was saddened by this statement. But she did not feel that any comment was justified. Mrs Baines went on:

'If something's wrong and you know it, the only thing to do is to walk away and forget it – if you can't do anything about it, I mean. The scalding could have been just Ethel's tale – we all know what girls are, specially at that age – but whatever Sydney is or isn't, he isn't a liar. Wesley's strict about some things, and lying is one; he walloped Sydney the first fib he ever told. So if Sydney says Ethel's fingers were *put* in the mangle, that's enough for me.'

'Yet the girl and her granny seem to be upon the best of terms.'

'That's what I say. There's something *wrong*. I don't know *what*. I don't much want to. I only want to get shut of it all. And it may be I'm too late.'

They had passed the Post Office and the mouth of Curlew Lane, and reached the gate of a neat cottage, fronted by a garden which, unlike any other of its kind, had order and pattern. The vegetables, the gooseberry and currant bushes were all confined to the part nearest the road; separated from this utilitarian portion by a rustic pergola of roses was a piece of lawn upon which stood a birdbath and a garden table and some chairs.

'I most sincerely hope that when the doctor comes, he'll find nothing much amiss with Sydney,' Miss Mayfield said, preparing to take her leave and turn back.

'Oh, come in. Please. It'd be such a help if you'd just go up and see Sydney and tell him you'd seen Ethel and she was all right. He's been on the fret'. Wanted me to go round and make out I'd gone to change the bandages! But, to tell you the truth, I didn't dare show that much interest. Besides, whatever I said he'd think I'd made up to comfort him. He'd believe you.'

'Well, of course. If you think I could do any good . . .'

The front room of the cottage was entirely devoted to Wesley Baines' work. Tools, pots of paint, panes of glass and plumbing spare parts were ranged on shelves across one side of the room. There were two benches, a large one with a lathe and a smaller at which Wesley sat, repairing a shoe. He had a scooped-out, thin, bony face which made Miss Mayfield think of pictures she had seen of Abraham Lincoln His thick fair hair was a good deal lighter than his weathered skin, his eyes a mild periwinkle blue.

'This is Sydney's teacher, Miss Mayfield.'

He stood up, so tall that his head only just cleared the low ceiling, very thin, awkwardly put together. He reached out a huge horny hand and said heartily:

'Glad to see you, Miss. Heard a lot about you, we hev, from Syd.'

'Have you looked at him?'

'No more than two minutes ago. Seemed to be dozing nicely.'

'Give Miss Mayfield a chair,' Mrs Baines said. 'Excuse me, Imust just *see* . . .'

She opened a door to the left of the fireplace, which faced the door, and revealed a stairway, steep and narrow but built of solid oak, uncovered and highly polished. Wesley Baines opened the door on the right, and Miss Mayfield caught a glimpse of a living room which, like the garden, differed from the village pattern. The gate-legged table, the Welsh dresser were reproductions – perhaps shoddy – of the real thing, but they were pleasing to the eye; so was the unutilitarian chintz which covered the chairs and curtained the window, a white ground, scattered with bright flowers. Some white-painted shelves held a collection of books; the floor was bare except for two bright rugs.

Wesley Baines brought in one of the chintz-covered chairs, and Miss Mayfield had just sat down when Mrs Baines came blundering down the stairs. Her nose and a band all about her mouth were chalky white.

'Dozing nicely,' she said in a voice of intense bitterness . . . 'The child's in coma! Dr Macdonald . . . My purse . . .' She snatched it up and rushed for the door. Wesley Baines reached out a long arm.

'Em, love. You said you'd ring him on your way to the school. Didn't you?'

'Of course I did. He said he'd be here at five, but . . .'

'Then he's on his way now. Ringing him again won't do no good.'

'Oh, he's like you, thinks I'm fussy, said five just to put me off. I'll give him five . . .'

She pulled herself free and went through the door and along the garden path, running with the clumsy speed of some creature out of its own element.

Her husband stared after her.

'He just looked sorta sleepy and peaceful to me,' he said in a puzzled voice. 'Whass she mean "in coma", d'you know?'

'Unconscious, I suppose. I don't really know, Mr Baines, but I'm sure your wife would; there'd be some difference in the pulse, or the breathing.'

'Went to bed last night as right as rain.' He picked up a strip of leather and bent it this way and that between his fingers. 'Daunts me,' he said, using what Miss Mayfield had already learned was the Walwyk term for something puzzling, beyond easy comprehension.

'I hope the doctor will soon come and give you some comfort, Mr Baines.'

He looked at her and said calmly, though he still worried the strip of leather:

'Tell you the truth, I ain't as upset as Em is. Syd's a good strong healthy boy; he'll pull through whatever it is. The fact is, Em's nervous these days. Used to be as steady as a rock, but ever since she had them shingles she've been fanciful. Take the other night, now; got herself all worked up because Syd'd been round to the Rigbys'. Mostly, if there's punishment to do, *I'm* the one to do it. But this time, no! She'd towd Syd to steer clear of Ethel Rigby and he hadn't, so he hev lines to write, just like in school, if you'll pardon me mentioning it, Miss. Maybe you don't howd with writing lines; I don't meself. When it's writ once, thass writ, and however many times you do it over, it don't make it more so. A good wallop is the best way. But Syd got lines to do, and if I towd you *why* – Em's real reason, I mean – you'd laugh.' He leaned over the bench, and his wide thin-lipped mouth stretched in a grin. 'Em got the notion that owd Granny Rigby can put a spell on you. What d'you think of that? Trained nurse and all. On'y, for mercy's sake, don't mention I towd you; Em'd never forgive me.'

'I won't. I take it that you, Mr Baines, don't believe such a thing to be possible?'

'It stand to reason it couldn't be. Would God put such power into any mortal hands? And for Em to think that! She's always been on about village people being so ignorant and backward.' He broke off and assumed a listening attitude. 'Ah, I thought so. That'll be the doctor.'

The car stopped with a jerk at the gate; the doctor climbed out, grabbed his bag, slammed the door and came loping up the path as though he had not a moment to spare. Inside, he recognized Wesley with a curt 'Good after-noon,' glanced at Miss Mayfield and dismissed her as of no importance, said 'Upstairs, I take it,' and dashed for the stairs. Immediately behind him came Mrs Baines, breathless.

'Saw the car,' she gasped, and followed the doctor.

Overhead the floor boards creaked; a murmur of voices, the words they spoke indistinguishable, reached the listeners below. Wesley Baines began to look anxious and fidgeted more violently with his piece of leather.

'Looks like Em was right,' he said at last. 'Must be more than some little thing.'

Miss Mayfield could think of nothing more helpful to say than:

'Try not to worry Mr Baines.'

Presently, the doctor came down the stairs; he now looked anxious as well as pressed for time.

'Where's the nearest phone?'

'Post Office. Can I go for you?'

'They'd take no notice of you. I want a bed in Wandford Hospital.'

'Is . . . is it serious, then?'

'I don't know. You,' he said, looking at Miss Mayfield, 'give her a hand. She's very distressed.'

Miss Mayfield went upstairs and into Sydney's room, where Mrs Baines stood holding a folded blanket against her chest and crying quietly and despairingly.

'I'll pack what he needs if you'll just tell me where things are,' Miss Mayfield said.

Mrs Baines nodded towards a chest of drawers. Miss Mayfield gathered together two pairs of pyjamas, a brush and comb and some handkerchiefs; she saw a red dressing-gown hanging behind the door, took it down and folded it and reached for the slippers that were under the bed. During all this time, Mrs Baines did not move; the tears dripped from her quivering cheeks on to the blanket.

'He'll want some washing things,' Miss Mayfield said. Mrs Baines spoke then, in a choked voice:

'All so useless.'

'I don't think so. Taking him into hospital is surely a hopeful sign, Mrs Baines. And you ought to start wrapping him, you know. The doctor was only going to the Post Office.'

'I know.' She moved, unfolded the blanket and then said, 'The bathroom is across the landing; Sydney's face flannel has the red border, and his toothbrush is red, too. His father'll get something to put it all in.'

Wesley Baines opened a cupboard and produced a suitcase, and Miss Mayfield put into it the things she had collected, and by that time Dr Macdonald — now frankly trotting — returned.

'I thought you'd be ready,' he said, looking at Miss Mayfield reproachfully.

'I suppose I'd best carry the boy down,' Wesley Baines said in a confused way.

'He can't walk,' Dr Macdonald said crossly. He took his bag and hurried out to the car, the back door of which he opened, and then stood by it, impatience screaming from every line of his face and figure. Wesley Baines lumbered upstairs and came down immediately, carrying Sydney's blanket-wrapped form as easily as a child would carry a kitten. Mrs Baines, still crying, followed and then, at the end of the path, passed her husband and ran and climbed into the car.

'Here, give him to me,' she said.

'Are you going, Em?'

She scorned to answer that, and repeated, 'Give him to me.'

'How about me coming, too, then?'

'I hardly think so,' Dr Macdonald said a trifle testily. 'Mrs Baines may be of some use . . .' The unspoken words 'but you'd merely be in the way' hung on the air. He threw himself into the driving seat and pressed the starter.

'Goodbye, then, Em. Let me know,' Wesley cried after the moving car. He stood there looking so big and helpless that Miss Mayfield was moved to pity.

'How about you, Mr Baines? Can you manage? Food, for instance. Would you like . . . Would you like to come and have supper with me this evening?'

'Thass mighty kind, Miss. But I reckon I ain't going to hev much appetite, not till I hear.'

'They have such wonderful cures nowadays, all these marvellous new drugs. I think perhaps the doctor was in a hurry because he'd thought of something, some treatment, so he didn't bother to say the few words that would have relieved your worry. And, of course, Mrs Baines being a nurse, she may worry too much, like . . . like teachers worry most about their children's progress at school.'

He shook his head at that.

'No; Em was right and I was wrong. I made light of it. All so sudden . . .'

'Well, I do hope you'll soon have news, good news. And if at any time you want a meal, remember you're very welcome to share mine.'

'Thank you, kindly. But I'm used to fending for myself. Em's often called on, you see. You been a great help.'

He turned in at his gate and Miss Mayfield set out for home. She had taken only a few steps when she remembered that she had left her handbag, containing her keys, on the workbench. She turned back.

The cottage door was open; and by the cobbler's bench Wesley Baines was kneeling, his head bowed, his big hands clasped before him like a good child's. Miss Mayfield reached in and retrieved her bag without his being aware of her presence. As she went softly away she was a little eased of her concern for him. He had his source of strength and comfort.

7

Sydney had been taken into hospital on Wednesday, and by Saturday there was still no change in his condition. Every evening at six o'clock Mrs Baines telephoned to the Post Office, and one of the Flack sisters ran along and reported, first to the anxious father and then to the village in general. It was therefore known to everyone that Sydney's illness remained a mystery, that he was being kept isolated in a small room by himself and that his mother was being allowed to help with his nursing.

On the Saturday evening there was no call from Wandford, and the Postmistress, with a few of her cronies, was watching the clock and beginning to predict the worst when a hired car entered Walwyk and stopped by the Baines's gate. Mrs Baines alighted alone and sent the car away. She looked so terrible, everyone said, that they were sure Sydney was dead. They were also sure that the only decent thing to do was to wait a few minutes while she broke the news to Wesley and then go to commiserate – and learn the details.

They found her, dry-eyed but pale and wild-looking,

'getting out her cooking things as though she'd gone crazy', Ella Flack reported. No, she said, Sydney was just the same; but she had to give a thought to Wesley, too, hadn't she? How was he going to live through the next week with no food in the house?

'We asked him to eat along of us,' Ella Flack said. 'Everybody asked him. He said even Miss Mayfield asked him to supper. You shouldn't have bothered.'

Mrs Baines said, well, she had bothered, and now she must get on with it.

When the meal was cooked and eaten, Mrs Baines said that she was going for a walk. She needed some air after being cooped up for so long. Wesley offered to go with her, but she said she'd go alone, and having some work on hand, he settled down to it and never even glanced at the clock again until Canon Thorby arrived, hilariously excited, crying, 'He's better, Baines, better! They rang through just now and said he was conscious and complaining of hunger. Where's your wife? . . . I long to see her face when she hears.'

'Thank God! Thank God!' Wesley said, before replying as to Emily's whereabouts.

'Indeed, yes, thank God,' said Canon Thorby, trying not to sound perfunctory. 'But they told me your wife had come home. Where is she?'

'Gone out for a breath of air.'

They waited together until she returned. Canon Thorby was disappointed by her reception of his news. Showing no surprise, she asked, 'Did they say when he could come home?'

'Not precisely. But Baxter shall drive you in first thing tomorrow morning, and then you can make arrangements.'

All this account of words spoken and things done reached Miss Mayfield by the village grapevine, which had been given most of it by Sydney himself. In Sydney's presence, Wesley Baines had attempted a clumsy teasing of Emily's way of receiving the news. And she had asked, well, how had *he* received it, and he had told her what he had said and what Canon Thorby had said.

Sydney had slept well on Saturday night, had eaten an enormous breakfast on Sunday morning; his temperature was normal, he had no pain; he was allowed to go home. On Monday, after two more enormous meals and a good night's sleep, he had announced his intention of going to school; and there for the whole day, unchecked by Miss Mayfield, he had been the centre of attention, with his 'My mum said to my dad,' 'My dad said to my mum' and 'Canon said to my dad.' No other child in Walwyk had ever been in hospital, and pressed for details about procedures there, Sydney was a disappointing informant.

'Most of the time I was asleep, see? Like the girl in the Bible.' But he had noticed that his bed had had wheels on it; and his Sunday breakfast egg had had a sort of woolly hat to keep it warm.

By the next day the excitement had died down. Miss Mayfield, eyeing Sydney carefully, concluded that he seemed to have suffered no damage. His mother's strange, almost distraught accusations against Mrs Rigby seemed like some detail from a nightmare remembered in bright sunlight. If only, she thought, I could be sure that Ethel's accident was an accident, I could be happy again.

On the Tuesday afternoon, she made an excuse to keep Sydney after school. When they were alone, she said:

'Have you seen Ethel since you were back, Sydney?'

'Yes. I went round yesterday afternoon. I thought she'd be in a muddle for rabbit food; but she wasn't. She'd gathered their food with her one hand.'

'I went to see her after we had our talk last Tuesday.'

'I know, Miss. Ethel told me.' His face took on a stubborn almost sullen expression.

'I thought Ethel and her grandmother seemed to be good friends. Sydney – I don't want to worry you or anything like that – but are you positively sure that what you said about the mangle was right? You were outside, you know. Perhaps you didn't have a good view.'

He turned his head and, biting at his lower lip, stared at the wall. He took two deep, quick breaths, like someone who has been running; then he moved his head and looked into Miss Mayfield's eyes with a desperate, trapped expression.

'I'm going to say it. Ethel said not to. Ethel said next time . . . Miss, what I said was *true*. Honest to God, Miss Mayfield. I saw her do it. But there's something Ethel is more afraid of. Something Ethel is real afraid of; she can't even tell me. So Ethel said, please don't say about it, or take any notice, because there's nothing anybody can do.'

'Did you tell Ethel that you had told me anything?'

'No, she told me. The minute we was out getting the greenstuff, she said, "Did you send Miss Mayfield round to Gran's?" And I said yes I did. And then she told me about the cake and drinking the wine. And she said never, never talk about her or her gran again.'

'Did she tell you why?'

'No.'

'Have you' – it seemed strange, a little unseemly, to ask such a question of a twelve-year-old – 'have you any ideas of your own about it, Sydney?'

He nodded.

'Ethel is afraid of something that might happen if her gran got angry.'

'Might happen to Ethel?'

'No. Ethel never said . . . but I think it might be her rabbits.'

With disconcerting suddenness and clarity, the voice in Miss Mayfield's mind said, *Or her friend Sydney.* And that would explain the vehemence with which Ethel had denied being fond of Sydney.

Miss Mayfield decided to venture one more question.

'And you've no idea, Sydney, what lies behind it all? No idea of what it is that Ethel's grandmother wishes her to do?'

'No, Miss. Ethel never said. She said it was something, and that she'd never do it, even if it did mean giving up the rabbits.'

'Well, thank you, Sydney. You've been as helpful as possible. And I promise you that I shall keep a sharp eye on Ethel.'

'Without her gran knowing, please, Miss. Ethel said poking and prying just made things worse.'

'I'll be very careful.'

When he was gone, Miss Mayfield tidied her desk, performing the routine task absent-mindedly. The talk with Sydney, unilluminating as it had been, had darkened, rather than lightened, her mood. She might say to herself at one moment that she was placing altogether too much importance upon the subject, but something mysterious remained, and the next moment there she was again, asking herself, why this, why that, why, why, why?

On Wednesday her attention was diverted by a visit from Her Majesty's Inspector of Schools, Mr Culpeper. It was not, as in Alchester, an unheralded try-to-catch-you-out visitation. Canon Thorby, arriving at ten o'clock to give his Maths lesson, said:

'Oh, by the way, Mr Culpeper, HMI, is over at Renham this morning; he's coming to lunch, and afterwards I'll bring him in to meet you. You'll like him; he's a good chap.'

Experience caused Miss Mayfield to doubt that; good chaps did not become inspectors. Inspectors were all cranks – at least in Alchester. They didn't wish you to teach a child to write a decent letter and address an envelope properly; they wanted more self-expression, something called Free Drama or Eurhythmics; they had almost religious attachments to some unusual form of handwriting, script, or italic; they thought history could be taught by the making of a puppet theatre, geography by the installation of a rain gauge, and that disciplinary problems could all be solved by the setting up of a class committee before which the behaviour of the teacher could be criticized as freely as that of the most disturbing element in the class. None of these quirks – some of which Mr Culpeper *must* share in order to have reached his present rank – seemed to Miss Mayfield to contribute to good chappery'.

However, within five minutes of meeting Mr Culpeper she was willing to forgive him his profession. He was the exception which proved the rule. He was a good-looking man, in his forties, with dark hair and dancing brown eyes; and he was a gentleman, Miss Mayfield concluded in her old-fashioned way. She remembered that Matthew Arnold had been a school inspector.

They chatted easily for half an hour, and then she was able to bring up the matter of the eleven-plus examination, and was pleased to hear Mr Culpeper say:

'It's a thing I feel strongly about. Every child should take it, even those at the most expensive prep schools; it's a safeguard against a change of circumstances. I don't think Canon Thorby is at all averse to the idea, but Mrs Westleton was dead against it. I think she feared that a Walwyk eleven-year-old might fail to pass and that the failure would reflect on her. It was an odd thing; she was here for many years, immensely popular – you could almost say well beloved – but she was, personally, most unconfident and insecure, I once broached the subject of the eleven-plus to her and she was so upset that I promised Canon Thorby never to mention it again. I'm so glad you brought it up.'

'Well, you see, there is a case . . .' and she told him about Mrs Baines's wish to leave Walwyk and the problem it evoked regarding Sydney's future.

'Now, he,' said Mr Culpeper, 'sounds the perfect candidate for what is known in Wandford as Old Bogey's Brass. In 1852 a prosperous farmer at Catermarsh, named John Bogey, founded a scholarship open to any boy of Catermarsh, Renham or Walwyk – candidates to be taken in that order – who wished to go to Wandford Grammar School, where John Bogey, had himself been educated. I don't think there has been a candidate for it for the last eighteen or twenty years; the people it was meant to benefit – the ambitious poor – don't take readily to the idea of a boarding school; and there are nowadays so many alternatives. Unless this lad you mention is demonstrably certifiable, the scholarship is his the moment he applies for it. In fact, the trustees were considering the possibility of converting the funds to other uses. They'd be delighted to have a candidate. May I send you the papers?'

They arrived on Friday morning in a long foolscap envelope. After tea, on that afternoon, Miss Mayfield went to call upon Mrs Baines, filled with something of the excited feeling which is the result of having been able to present to somebody exactly the thing desired. Nine days before, Mrs Baines had expressed two wishes, that Sydney should recover from his illness and that the family should be able to move from Walwyk. Sydney had recovered; and here was Miss Mayfield bringing the glad tidings that the move would not ruin – but, rather, improve – Sydney's educational prospects. She thought that this would be a very happy visit.

It went wrong from the very beginning. Mrs Baines opened the workroom door, and Miss Mayfield was shocked by her appearance. She had heard that Mrs Baines had looked dreadful upon her return from Wandford, but that was almost a week ago; and she still looked dreadful in the way peculiar to big, strongly built women who lose their flesh. She was as neat as ever, in a bright red-and-white patterned dress, with a string of red beads and matching earrings, but she was hollow-cheeked and so fundamentally pale that the applied colour on her cheeks and lips stood out like a clown's paint.

She said, in a cold, dull way, 'Come in, Miss Mayfield,' and ushered her through the workroom into the cheerful, bright sitting room.

'I haven't seen you since that dreadful afternoon,' Miss Mayfield said. 'It was a wonderful recovery, wasn't it?'

'I should have come and thanked you for helping me that day; I know that,' Mrs Baines said in a voice the reverse of grateful.

'I didn't do anything.' She produced the envelope. 'I have made a discovery that I hope will please you. About Sydney, you remember?'

'Oh, that! I've given up all thought of moving.'

'I see. Well, all the same, I think that you might be interested in this.' Miss Mayfield spread out the papers and explained the situation.

'Mr Culpeper was certain that he would get the scholarship,' she ended, 'and, you know, I'm not sure that in the end it might not be to Sydney's advantage to go to a bigger school, where there were boys of his own age, more fun, and more competition. . . .'

'You could say that of all of them.'

'I do say it.'

For the first time, Mrs Baines spoke with some expression in her voice; she said, with a sudden and alarming spitefulness:

'You'd be out of a job!'

'Out of Walwyk, but not unemployed, I hope. I admit that from my point of view it is a very pleasant post, but that is not the first consideration. The Walwyk school has many advantages, but I don't think we should be blind to the disadvantages. Lack of classmates of one's own age and sex is a great drawback.'

'Ah, now you're thinking about Ethel and Sydney. Well, I'll admit I was wrong there. Ethel's all right.'

'If you mean as a companion for Sydney, I never doubted *that*. Or did you perhaps mean that you've changed your mind about the relationship between Ethel and her grandmother; is that *all right*?'

Even in her own ears, the question sounded forced and contrived. Mrs Baines received it with a look of naked antagonism.

'We all make mistakes,' she said.

'Indeed we do. But you vouched for Sydney's truthfulness, and he saw . . .'

'He stood outside and *thought* he saw. There's the long and short of it, Miss Mayfield. A lot of to-do about nothing.'

The voice in Miss Mayfield's mind made its comment with its usual clarity. *Mrs Baines has changed sides*, it said.

'I'd be happy to think that you were right. Let's leave all that. Let's think of Sydney and his future.'

'If he went to Wandford Grammar, he'd have to be a boarder.'

'A weekly boarder. You'd see him every Friday evening and—'

'I wish,' Mrs Baines said, interrupting rudely, 'you'd *think* before you go rushing at things. How'd he get home on Friday? Walk from Renham bus stop? In winter, snow and fog. Even you, Miss Mayfield, can't believe that Canon Thorby is going to send the car to fetch home a boy who didn't think his pet school was good enough for him.'

'Well . . . no; I admit I hadn't considered every little detail.' To her immense surprise, she found herself growing angry. 'I only received these papers this morning. Nine days ago *you* came to me, asking what would happen to Sydney if you decided to move. I made what inquiry I could and bring you the result . . . Why are you so cross with me?'

Mrs Baines said quickly. 'Because you are so interfering.' Having said that, her face, her manner underwent a change, and she continued in a pleasant but false way:

'I know you mean well. That afternoon I was silly and hysterical and said a lot of things I didn't really mean. All about moving, and so on. And then, with Sydney ill, everybody was so kind and helpful, I realized where I was well off. It'd be silly to move. Sydney can stay here and do like Juliet Reeve is doing, if he's clever enough. I'm sorry you took so much trouble and I'm sorry to seem so ungrateful . . .'

'That doesn't matter in the least; I took no trouble at all. And, of course, it is for you to decide. Look, I'll leave the papers with you; you might . . .' She stood up, and Mrs Baines rose hurriedly and went with her to the door. There, in the bright light, Miss Mayfield noticed again how very unwell the other woman looked.

'You don't look at all well, Mrs Baines,' she said gently. 'I'm afraid the strain has told on you.'

'You should never say that kind of thing; it makes people feel sorry for themselves.' She softened this remark by giving a glimmer of a smile, quickly quenched. 'I'm all right,' she said.

They exchanged good evenings, and Miss Mayfield walked towards the gate, at which, just before she reached it, Sydney appeared, holding a handleless basket, covered by a piece of sacking, clutched against his stomach and a bundle of cow parsley under one arm. Thus burdened, he fumbled at the latch of the gate, and Miss Mayfield hurried forward and opened it for him.

'Hullo, Miss,' he said cheerfully. 'Look what I've got. Ethel just gave it to me.'

He nipped the bundle of greenstuff closer to his side and pulled loose the corner of the piece of sacking. Miss Mayfield caught a glimpse of a rabbit, a young one, prettily marked with black and white, crouched in the basket, its eyes bulging with fear. Before she could say 'How pretty', it had leaped, landed with a soft plop and was away among the gooseberry bushes.

With some presence of mind, Miss Mayfield closed the gate. Sydney gave a yelp, dropped the basket and the cow parsley and set off in pursuit. For the next ten minutes they stalked the rabbit, swerving, dodging, heading it off, not speaking, and moving as quietly as possible so as not to alarm it. At the end of that time they had worked down along the side of the cottage, and then to its rear. There, in an angle formed by the out-jutting scullery against the back wall of the sitting room, Sydney recaptured his rabbit, and Miss Mayfield, completely winded, leaned against the wall to recover her breath. From where she stood she had an uninterrupted view of the room within. Mrs Baines had spread out all the papers concerning the scholarship on the table and was sitting with her elbows on them, her head propped on her hands and her face wearing an expression of such utter misery and despair as Miss Mayfield had seldom seen.

Mastering her breath at last, she said, 'Sydney, you should feed the rabbit now; that would help it to settle down. I'm just going to have another word with your mother.'

She entered by the back door, stepped across the scrupulously tidy scullery and through into the sitting room.

'Mrs Baines,' she said, 'I can see that something about all this is causing you great distress. Couldn't you tell me and let us see . . .'

Mrs Baines jumped up, sending her chair screeching backwards. Her face flushed, her voice coarsened with fury.

'Get out! Don't ever come in my house again till I ask you. It's all your fault. Poking and prying. Nosey old maid. Bothering about Ethel Rigby. What's she worth compared with my boy? A tart's brat, doomed before she was born. And on her account look where you've landed me, that was always a decent woman. I'm the one that has to pay for your blundering, I'd like to . . .'

She stopped suddenly, and the angry colour seemed to fall away from her face; she stared beyond Miss Mayfield towards the scullery door. Miss Mayfield turned, expecting to see either Sydney or Wesley, her mind already fumbling for some feasible, smooth words that might explain this angry tirade. There was nobody there, nothing there, until she dropped her gaze to below the level where a human being would stand; and there, just in the doorway, was the cat which was called Vesper in one place and in another, Smut.

Later on, looking back, she was to say to herself that at such-and-such a point she *knew* what she suspected, and that point, like the horizon to a traveller, seemed to move onwards with her own advance through time. Actually, she knew at that moment, but presently dismissed what she knew as too preposterous for belief.

She felt sick with the kind of sickness which descent in a badly managed lift can induce. And she knew that what she suspected must be concealed.

'My cat,' she said, in a bright false voice. 'He follows me everywhere.'

In an equally false, though not bright, voice, Mrs Baines said:

'I'm sorry I spoke as I did. To tell the truth, you've upset me. I want the best for Sydney – and you may be right, this may be best. But he's only just back out of hospital; I *can't* part with him again, it's not to be expected. But, on the other hand, what you said made me feel guilty. That's what I meant about always having been a decent woman; you've made me feel selfish. That's why I snapped out at you.'

Oh no, Miss Mayfield thought; plausible, but no! And the outburst against Ethel, completely unexplained.

She said, 'You must forgive me – and my cat.'

Halfway along the garden path she met Wesley Baines, who carried his carpenter's bag. He greeted her with a genuine smile.

'Sydney and I have been having a rabbit hunt,' she said and described it.

'So he got it, did he? I made him a hutch. Week or two back, Em wouldn't hear of his keeping a rabbit, but she's come round.'

'One is manageable; it is the families which make the problem,' Miss Mayfield said.

'You're right there. And one we're sticking to, if I have any say.'

Letting herself into her house, she felt, on this evening, for the first time, what Canon Thorby had called isolation. She longed for someone to whom she could have talked, exposed even the most fantastic ideas without being thought a fool. Rose would have been the perfect person;

94

her self-denying, almost saintly life had not blinkered a lively and inquiring mind. She would have listened, gone with Miss Mayfield to the imaginative limit and then produced her own logical explanation of it all.

There must *be* a logical explanation.

Janet Lovelace, on the other hand, would have listened to the whole story purely for its entertainment value, added several fantastic suppositions of her own in order to enhance it and then destroyed the whole structure with a burst of hearty laughter, saying, 'What nonsense!'

It must *be* nonsense.

But there was no one to talk to, and her thoughts went round and round in her head, getting nowhere, like circus horses. At last she took a piece of paper and wrote on it in small letters, so light as to be almost invisible, two lists, side by side. Oh the left-hand side she put down what she knew or believed; on the right, her suspicions.

Mrs Baines has changed.	Mrs B. believed Mrs R. gave gave her shingles and made S. ill. She came home on that Saturday and made a bargain.
Ethel says her grand-mother wants something of her.	Some participation in some-thing occult?
Ethel has rabbits and is fond of Sydney, but denies it.	Rabbits and Sydney threat-ened; so Ethel pretends.

She stared at the paper for a moment and then on the right-hand side, hardly touching the paper at all, wrote:

Granny R. is a witch and the cat is her familiar.

'Really,' she said to herself in an expostulatory tone; and spent several minutes tearing the paper into fragments smaller than confetti. Even these she was careful to mix thoroughly with the wet tea-leaves before putting them into the dustbin.

8

ON THE FOLLOWING MONDAY MORNING ETHEL
Rigby returned to school with a handkerchief drenched in
eucalyptus, to support the legend of the cold, and some
inconspicuous pieces of surgical plaster on her fingers.
During the day the frequent – and, Miss Mayfield thought,
unnecessary – application of the handkerchief to her nose
turned it pink, and once, looking at her, Miss Mayfield was
reminded of the theory that people become like the pets
to which they are devoted. There was something rabbity
about Ethel's pale prettiness.

By three o'clock in the afternoon Miss Mayfield had
become irritated by Ethel, who throughout the day had
been markedly inattentive. The Walwyk school furniture
was surprisingly modern and functional; each child had a
desk with an adjustable top which, could be made to slope
or lie flat at will, and between this top and the floor, on the
right-hand side, were three open shelves for the accommodation of exercise books, pens, pencils and paints. On
four separate occasions during that Monday Miss Mayfield

– whose eye returned to Ethel more often than she realized – caught the girl taking out, looking at or hastily replacing some object from her top shelf.

On the fourth occasion she felt that some mild rebuke was called for, so she said:

'Ethel, you have missed almost two weeks' work, and you should be working hard to make up. Whatever it is that is diverting your attention, please leave it alone, or I shall have to ask you to put it on my desk.'

Ethel turned scarlet and behaved impeccably for the rest of the session.

At four o'clock, with the class dismissed, again without fully realizing what she was doing or why, Miss Mayfield looked at Ethel Rigby and noted that she was empty-handed. And the moment the door was closed and she was alone with her pile of books to be marked, Miss Mayfield went to Ethel's desk.

The top shelf held nothing which might not be expected to be there, nor did the second, and the third seemed unrewarding, too, until Miss Mayfield, reaching in to pull out a paintbox, felt the back of her hand brush against something that was fastened to the division between the second and third compartments. She closed her fingers about it – it felt like a small box – and pulled. There was a ripping sound, and there in her hand was a little cardboard box, with the ends of the surgical plaster which had held it to the top of the compartment falling limply on either side.

She noted, with a curious detachment, that her fingers had begun to tremble and had turned hot, damp and limp. She had been curious to know what it was that had been distracting Ethel's attention, and she had looked for it and found it. But now . . . now she was reluctant to push forward with her investigation. She stood there holding the little box slightly away from her, as though it might explode.

At last she opened the lid and saw some harmless cotton wool. The thought came to her that this was something which a girl, a pupil of hers, treasured, had wrapped in cotton-wool and tried – not without skill – to hide. What right had she to pry? What right? What reason?

Using the very tips of her finger and thumb, she lifted the cotton-wool covering and looked down at the object thus revealed without any surprise, with, indeed, a momentary satisfaction – I knew it! I knew it all along!

It was a little figure made from a length of softened-down candle, greyish white in colour and semi-opaque. It was male – indeed, its sex was exaggerated out of all proportion – and it was in two parts; the whole of the top of its head had been cut off and was still separate, like an Indian scalp, but pressed into position by the bolstering of the cotton-wool in which it lay, cotton-wool that was specked and flecked with little bits of something that looked like the broken brittle remains of some green leaf.

The voice in Miss Mayfield's mind said, *This is Sydney. Granny Rigby made it and severed the top of the head. Cut off his consciousness. Ethel put the whole thing together and wrapped it in cotton-wool to keep it safe.*

What madness is this? This is the year nineteen hundred and fifty-nine. Nobody has believed in witchcraft for at least two hundred years; the laws against it have been repealed; and here I stand, an ordinary God-fearing village schoolteacher . . . with the evidence *in my hand*.

But it's a joke, a well-worn joke; make a wax model and stick pins in it. Janet Lovelace had a record of some of the numbers from a popular West End revue: a man parked in a place inconvenient to another man, who said he'd make a wax model of the intruder's big end (whatever that might be) and stick pins in it. In the record you could hear the hearty laughter that greeted that joke. Yes, it was a joke nowadays.

Not to Sydney. Not to his mother. Not to Ethel. And not to me. God help me, not to me!

She remembered how she had prayed, very humbly, either to be given some sign in this bewildering situation or to be given the strength of mind to dismiss it.

Was this the sign?

Equally urgent was the question: What to do with it? She was tempted to take it and lock it away somewhere, so that at some future date, if she ever needed it, she could produce it. But why should she ever need it? And had she the right to take it? It belonged to Ethel just as much as any other piece of property.

In the end, she replaced the cotton-wool, closed the box and fixed it back into position with the ends of sticky tape. Then she tried to forget it but couldn't, and found herself, almost every day, under a neurotic compulsion to check on its presence. Day after day, as soon as school was dismissed for the afternoon, she would go to Ethel's desk and push in an exploratory hand. The little box was always there. Ethel, having hit on a safe hiding place, was content to leave her secret there.

More than a week passed before anything noticeable happened.

At the very beginning of the term, Canon Thorby had spoken, about the Fête which was held every year on the third Saturday in July in the Rectory garden.

'Ostensibly,' he said, 'it is to raise funds for the National Children's Homes. My mother started it when it was called Waifs and Strays. I personally would rather write a cheque and be saved the bother and mess, but I can see that it is a social occasion justifying a new frock. We have coconut shies and bowling for a pig and a buried treasure and all the usual things, including – and this is where you come in – some kind of entertainment by the school children.' He put on a half-comic, half-serious look of appeal. 'And *please*, dear Miss Mayfield, could it not be animated nursery rhymes this year? Mrs Westleton's inventiveness stopped short there, and apart from comparing this year's Miss Muffet with last year's – always to her detriment – interest is completely dead. Of course,' he added hastily, 'I know it is difficult to find anything which makes use of such diverse ages and sizes. Nobody must be left out.'

She said, rather tentatively, 'Once, in Alchester, we did little scenes from history – very simple: Raleigh spreading his cloak for Queen Elizabeth; Charles the First going to his beheading, and so on. Do you think they'd find that kind of thing dull?'

'If you but knew! No, I'm sure they'd be delighted. You'd need a lot of costumes, but you can always hire those.'

'We could make *some*. You see, that wouldn't link it with the sewing as well as the history lessons. I really am a great believer in correlation, though I believe that is frowned upon now as being old-fashioned.'

'I think that is a splendid idea – just so long as you don't undertake too much and make a chore of it.'

The girls had taken eagerly to the idea of making costumes instead of dull everyday garments. Audrey Head, whose mother was the village dressmaker, proved to be an expert and rapid worker on the sewing machine, and during the sewing lesson with which the week always closed, on a date which Miss Mayfield remembered – the twenty-ninth of May – Audrey was very anxious to have a fitting. One of the garments sufficiently advanced to be fitted was the black one in which Ethel Rigby, as Mary Queen of Scots, was to appear.

Miss Mayfield, who was eager for the girls themselves to take the responsibility for the costumes, remained in the background while they bustled excitedly about, bossed by Audrey, who presently said:

'Come *on*, Ethel. This is yours.'

'Can't I try it on over my jumper? Save pulling my hair about.'

'No, you can't. This is going to *fit*. Bother your hair; I'll lend you my comb afterwards.' With the black dress, looking very long and limp, hanging over her arm, Audrey advanced purposefully towards Ethel, who backed away.

'I don't want you pulling me about, Audrey Head,' she said sullenly. 'Here, give it to me.'

She snatched the dress and retreated until she was standing with her back to the wall, and there she carefully removed her jersey and skirt and stepped into the dress, contorting herself in order to work the long zipper at the back of it. Miss Mayfield and Audrey, in conference, had decided to allow the anachronism in order to facilitate ease in changing.

Over Miss Mayfield's mind there rippled a thought which had nothing to do with Ethel in her capacity as old Mrs Rigby's granddaughter; it was a self-congratulatory thought. I chose well, she said to herself; she *is* just that degree less buxom than any of the others; she might very well have 'sat out her twenty years at Fotheringhay'. All the girls, indeed, were altered by their costumes, but Ethel was transformed into beauty and a kind of sad dignity.

Miss Mayfield said:

'I never thought, until now, that you should wear a ruff, Ethel; I'm not sure that anyone would, in the circumstances; but you must have a big upstanding ruff, and you must take it off – rather slowly – and that will be a kind of symbol of resignation.'

'I ain't absolutely sure that hem is level,' said Audrey with self-important self-criticism.

'I am not,' Miss Mayfield corrected her.

'You neither?' said Audrey, misunderstanding. 'Turn round, Ethel. No, not like that – slowly. I'm right; it cocks up on the left.'

She went down on her knees and busied herself with the pins.

Miss Mayfield, under cover of watching this operation, went close, took a position slightly behind Ethel, and when Audrey said, 'There, that'll do. Nothing else wrong that I can see,' Miss Mayfield leaned forward and ran down the zipper.

With admirable self-control she only said:

'All right, Ethel, you can get dressed. And now, Audrey, what about your own?'

Half an hour later she sat alone in the deserted school-room, brooding.

Once – and although it was in time so recently, it seemed half a lifetime away – Canon Thorby had told her that if ever she needed a woman confidante, his sister was the one to go to. And now, little as the idea appealed to her, it seemed the right thing to do . . . And I shall take that little doll, just to prove that I am not imagining things, she thought.

She rose and went through the now familiar motion of feeling under Ethel's desk. The box had gone. Between the Thursday afternoon and Friday, it had been removed. All that remained to show that it had ever been there was a slight stickiness where the tape had adhered for so many days.

I was a fool not to have taken it while I had the chance, she told herself bitterly. Then she had a second thought; far, far better to approach this on the level of fact, not of fancy. What she imagined and what she suspected had no part to play here at all.

She went home, made a rather stronger pot of tea than usual and forced herself to drink it calmly. Then she washed her face in cold water and combed her hair. It was just half-past five when she rang the bell at the Rectory and was admitted by Reeve, who, when she asked for Miss Thorby, said nothing to indicate that Miss Thorby was not receiving that afternoon. However, shown into a room which she had not entered on her first visit and which she saw was a library, she was greeted by the Canon, who said with a kind of mock plaintiveness:

'Please, will I do?' He then added, in his ordinary manner, 'Poor Isabel has one of her incapacitating headaches and is lying down.'

'I'd rather tell you about it, really; but you did once tell me that Miss Thorby . . .'

'I quite understand. Oh dear me, you do look troubled. Sit down and tell me everything.'

'This afternoon we were fitting on the costumes for our scenes at the Fête, and when it was Ethel Rigby's turn, I found . . .'

'That you'd run out of material? Dear Miss Mayfield, let that be the least of your worries. I told you to hire what was needed.'

'Ethel Rigby,' Miss Mayfield said in a dogged voice, 'had had, very recently, a really savage beating.'

'What? Ethel Rigby?'

'Ethel Rigby. And I think I should tell you that I have, before this, been told that her grandmother ill-treats her.'

'Old Phoebe Rigby ill-treat Ethel! Miss Mayfield, that

is palpable nonsense; there isn't a more doting, indulgent . . .' He sought for some final, clinching adjective.

'I know. I've heard all that, Canon Thorby. And I know it *looks* that way. The girl herself *connives* to maintain that impression. But I can't believe it, not after what I saw this afternoon.'

'Oh, well,' he said, 'we can soon settle the truth of this. I'll go straight round there and see for myself. You can come with me or not, just as you prefer.'

'I'll come. I'm the one who made the accusation.'

There's probably some – I won't say reason; physical violence is never reasonable, but some justification. Though there again I must admit that Ethel never struck me as a girl who needed chastisement. If Reeve, now, took a stick to that baggage Juliet, nobody could blame him; Ethel always seems a bit spiritless; but, of course, how they seem in public and how they behave at home are very different things.'

'Nothing,' said Miss Mayfield flatly, 'could possibly have earned a girl such a thrashing.'

'Dear me, as bad as that?' He looked at her sideways from his greater height. 'You'll excuse me asking this, won't you – is this your first brush with this kind of thing?'

'Not quite . . .' She told him about the cases in Alchester, adding, 'Africans are extremely indulgent to their children when they are young, but they have some . . . some very brutal customs, which I had to learn to live with. I'm not unduly squeamish.'

'No, of course. I was forgetting. You have such a delicate, Dresden-china air, you know; one thinks of you as having been in a glass cabinet all your life. And I suppose the very reverse is true.'

Mrs Rigby said, 'Good evening, sir,' and then, with greatly diminished cordiality, 'Good evening, Miss,' and ushered them into the parlour, She knows why we are here, Miss Mayfield thought; and was glad of the Canon's support.

The old woman, having seen them seated, sat down herself on one of the hard straight chairs and folded her hands in her lap.

Canon Thorby, maintaining an easy and affable manner, went straight to the point.

'Mrs Rigby, Ethel had cause to remove her dress in school this afternoon and Miss Mayfield saw, to her consternation, that her back shows marks of a beating. A pretty severe beating.'

'Be a funny thing if it didn't,' Mrs Rigby said with no sign of being abashed or repentant. 'Laid it on good and hard, I did. She'll bear the marks for a week, I reckon.'

'May we know why you beat her?'

'You may. You'll understand, sir. I'm not having her go the way Maud went, at least not for lack of a hiding to bring her to her senses.'

'Not that old trouble already?'

'Sorry as I am to say it, that is so. I'll name no names for the present, and I've knocked sense into Ethel I *think*, but if I have any more bother, I shall ask you to hev a word with the chap. Everything else apart, she's only fourteen and, sometimes I think, not all that bright.'

'I'll do more than have a word,' he said sternly. 'To

PETER CURTIS

revert to Ethel. Don't you think she is a little old to be
whipped? Have you tried other persuasions?'

'I've talked till I was black in the face. Now, you're both
clever people, you tell me; what do you do with a girl of
fourteen who turns round and says, "I'll do what I like"?
Specially' – her voice almost broke – 'when you know what
happened before and can look back . . . and remember.'

'I know, I know,' Canon Thorby said hastily. 'It is a
very trying situation. You know, you may be a little over-
anxious. History seldom so exactly repeats itself. Would
you mind if I had a word with Ethel?'

'Why should I? She's right here.' She opened the door
into the back room and called. Ethel came in, carrying her
knitting. It was some of the dish-cloth yarn which,
smeared with aluminium paint, was to be chain mail in
some of the scenes. The elder girls had been entrusted to
work on it at home.

'Hullo, Ethel,' the Canon said. 'I should like you to tell
me, in your own words, exactly what happened last
evening.'

'What about last evening, sir?'

'Weren't you punished?'

Ethel swung round on her grandmother and said
venomously:

'What did you want to go telling about that for? You
hit me, didn't you? Wasn't that enough? D'you want to
make me look a fool in front of everybody?'

'It was I, Ethel. I saw your back when I unzipped the
dress this afternoon. I thought something should be done
about it.'

'Oh.' From lowered sulky eyes Ethel shot Miss Mayfield a look of hatred.

'If you'd looked a little closer. Miss,' said Mrs Rigby with cold politeness, 'you'd have seen that something was done. She had lotion on the stripes last night and again this morning; She's my own flesh and blood; I don't like hurting her. But running round and answering back I just will not have.'

'Ed Woodly only walked down the lane with me, if you call that running round,' Ethel said insolently.

'That,' said Canon Thorby, 'is no way to speak to your grandmother. One of these days, when you are older and have more sense, you'll realize how much you owe her. You should be ashamed to cause her such anxiety.'

'She is, sir. She is,' the old woman said defensively. 'Thass why she spoke so sharp.' She turned to Miss Mayfield. 'There's only so much that schools are responsible for, you know, Miss, and others we have to take care of ourselves as best we can.'

'You're right, up to a point, Mrs Rigby,' Canon Thorby put in. 'I'm sure Miss Mayfield would be the first to . . .'

To what? Confess herself mistaken? Apologize? I will not. I'm still not *convinced*. I don't know why, but I'm not; made to look a fool again, but not convinced.

'I think any teacher – or anyone else, for that matter – who saw such marks on a child is morally bound to do something.'

'Well, what are you going to do?' Mrs Rigby spoke quietly, but insolently for all that.

'I asked Canon Thorby's advice. And I feel bound to

mention that he has no knowledge of the extent of the lacerations.'

'That's easily remedied. Ethel, off with that jumper.'

'Look,' Ethel said, 'I sauced you and you give me a hiding. I ain't going to be made a peep-show of.' She put the knitting on the table and doubled one hand into a fist and, bending her arm behind her, gave herself a clout between the shoulder blades. 'Don't hurt,' she said.

But that was a lie; Miss Mayfield had seen the skin go white and tight around her mouth and the root of her nose.

'There been about enough fuss over this,' Ethel said, and opened the door of the back room, went through and slammed it smartly behind her.

'You see,' Mrs Rigby said.

'Yes. You have your hands full. One thing rather stands out, though, doesn't it, Mrs Rigby? Beating her doesn't seem very effective.'

'Well, sir, it was a try. I've still got a trick or two up my sleeve. And, sir, I don't want you to say I complained about Ed Woodly; it was Ethel brought his name in. I daresay I was hasty. They weren't up to any real harm, but you know what he is, bad as they come; and when she turned cheeky, I did lose my temper and laid on a bit harder than I meant.'

When? Miss Mayfield wondered, trying to visualize the scene. The beating had not been administered through Ethel's clothing, of that she was almost sure.

'By the way,' Mrs Rigby was saying, 'I wrote out that recipe for pot-purry Miss Isabel asked me about when mine took the prize. Now you are here, p'raps you'd take it; we shall soon be saving up the rose petals.'

She went to the cupboard and returned with a piece of paper, which the Canon folded and placed carefully in his wallet. He rose as he did so.

'Don't go forgetting it, now,' she said, smiling.

'I'll try not to. Well, Mrs Rigby, I'm sorry about all this. I shall take the first opportunity of saying a few words about obedience and respect to parents and elders, and I'll have a tactful word with Master Woodly, too. He'll find himself out of a job if he doesn't mend his ways.'

'Please, sir, not over this bit of silliness. Why, I've known his mother since she was about as old as Ethel is now; together in service, once we were. I wouldn't have her heart broke just for a bit of thing like this. Mind, he's bad, no denying that – with girls, I mean – but he's good to his mother, and I wouldn't on no account . . .'

'All right, Mrs Rigby, we'll forget it, this once. And go easy on Ethel, will you? She's at a difficult age and I'm sure there's no real vice in her. Goodnight.'

As they walked along Curlew Lane, he said:

'Well, do you feel happier about it now?'

After too long a pause, she said, 'I suppose I have to be.'

'Old Phoebe let her temper get the better of her, that's plain, and I think she's ashamed of it but too proud to say so. You'd understand why she is a little unbalanced about boys if you knew her whole story.'

'Miss Benson did give me a bare outline.'

'A whipping, you know, is quite different from

prolonged neglect or the deliberate sadism that one reads about. There was a time when the highest people in the land beat their children.'

'Lady Jane Grey. Margery Paston. I know. What bothers me is Ethel's attitude.'

'Rude and defiant, I agree.'

'I didn't mean that exactly – though the rudeness and the defiance seemed to me to be out of character, assumed. No, what mystifies me is the way she *sides* with her grandmother.'

'Surely that is an indication that there is nothing very much wrong in their relationship.' He was silent for a moment, and Miss Mayfield could hear the soft sad cry of the wood-doves from the trees beyond the allotments. 'I haven't spent all my life in this peaceful backwater. For four years, immediately after my ordination, I was a curate in a very poor parish in East London. A case or two of cruelty to children came to my notice there, and I assure you that no child, even in the safeguarding presence of strangers, would have dared speak to the person who had ill-used it as Ethel Rigby just spoke to her grandmother.'

'Unless it had been told to, as part of the deception, so the people who asked questions should come away saying exactly the thing which you have just said.'

He stopped still on the path.

'How very shrewd!' he exclaimed. Then, walking on, he said, 'It might be true in some cases, I suppose. But not in this. They had no time to concoct a tale. The old woman opened the door and called Ethel in. Ethel's performance was quite unrehearsed, I am sure. I can't seriously imagine old Granny Rigby laying on the stripes and saying, "If anybody asks you, whack, how you came to be beaten, whack, you're to say, whack whack, that you'd been running round with boys." Can you?'

'Not when it's put like that,' she said a trifle wearily. 'But there could be a kind of over-all understanding that any inquiry was to be fobbed off, lest something worse should happen.'

There was a slight grit of impatience in his voice when he next spoke:

'I do think, you know, that you're making it all unnecessarily complicated. I've known Phoebe Rigby all my life. She isn't a sadistic, scheming, deeply cunning child-beater; she's a poor simple old woman whose one darling daughter ended up on the streets and who is terrified of her granddaughter going the same way. By the same token, she's known me a long time, too, and when I say "Go easy on Ethel", she takes it as the order it was meant to be. I have my village well in hand, Miss Mayfield, casual as I may seem. Now, let's speak of a more cheerful subject. How are the scenes from history shaping up?'

They had by this time almost reached her house, having taken the little footpath directly across the Green.

'Most of the children are word-perfect. But, of course, it's the *spectacle* we count on to rouse interest; it's to look at more than to listen to. The colours really are rather nice. As a matter of fact, I have the sketches I made for them indoors at this moment. Would you like to see them?'

She was faintly aware of being sycophantic; she had annoyed him and wanted to get back into his good graces.

'I'd like that very much,' he said.

They entered her house and went into the sitting room, where she spread the gay drawings on the sofa, and floor. Canon Thorby sat down in a chair and once again suffered one of his physical collapses. Miss Mayfield realized that the little episode just ended had exhausted him; his colour had faded, all the lines of his face sagged in an immense weariness. She remembered Miss Thorby's headache. His life probably contained unsuspected strains and stresses.

She said, in a voice which she did not know was almost maternal:

'May I get you one of your own drinks, Canon Thorby?'

'That would be very kind indeed. I've had rather a brute of a day. And this . . . Absurd as it seems, I always loathe having to take anybody to task. I know it has to be done, and I do it, but it does go against the grain.'

'I can see that.'

He shot her a glance. 'Most people aren't so perspicacious; they think I go through life like a well-upholstered steam roller.' He smiled.

'Would you like sherry?' she asked, anxious to minister to him.

'Not, alas, the sherry which I, remembering Mrs Westleton's taste, provided for you. I like only dry sherry, so if you'll give me brandy and soda again, I shall be very happy.'

When she returned to the room, he had revived again, and began to talk with great enthusiasm of her drawings.

'They're absolutely beautiful. I'd no idea you had such

talent. They're professional. What do you intend to do with them?'

'They've served their purpose. The costumes are now in the making.'

'Well, they're certainly not going back into that portfolio, to blush unseen. With your permission, we'll have them framed. And then, for a start, we'll exhibit them at the Fête. . . . Yes, in the Orangery, where the teas are served. . . . Just to show off what talent we now have in Walwyk. And then, after that – well, we'll see. . . .'

Miss Mayfield, who had a modest estimate of her own skill, decided that he was being exaggeratedly complimentary to make up for having been a little out of temper with her.

9

'I WANT,' SAID MISS MAYFIELD, WITH THE DIFFID-
ence of one aware of being in alien territory, 'a bottle of
sherry. And it mustn't be sweet.'

'A dry sherry,' said the young man behind the vast
mahogany counter, speaking like an actor throwing away
a line.

'Yes. At least . . .' She was not sure that she had heard
aright. 'Not sweet,' she repeated, in order to be on the safe
side. 'And I want the best.'

'Tío Pepe? Amontillado?'

'Whichever is the better. I know nothing about it,' she
added unnecessarily.

Just then a door in the glass-and-mahogany partition
behind the counter opened and Mr Walter Freeman, sole
survivor of the families of Freeman and Marsh who had
given their names to the business more than two hundred
years earlier, stepped down into the shop. He was in his
sixties, a dandy, in an unobtrusive way, and he had been in
his youth, and for some years after it had fled, a bit of a

dog with the ladies. He had kept his eye for the type which appealed to him, and in some details Miss Mayfield complied with it. He liked little, fair, helpless women, and Miss Mayfield, who was small and fair, was, at that moment, looking the very epitome of helplessness. Regretfully noting that she was also dowdy, he nevertheless said, 'All right, Rowton,' and to Miss Mayfield, 'Perhaps I could help you.'

She was obliged to expose her ignorance for a second time, and this time was conscious of it, so that a faint pink colour rose in her cheeks.

'It's quite a decision,' Mr Freeman said gravely, 'and not one to make in a hurry. Would you like to come this way?'

He lifted a section of the counter, opened the door behind it and, with an air, conducted her into a big, comfortable room which in decoration and furnishing had scarcely changed since the original Walter Freeman and his cousin Richard Marsh had sat there.

'Do sit down,' he said, pushing a big leather chair an inch forward. Miss Mayfield did so, under the impression that sherry was sold in this special department, where – as in some clothes shops – it was not the done thing to have the goods on view. She was confirmed in this thought when Mr Freeman went to a cupboard. However, no bottles of sherry were revealed, but several decanters and some glasses.

'The only way to choose a sherry exactly to your taste is to sample it,' he said. 'Now, a dry sherry you said, I think.'

'But it isn't for me. I never drink it. It's just that

someone comes to see me now and again and I would like to have some sherry to offer him, and all I know is that he doesn't like it sweet.'

Mr Freeman, who was a busybody and liked knowing things about people just for the sake of knowing, said cunningly:

'I suppose the gentleman wouldn't, by any chance, be one of my customers.'

'I don't know. It's Canon Thorby, of Walwyk.'

'Then I can indeed advise you. Ever since the end of the old smuggling days we have had the honour to wait upon the Canon's family.'

He brought out the archaic phrase with no diminution of his dignity.

'This,' he said, taking up a decanter of a pale, almost straw-coloured liquid, 'is Canon Thorby's favourite. Are you sure that you would not like to make its acquaintance?'

'Thank you. Quite sure.'

Regretfully, he closed the cupboard.

'Walwyk is a most picturesque village, I understand. It sounds strange, perhaps, to have lived so near for so long and never seen it. But it's not the road *to* anywhere, and so . . .' He spread his hands in a gesture that finished the sentence.

'It's very pretty. And part of its charm perhaps depends upon it not being on a road to anywhere.'

'You have lived there long?'

'Only since the beginning of the term.'

Mentally, he snapped his fingers. Of course, Mrs Westleton's successor. School-teacher – and, poor dear, how in the world could she keep the modern young in order? – old maid, and like the rest of them, dazzled by the Canon, spending her hard-earned money on the 'best' sherry; for him. How very pathetic!

Two very different emotions dictated Mr Freeman's next action. One was a feeling of competition, hardly conscious; he was slightly older than the Canon, but dash it, he was well preserved and could be just as charming he was sure. The other feeling – and it was conscious – was of pity; he immediately forgave Miss Mayfield her dowdiness, attributing it to poor pay and the preference which everybody showed for drably dressed schoolteachers. Mentally, he reclothed her in the softly folded chiffon, the becoming flowered hat of his own 'best' period. She would be charming.

Aloud he said, after a glance at his watch:

'Since you don't drink sherry, perhaps you would like some coffee. Absolutely no trouble at all; they make it next door . . .' He opened another door, towards the rear of the premises; and spoke to someone invisible, telling them to pop next door and bring coffee for two, 'in a pot, mind, none of their sloppy cups. And a plate of macaroons.'

'So you live in Walwyk,' he said, resuming his seat and the thread of the conversation. He then mentioned Mr Frisby, and Miss Mayfield thought this was the moment to mention her mild little joke about the 'Frisbian' cattle. Laughing heartily Mr Freeman rose again to take in, from a huge bare-armed man in a green apron, the tray from the cafe next door.

'I once had a somewhat unusual meeting with someone

from Walwyk,' he said in a reminiscent voice. 'I've just remembered it. Quite a while back, during the war. Yes, it must have been during the war, because I was traveling to Wandford by train – we have another business there. I was on the early train, and I heard some kind of altercation going on, and what sounded like a woman crying, so I went along and found the ticket inspector and a young woman who had no ticket and no money. I . . . I supplied the deficiency and afterwards talked to the girl – she was about eighteen, I suppose. She told me she'd lived in Walwyk all her life and hated it.'

'Why did she hate it?'

'Oh, she said life was so dull. That didn't seem to me to be quite an adequate reason for leaving so precipitately that she had brought neither money nor luggage; but if she had another, she kept it to herself.'

'You wouldn't, of course, remember her name?'

'Her name?' He sounded surprised. 'No, she never told me that, unfortunately, as it turned out. You see, I insisted upon fending her some trifling sum – she really was too pretty to be cast on the world penniless – and she must either have known me by sight or made some inquiry; for about five or six months later the exact sum was sent to me by Postal Order. No name, no address, just the Wandford postmark. I should, of course, have sent it back had I known where to send it.'

'What did she look like?'

Once more Mr Freeman was surprised. He had told his little story partly to keep the conversation going and partly to show himself in a kindly light. His listener seemed to be extremely, almost unduly interested.

'She was pretty, as I said. Oh, and delicate-looking. In fact, she did say that she had tried to escape Walwyk by joining one of the women's forces, but had been rejected as physically unfit. Pale . . . fair-haired . . .' He frowned in his effort to remember. 'Oh, and she had those slightly projecting teeth which don't sound attractive but actually can be, in the right face. Why? Do you know anything of her?'

It sounds like Maud Rigby. Oh, how I wish she had told you her *real* reason for leaving home. It would have helped me to . . .'

In what way would it have helped you?'

I might have been nearer to understanding something.' She looked into his kind but worldly-wise eyes and thought, Here is someone in whom I could confide. 'I'm sorry I blurted out the name. If I hadn't, I could have told you what is worrying me, keeping it all anonymous.'

'Anything you told me in confidence would be perfectly safe with me,' he said. And that was true. He was a busybody, but not a gossip. He went on, 'Of course, if anything is really troubling you, you should consult Canon Thorby. He is the uncrowned King of Walwyk. I don't mean that unkindly. He's actually very sensible and well-meaning. We meet on one or two committees.'

'Canon Thorby . . .' she said, and stopped, wondering if she was on the verge of being disloyal. 'He does know the village and the people very well, naturally. But sometimes a stranger . . . It's like families not noticing how one member has aged, or looks ill, and then someone else comes in and sees. Mostly we see what we are used to – or what we wish to.'

'And what have you seen?' he asked, going straight to the point.

She smiled at him, and he noticed that when she smiled, a delightful little crease, shaped like a half moon, appeared in her upper lip, and there was a tightening in each cheek which, once upon a time, had been the site of a dimple.

'That's my trouble,' she said. 'Even I am not sure.'

'Suppose you tell *me* and see what I think.'

She was surprised to find what a thin, poor story it sounded, put into careful words, honestly confined to facts. Nothing really. She was miserably certain that she was being a bore. She mentioned the little wax doll, because that was, after all, a fact. And as she mentioned it she glanced at Mr Freeman. He was steadily, obviously staring at his coffee cup, avoiding her eye. A nice man, she thought; he didn't want his amusement or scepticism to show in his eyes.

Actually, for Mr Freeman, time had run backward, fifty-eight or -nine years, and he was again what they had called him even then – the child being father to the man – 'a little jug with big ears'; and he had learned that a child, by staying very still and looking sleepy, could often hear fascinating things. He was in his grandmother's house at Catermarsh and it was the Michaelmas rent day, which his grandparents, old-fashioned as they were, always celebrated by giving their four or five tenants and their families a supper – roast geese, apple pie and cheese. The party was over; he had his head on his grandmother's knee, and she stroked his hair as above him the grown-ups talked about strange goings-on over the river in Walwyk. He had understood almost nothing, but he had sensed the atmosphere, something dark and sinister and shivery, not entirely dismissed by his grandfather's sturdy verdict of 'Complete nonsense. Talk about heathen! We're worse than heathen to give such things a moment's thought!'

Mr Freeman had, in fact, not given such things a moment's thought for many years, and what exactly was spoken above his drowsy head in that faraway time was all so vague that he could not have given any account of it. Nor, he decided, would he have done had it been possible. Poor little woman, she had to live in the place; she was already anxious, and it would have been cruel to add anything that might make her nervous. So he spoke soothingly:

'From what I know of Canon Thorby, he's not the man to let any cruelty go on in his village – a chained-up dog always finds a champion in him. If he thinks the relationship between the girl and her granny is all right, I think you need not fret. Perhaps you haven't yet come to understand the East Anglian temperament; there is a fanatical family loyalty. I expect that had you come on the old woman actually beating the girl and tried to restrain her, the girl would have kicked your shins. Yes, indeed, I know a case where it happened. To me, in fact, in Selbury High Street, if you please!'

'Does the East Anglian temperament explain the doll?' Anxious not to seem tediously serious, she asked that question with a half-smile; and again he thought,

Charming; all she needs is a little encouragement and some attractive clothes. He lied valiantly.

'Oh, the mommet. That is the word, or something like it. Well, perhaps not strictly East Anglian, but rural. Until very lately they've been in the habit of making all their own toys, you know. Out of the most unlikely materials. Have you ever seen a corn-dolly? You will, in Walwyk, this harvest-time, made out of straw. I should imagine – correct me if I'm wrong – that the girl in question isn't very mature for her age mentally, though perhaps rather tall?'

'That is so.'

'Then she is officially too old now to have a doll of the ordinary kind, but she hankers for one. So she made herself a little tallow treasure and was secretive, about it. I offer you this explanation because I can remember my younger sister, who was tall, not being allowed to take the doll's perambulator out with her on walks, while my older sister, the senior by quite eighteen months, but short, was allowed to. My father said it was manifestly unfair, but my mother was adamant; she said Florence would *look* so silly.'

He smiled. Miss Mayfield thought, Well, I have told my story to an outsider, and the verdict almost agrees with Canon Thorby's. Perhaps I *am* fanciful. But I didn't mention – how could I? – the gross feature of the little image; or is that also a feature of East Anglian dollmaking?

'I'm afraid I've wasted a great deal of your time,' she said. 'But it has been a relief to talk to somebody.'

It worked, just as of old.

'I very much hope that this, our first talk, will not be the last.'

'I hope that perhaps one day you will come and see Walwyk for yourself. You really should, you know. It would give me great pleasure to make you some coffee, or tea. Or to offer you,' she gave him her full smile, 'a glass of the Tío Pepe, or is it Amontillado?'

'Tío Pepe. And you may be absolutely certain that I shall take you at your word.'

Hurrying away to do the rest of her shopping, the bottle of sherry lying modestly at the bottom of a brown paper carrier bag which did not invariably accompany single-bottle purchases, Miss Mayfield thought that Mr Freeman was a kind and sympathetic man, but he was not what she was looking for.

What am I looking for, then? Someone to share my fancies, suspicions, fears?

The answer to that was Yes!

10

THERE WAS A STRETCH OF UNEVENTFUL DAYS. MAY ended and June began, and when the month was eleven days old Miss Mayfield was in her garden, removing some quick-growing suckers from her rose bushes, when Wesley Baines opened her gate. In one hand he carried a pair of shoes which she had left with him to have rubber tips put on their heels

'Oh, Mr Baines,' she exclaimed, 'you shouldn't have bothered to bring them. I could have come, or Sydney could have brought them.'

'I know,' he said in his slow deliberate way. 'They're the excuse, like. I wanted to have a word with you, if you can spare the time.'

'I've plenty of time. Do come in.' She imagined that perhaps he had seen the papers concerning the Bogey scholarship and had come to talk to her about it.

Even at that minute Wesley's concern with a well-done job took precedence of his immediate worry.

'If you don't mind me saying so,' he said, pausing and

looking at the rose bed, 'just clipping them off like that don't do no good. It just make them stronger. You want to haul it out, like this, see. . . .' He hauled out almost a foot of underground growth. 'Then you got it right near the root.'

For a moment it looked as though he were about to tackle the job himself; but he pulled himself away and entered the house. The ceiling of her sitting room was at least three feet higher than that of his workroom, yet he seemed larger than ever against the new background. She took the shoes from him and asked him to sit down. He did so, on the very edge of one of her armchairs, so that his knees stuck out far over the hearthrug. He dropped his hands between them and began pulling at his fingers.

'Well,' she said, in as cheerful a manner as she could assume, 'and what can I do for you, Mr Baines?'

'Just don't laugh at me,' he said simply. 'I know what I've come to ask you sound very queer. But there it is. What can I do but ask? It ain't easy, though.' He pulled at his fingers as he had pulled at the rose sucker.

'Is it about Sydney?'

He weighed this. 'Well, I suppose, in a way. But more about Em.' He decided to take the plunge. 'Miss Mayfield, there's something wrong with Em, and you're mixed up in it.'

'Oh, in what way?'

'I'll just tell you what I know and then maybe you can sort it out. Now, f'rinstance . . . Up to the time Sydney was took ill, she seemed to think very highly of you. You'll hev noticed, maybe, that Em ain't as ignorant as most, and she used to grumble good-tidily about Mrs Westleton – she was here afore you. So then Sydney'd come home and say something you'd said or done, and Em was pleased, saying what a change and how lucky we was. Things like that. Well, then Sydney was ill and nobody could be kinder than what you was. Helped pack his duds. Arst me in to supper. But now – and this don't sound a very nice thing to tell a person, but I must, to make it clear – *now* she ain't got a good word for you.' His periwinkle-blue eyes met Miss Mayfield's in a look both troubled and apologetic. 'I say to her, "Em," I say, "whass come over you? Whass got into you?" And she don't give me no sensible answer. That is, not when she's awake. But she've took to talking in her sleep. And thass where you come in.'

'You mean she talks about me in her sleep?'

'Thass hard to explain. You ever slept alongside anybody that talked in their sleep, Miss?'

'Not that I can remember.'

'Well, that ain't like talking. They mutter and mumble and sort of call out. Em'll say, "Miss Mayfield, don't!" or "Don't do it, Miss Mayfield." She'll say you're – excuse me, Miss – nosey. She'll say things about minding your own business and leaving her alone.'

He had given an expurgated version of his wife's sleep talk. She had used words and phrases which she must have picked up while nursing rough soldiers. They had shocked him very much.

'I can think of a possible explanation of *that*, Mr Baines. Probably I do deserve to be called nosey. You see, I busied myself about the possibility of Sydney's trying for a scholarship; I told your wife I thought he *ought* to try. I have a strong feeling that with half her mind she agreed with me and wanted him to; but she couldn't face the idea of his being away from home, so she rejected the idea. But I should think some conflict was set up in her mind, and that results in her sleeping badly and in her unconscious state throwing all the blame on me.'

She thought she spoke plausibly and convincingly. Wesley Baines listened carefully, with frowning attention; but he would not accept it as an explanation of the problem. Under her eyes his expression changed, became harder, less diffident. He edged himself even farther forward in the chair.

'That *sound* all right. It might explain, in part. There's more to it, though. Now I'm gonna ask you a real rude question. Did you ever – accidental-like and meaning no harm, I know – but did you ever say or do anything to draw Em's attention to the fact she'd married beneath her?'

'Why on earth should I? Her astonishment was genuine. 'I wasn't even aware that she had. I don't think she has, if you want my frank opinion. What outdated nonsense!'

'No,' he said, 'less be fair. Em, as a nurse, ranked as a officer; I never got beyond sergeant, never wanted to. And even common ordinary nurses don't look to marry labouring chaps like me; doctors is more their line. Mind you,' he spoke with great earnestness, 'I never put on no false front; I towd her just how we'd live and where and what I did fer me living. And she could tell, just from looking at me and listening to me. And till lately, till you come, here, in fact, we've been wonderfully happy. And now thass all gone wrong.'

'Since I came? Or since Sydney was ill?'

'Afore he was ill. She was all on the hanker to move, that was the first thing. After nearly fourteen years, mark you, all at once she don't like the place, nor the neighbours, nor the house. She's on and on about being a woman with a profession what can earn her living anywhere, a woman thass wasting her training and her skill. Now, Miss, you're a woman with training, and you're putting it to use. You're sure you never even hinted to Em she was wasting her life? You might not be so wrong, at that, if you look at it squarely.' He looked about the room. 'Maybe you didn't hev to say anything. Maybe the sight of you, doing your rightful job and living so nice, was enough to set Em thinking how she could hev lived and been looked up to if she hadn't gone and married a cobbler.'

'That is utter nonsense. For one thing, any woman who is married – even if her husband is deaf or drunk or crazy or cruel – in her *heart* is convinced that she is superior to *any* unmarried woman. For another, you're not a cobbler; you're a skilled craftsman. And also I have only had two conversations with your wife, both about Sydney and his education. If this other matter had ever come up, I should have said what I truly believe, that any woman who makes a home and brings up a child is doing the job God created her for.'

He gave a deep, heavy sigh.

'Then we're no nearer. I hoped you'd tell me something that I could put on the table and hev out with Em. You see, I *know* something's gone amiss. Take this sleeping. I just happened to mention she was tossing and turning and muttering. My owd mother was a great believer in a lime pillow for bad sleeping, and there's a lot of sense in some of them owd notions – arter all, people used to live and keep healthy without doctors in the owd days. So I said, "Come the limes in bloom, Em, and that ain't far ahead, I'll make you a lime pillow." No harm in that, is there? And what happens?' He answered his own question. 'She go flouncing off and make herself a bed in that little place over the scullery, no bigger'n a dog kennel. My Em!'

'Oh dear,' said Miss Mayfield, embarrassed. 'Still, it was the sensible thing to do, wasn't it? It ensures that you get a good night's sleep.'

'I ain't worrying about myself. Thass Em. There's another thing, too. Maybe I shouldn't mention this . . .' Suddenly, the pupils of his eyes dilated, flooding the blue, and Miss Mayfield knew they were now near the heart of the matter. 'All this running round to owd Mrs Rigby's. That ain't so long ago since she couldn't bear the mention of the owd crone – called her a cruel owd witch and all sorts. Now, every so often, when Syd's abed, she'll say, "I'll just pop round and hev a chat with Mrs Rigby." I can't get outa my mind that down Curlew Lane there's a cut through the wood to Tharkell's place. She nursed him once, and he give her a lovely handbag; and he do hev a way with him.'

Taking precedence of everything else in Miss

Mayfield's mind was a feeling of affront; really, people shouldn't come and sit down in one's home and say such things! So embarrassing, and quite uncalled for.

Then, seeing how wretchedly miserable and puzzled he looked, she rebuked herself for such a heartless and conventional reaction. She said gently:

'I'm sure you can put all thought of that out of your mind, Mr Baines. I know why your wife has changed her attitude towards Mrs Rigby. You as good as told me yourself. Do you remember? You said Mrs Baines believed the old woman could put a spell on you. I think she does believe it. I think she blamed Mrs Rigby for Sydney's illness, and thinks that in some way she cured him, so now she is grateful and friendly.'

Working at his hands as though bent upon dislocating every finger, he said:

'Ah, but, you see, that was one thing We did hev out. I tackled Em; about the third time she went round there, I said "No time ago you was saying she give you the shingles and poured boiling water over Ethel, and now you go visiting her." Know what she said? She said Mrs Rigby was a poor harmless old woman, and she'd sadly misjudged her. But that ain't true – at least not wholly. Em still hate her. I can see the look come over her face even when she say she's going round there. You don't live alongside a woman, close, for nearly fourteen years without learning *something*. Em don't feel any different about Mrs Rigby to what she did two months ago. She may *act* different, but even that I doubt. Two, three times every week, off down Curlew Lane. There's more to it.'

'I think so, too; but there's very little that I, or you, can do about it. I could tell you what I suspect; but that would do you no good; and in any case I have almost told you.'

She realized that brought face to face with a fellow human creature in misery, one's natural impulse was to say the comforting thing, to use words as an emollient.

'I'm now going to ask you a question. How old is your wife?'

'Em? She's forty-four.'

So old, Miss Mayfield said to herself. Just my age, and she looks ten years younger at least.

Perhaps the thought showed on her face, for the man said with a kind of pitiable pride:

'She don't look it, do she? Even lately, when she's sleeping so bad. But thass right; I was thirty-one and Em was thirty when we was married, and she didn't look a day over twenty.'

'Well, she is at or nearing the age when women often suffer little physical or mental upsets. Quite honest women go shoplifting, and . . .' Good heavens, she had almost said that chaste, faithful wives became flirtatious! '. . . and sensible ones get all kinds of fads and fancies. At the last school I was in there was a perfectly ordinary woman who took against tea – of which she'd always been fond – to such an extent that she couldn't bear the sight of a teapot. *She* went to a psychiatrist and he just told her to wait, and within a year she was drinking tea with the rest of us in the staff room. That is true. I saw it happen.'

He thought this over.

'Em's took against me, and against you, and against chapel, and took up with owd Mrs Rigby. And all on account of being forty-four?' Suddenly his hands were still.

'You know,' he said, 'God do work in a mysterious way. There I was, getting all bothered and thinking all manner of nasty things. And He put in my head to come and see you. I was on my knees, asking for guidance, and the idea of asking *you* sounded in my head as if somebody spoke the words. So I come, and I do believe you've give me my answer. I've been done by better than I deserved, thinking such evil thoughts and all.'

Her pity for him was enhanced by a faint sense of guilt.

'I wouldn't call it an evil thought, Mr Baines. Just a natural suspicion which any man might entertain. And strictly in confidence. I've already forgotten it.'

'Em was dead right in what she said afore she altered; we are real lucky to hev you with us. You've lightened my load. He stood up and evidently, as he did so, suffered a prod from his Methodist conscience. 'Of course, what God choose for us to bear we must bear; I know that, I don't want for you to think I was whining or groaning. We're in God's hands and His will must be done. Only, I'm glad and thankful that He saw fit to send me, through you, a ray of light. So I'll say goodnight, and God bless you.'

'I haven't paid you for the shoes, Mr Baines.'

'Thass nothing. So long as you live in reach of me, you don't hev to pay for shoes, nor no other job I can ever do for you, Miss.'

'That's very kind. And very rash. I might live here for another twenty years and grow very demanding.'

'I'm sure I hope you will.'

When she had seen him out of the door and returned to the sitting room, the cat, which she had not known was there, was just emerging from behind the sofa, yawning, showing its tiny white teeth, its curled pink tongue. It made for the door, turned towards the kitchen and when Miss Mayfield opened the back door for it, leaped the wall and disappeared.

The voice in Miss Mayfield's mind said, *Going home to report.*

Suddenly she was frightened, not of the situation in which she found herself, but of her own state of mind. I've caught the infection, she thought; I've just spent half an hour telling near lies, covering up for Mrs Rigby and Mrs Baines, concealing what I suspect. I've sent Wesley Baines off, cheered by my euphemistic words, and then I turn straight around and think *that* about a cat.

She had intended to have supper; instead she went and sat down at the elegant little Queen Anne writing table and wrote to Rose. She wrote as she would have talked had her friend been in the room with her, putting down everything – what she imagined, what she guessed at, what she feared – and then, as she would have in a conversation, contradicting herself and offering alternate explanations.

'It's very wrong of me to bother you with all this,' she wrote, bringing the long letter to its end. 'I've had three chances, lately, to say what I suspected, but each time I was talking to a man, so perhaps I didn't have enough confidence. I did mention the wax image once – to a nice man named Mr Freeman, in Selbury – and he saw nothing sinister about it, but of course I hadn't described it as I have done to you. Please, Rose, don't worry. I'm all right. I really need somebody to tell me that I'm silly and fanciful and should take myself in hand, or that I am right and should go ahead without hesitation.'

She stared at the last words and asked herself, Go ahead with what? Witchcraft was no longer a crime; the laws against it had been repealed long ago. Go ahead with the rescue of Ethel; that was the answer. Out of it all, all the mystery and uncertainty, only one thing really mattered – Ethel's well-being.

II

ON THE TWENTY-FOURTH OF JUNE, WHICH WAS A Wednesday, Berta Creek, for the first time, was late. Ordinarily she brought Miss Mayfield a tray of tea at twenty minutes to eight, and her punctuality had been unfailing.

On this morning Miss Mayfield suspected, not Berta, but the accuracy of her bedside clock, checked it by her wrist watch, and at ten minutes to eight, thinking that something must have happened to Berta, rose with the intention of making tea herself. Her morning tea was, she admitted to herself, more important than anything else she ate or drank in the course of the day. In Alchester, where she and Janet had to be stirring early because their flatlet was quite a long bus ride from the school, she had always made the tea by a quarter past seven. It was therefore with no sense of grievance that she rose and pulled on her dressing gown and stepped out on to the landing, just in time to meet Berta coming upstairs with the tray in her hand.

Berta said, without preliminary:

'Oh, Miss; something dreadful's happened. Wesley Baines. He drowned hisself last night.'

Berta Creek, in her eagerly sought-after account later on, said that Miss Mayfield fell against the banister rail of the landing. And that was true. Feeling her face turn stiff and brittle, her knees weaken, Miss Mayfield clutched at the rail and said:

'Oh no, Berta!' And then, immediately, 'How do you know?'

'I come right by the gate. Ed Woodly and Frank Revatt was just taking him in on a gate; his body, I mean. Couldn't walk by, could I? Had to stop and ask. Thass why I'm late.'

Miss Mayfield tottered into her bedroom and sat down on the edge of the bed. Berta placed the tray in its usual position.

'To say he drowned himself is terrible. What makes them think that?'

'He was laying in the edge of Puddler Pond, where it ain't more than a few inches deep. 'Course, somebody might hev held him down, or he could hev took a fit, but that ain't very likely, is it?'

Miss Mayfield lifted the tea-pot, but it wobbled so wildly that she set it down again hastily. Berta stepped forward and poured out a cup.

'I give you a turn,' she said. 'I never meant to. But I had a turn meself, seeing them carry him in. He did look awful.'

'Was a policeman there?'

'A policeman? How could there be? There's only Cobb, and he live at Renham.'

'Then they shouldn't have moved him,' said Miss Mayfield, with such passionate conviction in her voice that Berta looked at her with astonishment.

'They couldn't just leave the poor chap laying there, face down in the water, could they? 'Twouldn't be human. They took a gate off its hinges and brought him home.'

Miss Mayfield knew Puddler Pond. It lay on the edge of Ling Wood, a stretch of the original forest which still stood towards the rear of her own house, separating the village from the first of the fields belonging to the farmer named Maverick. She had made its acquaintance on a happy day during her very first week in Walwyk. Miss Benson had come to school limping; she had sprained an ankle playing tennis. 'Tough luck on my brats,' she had said. 'I'd promised them a nature walk this afternoon. We always make a picnic of our nature walks, and the poor little brutes have brought their fodder.'

Miss Mayfield had seen here an excellent opportunity to get to know the Juniors whom she would not actually teach, so she had offered to take the walk. 'Where shall we go? You have to guide me, you know,' she had said. After a shy pause somebody said, 'Let's go to Puddler Pond.' They had led the way, out of the village, turned in at a gateway in the left-hand hedge and walked a well-trodden pathway towards the trees. When they reached the wood they fell silent and seemed to huddle together. The Pond was dish-shaped, and all around it grew pink willow herb and cowslips and small wild purple orchises.

'There's lilies of the valley, too, later on,' someone said.

'I expect you often come here.'

'No fear!'

'Well, no. I suppose your parents are afraid you might fall in.'

'They know we wouldn't go near. The Puddler'd get us!'

She had asked who or what was the Puddler, and received three different, very definite answers. The Puddler was a Thing that lived in the water and would drag you down if you went too close; it didn't like to be disturbed. Puddler was, on the other hand, the ghost of somebody who had drowned in the dark water. Puddler was nothing of the sort; he was a man who had dug clay to make himself a house, long ago, and so made the Pond.

It had been plain to her then that for the children the place had the fascination of horror, of something forbidden, and that was why they had suggested it to her, the innocent stranger, when she asked where they should go. She had said that it was a damp, dreary place and suggested that the picnic should be enjoyed elsewhere; so they had passed on to a more cheerful spot and there vied with one another in pressing sausage rolls and hard-boiled eggs and currant buns upon the new teacher, who had come unprovided. It had been a very happy outing and one Which Miss Mayfield had intended to repeat before the end of the summer term.

Now, staring at the cup of tea which she dared not attempt to lift in case she should slop it, she said:

'Berta, have you a bicycle?'

'Yes. Back home.'

'Then I want you to take a note for me. To Miss Benson, you know . . . at Mr Frisby's. I want her to have it before she sets out for school. So never mind about breakfast; I can get it.'

'All right,' Berta said.

Miss Mayfield hurried down, snatched paper and pen and wrote:

'I may be a bit late. Start them off, will you please, and tell mine to get on with their own work. Juliet Reeve will supervise. I shan't be long. D.M.'

She folded the paper, gave the flap of the envelope a hasty perfunctory lick and stuck it down.

As soon as Berta had left the house, Miss Mayfield ran up to the bathroom, which was at the back of the house, and looked out of the window. There was no need, she saw, for her to go along the road and turn in at the gateway. She could go over her own back-yard wall – as Smut had so many times done – cut diagonally across a meadow and so, very quickly, reach the path which led to the Pond.

Having made certain of that, she ran into her bedroom and threw on the minimum of clothing. No stockings, no corset – a waste of time.

She scrambled over the wall and was in the meadow, which was knee-high with marguerite daisies. Crossing it, she was aware that for a few moments she was visible to anyone on the other side of the Green, but she hoped that they would be too much interested in the Baines's cottage to spare a look in her direction. Soon she was on the path which she had followed with the children on that happy afternoon. There was the gateway. No gate now. Ed Woodly and Frank Revatt had lifted it and used it as stretcher. She shuddered.

It was a warm bright morning and on field and meadow the sun lay golden. In the wood it was cool and shadowy. Even the little clearing in which the Pond lay, though it was open to the sun, seemed chilly.

Puddler Pond was shrinking and its edges were drying out in plainly perceptible stages. There was an outer rim of cracked and wrinkled clay over which a thin veil of quick-growing weeds was already spreading; inside it lay another circle, bare and beginning to crack; and inside that a ring of moist mud. In this, there was a hollow depression at one point, and Miss Mayfield judged that there Wesley's body had lain. When she looked more closely she could see traces of moist mud upon the dry circle and some of the greenstuff of the outermost circle broken; that was where Ed and Frank had dragged the body backwards. There were also several footprints, those nearest the pool's edge beginning to fill with water.

It was all very much as one would have expected, and standing there, she wondered why, upon hearing the news, it had seemed so imperative that she should view the scene for herself. She still felt that the men had been wrong in removing the body and that the place should be guarded; those footprints, for instance, might be important. Among them there might be one which did not belong to Wesley, or to the two men who had found him. But her strongest feeling was the half-fearful certainty that if she looked hard enough and patiently enough, she would notice something which anyone else might miss, but which would be, to her, of great significance.

She stood for some moments, staring and waiting; yet when she did notice something, it was so obvious that it seemed impossible that it had not struck her immediately. On her side of the pond the wild flowers and weeds which grew in the little clearing were all standing upright save in the place, where Ed and Frank had trod; on the other side, farthest from the edge of the wood, all growth had been trampled flat; the pink heads of the willow herb and ragged robin, the white flowers of the dead nettle, the yarrow's yellow and the blue of the bugloss were all stamped down into the grey-green mesh of smashed vegetation. And the sharp earthy odour of trodden grass and broken stems and leaves still hung on the air.

It's as though a herd of elephants . . . But this is England!

Moving reluctantly, as though each step pained her, she went round one end of the dish-shaped pond and stood upon the crushed vegetation. She saw nothing else until she was very near the water upon that side, and then, in the area of soft brown mud, she saw exactly the same sight as had shocked Crusoe on his island — the mark of a bare foot. On either side there were others, some complete, some the marks of the forepart of the foot only, the tracks of people moving lightly on their toes. Or dancing. Dancing. Dancing last night, Midsummer's Eve.

The faint feeling of guilt which had just scratched her when Wesley Baines took his leave strengthened and set its fangs into her. He was dead now. Because she hadn't been frank and honest. She'd *known*; and she'd said nothing. And now she knew, just as certainly as though she had seen it happen, what had taken place here last night. Wesley, with his suspicion or his curiosity newly aroused, had followed Emily here; he'd seen the secret thing and paid the price with his life.

And who will believe that? I have no proof. Nothing to show.

The wood had been alive with bird song. Suddenly through it came the sound – half bark, half howl – of a dog, which was immediately answered by another. All the birds were suddenly silent.

There was a moment of complete stillness, as though even the trees were holding their breath; and then there was a sound, a muffled shuffling noise, as though, just out of sight, something soft but heavy was moving towards her.

Some instinct made her turn, so that her back was towards the pond, her face to the trees. She could see nothing, yet the sound came nearer. The dog lifted its voice again, and again was answered.

Then, in the shadow of the trees, she saw movement; another, deeper shadow, on the move, close to the ground, grey, like thick fog advancing to engulf her.

She had a second in which to taste fear to the full, time to think that there was such a thing as Evil which could take palpable and visual form, and that she was here alone with it. And then she recognized the thing for what it was, a flock of sheep. She knew a second of relief, and then terror again, because the animals themselves were in the grip of panic. And she could see why. Leaping in pursuit, one on each flank of the moving mass, pushing it closer and sending galvanic waves of fear through the whole, were two . . . dogs?

She heard again Ed Higgins's voice saying that there were wolves in the Walwyk woods long after they'd all been killed off elsewhere.

By that time the sheep had reached the edge of the trees and came, straight towards the pond, pressing more closely and running faster now that no tree trunks impeded their passage. They surged, wild-eyed, towards Miss Mayfield, who stood absolutely still, certain that when they saw her – representative of the human race – they would break their solid front. And the first ranks did so. They appeared to be running blindly, but when they were so close that she could smell them – the woolly sheep smell mingled with the disinfectant with which they had recently been dipped – they broke rank. One sheep ran to the right of her, another, jostling madly, to the left. But they were the ones at the head of the stampede; those nearer the pursuers were more crazy. She might stand and shout and wave her arms; she was, by comparison, harmless, and they ran straight at her. One hit her smack in the thighs, so that she fell over backwards. She had enough presence of mind, or sense of self-preservation, to clap her hands over her eyes as she fell. The sheep which had charged at her ran over her; she felt its feet, surprisingly hard and sharp, hit her chest, her cheek, the back of one of her hands. She twisted herself over, putting her face to the ground, humping her back, and three other sheep scrambled over her, one of them hitting her in a way that almost dislocated her neck.

Then, like a beating, it was over. No more blows fell. Slowly, stiffly, she rose to a crouching and then to a standing position, and turned.

Some of the sheep had run straight into the water; others had veered, left and right, to skirt the pond. The two dogs – yes – they were dogs – had caught a laggard and had it down and were mauling it savagely. It lay on its back, as Miss Mayfield herself had so recently done, and one dog was at its throat, tearing as savagely as any wolf could ever have done; the other was slashing away, with bloody fangs, at a hind leg.

Her cheek and the back of her hand were streaming with blood; the clean handkerchief – the taking of which and the placing in her pocket or sleeve was so much a part of morning ritual that even on this morning, when she had come out uncorseted and stockingless, it had been performed – was tucked into her sleeve. She took it out, unfolded it and dabbed at her wounds. As she did so she looked towards the dogs again and felt sick and realized that one of the sheep had put its full weight on her stomach. She bent over and retched with the painful, empty-bellied sickness of the last stages of *mal de mer*. But her mind was active. One part of it noted that the sheep, lately so terrified, had sensed that the victim had been selected; the rest, the lucky ones, had circled the pond and reached the herbage on the far side. They were placidly feeding. The other part of her mind registered a recognition of one of the dogs. It was called Lassie and belonged to Mr Frisby. Miss Benson had once invited Miss Mayfield home to tea with her, and the dog had been there. 'Marvellous with cattle,' Mr Frisby had said, 'though it's a sheep dog, really.' Miss Benson had called it a sentimental booby with a complex about being a lap dog, and Mrs Frisby had said it shed hairs over everything.

The other dog was a great gaunt mongrel, like a greyhound with a rough coat. A complete stranger.

Something – she never knew what – made Miss Mayfield strike a blow for civilization, for the domination of the human animal. Standing there, streaked with blood, shaken and sickened by her battering, she put every ounce of authority she had ever possessed into her voice and called sternly:

'Lassie!'

The dog raised its head, looked at her and gave one half-apologetic wag of its plumed tail, and then resumed its revolting gorging. It would probably, at this moment, have done no more had its own master called. At least she had made certain of its identity. She turned and staggered away round the pond, threading a path through the placid sheep, noting that now all the weeds and wild flowers were trodden down, and no prints left in the mud anywhere, save those of small scampering hooves.

At the Rectory, Reeve opened the door in answer to her urgent ringing and stood for a moment gaping at her in dismay.

'Miss Mayfield! What happened to you?'

'Never mind,' she said. 'I must see the Canon at once!'

'He is engaged just at present.'

'Tell him I'm here, will you?'

'Of course, Miss. Meanwhile, if you would care ...' His gaze went to the door of the cloakroom, but at that moment the door of the study opened and out came a young man, very good-looking, though at the moment the pallor of shock under his sun tan gave his skin a peculiar colour. Behind him was Canon Thorby wearing a dark-crimson dressing gown.

'... absolutely right, Ed,' he was saying. 'Don't give it another thought. I'll get in touch ... Why, Miss Mayfield, what in heaven's name has happened to you?'

'Nothing that matters. Only, I must talk to you at once.'

She felt calm and purposeful, but as she spoke her lower jaw shook convulsively.

Canon Thorby put his large, warm hand under her arm, cupping her elbow.

'Come and sit down,' he said soothingly. 'Reeve, bring a pot of coffee, as strong as they can make it, and quick.' He pushed the study door closed and led Miss Mayfield to a sofa and gently lowered her. It was impossible even to hazard a guess as to what had brought her, so early in the morning, in such a state, one cheek bleeding and rapidly swelling, her usually neat hair broken from its chignon and tumbling about her shoulders, her cotton dress soiled and torn.

'Are you hurt?' he asked. 'Do you need a doctor?'

'Oh, no, no. All superficial. I just ...'

'Then, if you don't mind, I will make a telephone call first. Renham 4, please,' he said calmly into the receiver. In the seconds that elapsed before he was connected, he gave her a long reassuring look – not a smile, but a glance which told her that in a moment she should have his full attention and all would be well.

'Ah, Cobb? Canon Thorby here. I'm afraid that for once we *do* need you. We have what seems to be a case of suicide. . . . Yes, tragic, isn't it? . . . Wesley Baines . . . If you would. Thank you. I'll see you then. Goodbye.

'I don't think it was suicide. You mustn't . . . you mustn't start off with that idea,' she said.

'I'm afraid we must face it. Ed Woodly was just describing to me how he and another man, on their way to work, found the body. Not submerged, just the face, in quite shallow water. I'm afraid the inference . . .'

'I know how and where he was found. I've just come from the place.'

'My dear Miss Mayfield, whatever induced you? . . . Oh, thank you, Reeve.' He set about pouring the strong black coffee, rose and brought a cup to her, holding out the sugar. 'Take a lot. It's supposed to be good for shock. And you have had a shock, haven't you?'

'I'll tell you everything. I'll be as brief as I can.'

'Tell me first, what happened to you to get you into this state.'

'Some sheep knocked me down and ran over me. Two dogs stampeded them; one was Mr Frisby's Lassie. But, Canon Thorby, that is only a small part of the whole. You'll see when I tell you . . .'

'I'm not at all sure that you're in any state to tell anything, Those cuts – do you mean to tell me sheep's feet made those? Then it's doubly urgent that they should be washed and disinfected. Probably you should have an anti-tetanus injection. Miss Mayfield, let me send you straight in to Wandford, with Baxter.'

'You must hear me first,' she said, struggling with the vibration of her jaw. 'It's all to do with Wesley Baines.'

'Drink your coffee, then,' he said in a resigned way. He lifted his own cup and sipped it.

Anxious not to sound sensational or dramatic and struggling hard to keep her voice under control, she told him everything in dry precise little sentences, terse as a telegram. She began with the finding of the sheet of exercise-book paper with its simple sentence and ended with the finding of the print of bare feet in the mud half an hour ago.

When she had been speaking for two minutes, Canon Thorby abandoned all pretence of drinking his coffee, leaned his elbows on the desk and put his chin on his fists. And for a moment after she had ceased speaking, he remained in that position, regarding her steadily. Then he moved, sat back in his chair and said:

'You really believe this? You find it easier to credit that Wesley Baines followed his wife last evening, found her dancing barefoot with old Granny Rigby and her crew and was murdered than to believe that ever since the war he has been neurotic and melancholic and last evening drowned himself?'

'It sounds fantastic, I know. It is that knowledge which

has held me silent . . . for far too long. But I believe it. It fits in with everything else.'

'Ah, maybe. But one should beware of this fitting in with a preconceived notion. Take a simple example. Primitive man believed that thunder was the voice of the Almighty, raised in displeasure, and that the lightning was His sword; consequently, when lightning struck, it all seemed to fit in. We know better.'

'You don't believe me,' she said with a sinking feeling of defeat.

'I believe that everything you have told me you have said in good faith. I cannot believe the theory you propound to me. I dare not. If I gave one moment's credence to such superstition, I should be utterly unfit for the vocation I follow.'

'Why? Many churchmen have admitted the existence of witchcraft.'

'In the Dark Ages. Just as many doctors then believed in powdered bloodstone as a cure for haemorrhage. A doctor who prescribed it today would soon be in trouble.'

'That isn't a comparable analogy. Science may have disproved the efficacy of the bloodstone; it has not yet disproved the existence of evil.'

He gave her a look of respect and approval.

'You have a point there. Mind, I never denied the existence of evil; all I question is that it takes the form of mysterious illness caused by wax images, familiars in the shape of cats and midnight junketings in lonely places.' He pushed back the cuff of his sleeve and glanced at his watch. 'I wish I had time. There's a perfectly reasonable explanation of everything you have mentioned; even the marks of bare feet. I expect somebody went bathing in Puddler Pond. . . . Unfortunately, I have a busy day ahead of me; and I think you should be in bed.'

'I couldn't rest. Not with everybody going round saying that Wesley Baines committed suicide.'

'Miss Mayfield, nobody is going round saying anything. Naturally, the men who found him came to their own conclusions, which they are at liberty to express. In speaking to the Police Constable at Renham, I said we had what seems to be a case of suicide. That is all. Apart from your – what shall I call it? – rather far-fetched theory, have you any reason for doubt that it was suicide?'

Had she?

'It would have been so out of character.'

'It almost invariably is. Near relatives are always taken by surprise. "So cheerful, so contented," they say. Actually, in this case that is not so; I think nobody realizes what Mrs Baines has been through. All war casualties did not occur on the battlefield, you know.'

'Wesley Baines, on that evening I told you of, spoke of his faith in God. About bearing what God chose to send. Oh, I know it's very little to go upon, but it gives me a certainty that he wouldn't have drowned himself. And I'm so afraid . . .'

'Of what?'

'That with this general impression that he did kill himself, something vital might be overlooked.'

'Such as?'

'Any sign that he had been forcibly held down in the water.'

'Now, there, at least, I can put your mind at rest. In a case like this, a . . . a very careful and expert examination of the body will be made. The police are not fools; they're bound to be alert to the possibility of a fatality being rigged to look like suicide. You really need not worry. Look, you go home, sponge those cuts – have you any Dettol? – and lie down and put the whole thing out of your mind.'

'And you'll do nothing about all that I have told you.'

'Indeed, yes. I shall inform Frisby that his dog has run berserk. And when all this dismal business is over, I will go round to Phoebe Rigby's with bell, book and candle. And I promise to confiscate her broomstick.'

The tone of humorous indulgence was the last straw. Suddenly, to her dismay, she found herself crying, help-lessly, hopelessly, crying with such streaming tears and harsh indrawings of breath as she had not known in all her adult days.

Canon Thorby came over to the sofa and put his arm around her shoulders.

'Really, you mustn't; you mustn't upset yourself any more. The shock of the news, and then the sheep worrying . . . too much. Just leave it to me. I'll see to everything. It can all be explained, I promise you.'

Once having started to cry, she found it impossible to stop. He must have rung a bell, summoned some attention, for presently he removed his arm from her shoulders and took her hand and said, in a firm, authoritative voice:

'Miss Mayfield! Stop it! You are hysterical! Stop! Now, swallow this – it's only an aspirin. That's right. And a drink of water. Good.' Speaking rapidly, snatching his chance while she struggled with the aspirin, which refused to be swallowed, he said, 'Try to spare a thought for *me*. I'm quite upset myself, you know, and now I have poor Emily Baines to face.'

She said, 'I'm sorry. I'm sorry.'

He stood up, lifted her feet and swung them into the place where he had been sitting, pulled a cushion into place and pressed her gently backwards.

'You just lie there and rest. Everything is going to be all right.'

I've done all I can. I've done all I can. The words repeated themselves soothingly in her brain. Another voice attempted to contradict, *Telling him was only a first step; there are many more.* Yes, she agreed, many other things must be done. She made an attempt to shake off the lethargy which had laid hold of her. Something moved towards her like a grey cloud, and again she tried to rouse, but could not, and it came on and enveloped her, feather-light, soft as chiffon, and warm. She gave herself into its embrace with a feeling of blissful release and with a last sob fell asleep, like a child, the tears still on her face.

12

WHEN SHE WOKE, THE ROOM WAS FILLED WITH twilight. It took her a moment or two to remember where she was, and why. Then the whole burden of memory settled down on her pressingly. She stirred and sighed, and instantly Canon Thorby's voice asked softly:

'Are you awake?'

'Yes.' He switched on the desk light and twilight receded.

'How are you feeling now?'

She moved under the rug of soft blue wool which someone had tucked about her. Her head ached, so did her bruises, and she was stiff all over, but she said:

'All right now, thank you.'

'Well, you've had a good sleep, which always helps.' He came and stood by the sofa. 'I've been holding back dinner, hoping that you would dine with me. It would give us an opportunity to have a little talk – if you feel up to it, of course. But perhaps you would rather go home.'

'Oh no. There's a great deal I want to hear . . . and to say. I'm afraid I'm rather untidy, though.'

'Knowing women,' he said lightly, 'I imagined that would be among your first thoughts, so I sent to your house, and Berta Creek found a dress and some shoes and stockings. They're in the bathroom, first on the left at the top of the stairs. Shall I tell Reeve about ten minutes?'

In the luxurious bathroom she washed, donned the clean dress, took out what few pins remained in her hair and combed it and pinned it up again. The place on her cheek was so swollen that she looked lop-sided, the violent crying and then the long sleep had puffed her eyelids, a bruise she had not known was there was turning blue on her forehead. But it doesn't in the least matter what I look like, she thought, turning away from the glass.

Canon Thorby was waiting and took her into the dining room, where the table was laid with two places.

'Isabel is away at the moment,' he explained. He went on in a conversational voice. 'You'll be interested to know that the dog *was* Lassie. Poor Mr Frisby is very much upset. The sheep were Maverick's, and he is also upset, and angry as well. But, of course, Mr Frisby will pay for the mauled sheep. I feel very strongly that somebody should present you with a new dress. . . . All right, Reeve, back to the Third Programme; we can manage now.'

As soon as they were alone he went on, in a different, more conspiratorial voice:

'I couldn't think how to account for your state, so I thought as much of the truth as was possible was the best thing. I credited you with a recklessly heroic attempt to save the sheep. I suppose it is *just* possible, in the morning quiet, for some sound of commotion to have reached you, at the rear of your house?'

'It doesn't matter. I intend to tell the whole truth.'

Canon Thorby put down his soup spoon, very gently.

'I am to understand by that that you intend to make public all the wild surmises and theories which you expounded to me this morning?'

'Yes. What else can I do?'

'Well, you must, of course, do as you think fit. I hope you have considered the consequences. It is a story out of which the gutter press will make great capital, and your mental stability will certainly be questioned. You are prepared for that?'

She nodded. He took up his spoon and resumed eating.

'You must eat,' he said pleasantly; 'you're going to need all your strength.'

She took two spoonfuls which did not go down; they lodged behind her collarbone and stayed there.

'I'm sorry,' she said, and put down the spoon.

He removed her plate, then his own, and standing at the sideboard, said:

'This is one of Mrs Thatcher's daintier dishes, cold lobster soufflé, light as a feather. Do try a little. How very disappointing! I ordered it especially – with, I may tell you – several other things on my mind.' He helped himself and, sitting down again, gave proof that it is possible to eat and talk at the same time with ease and grace. 'Before we go any farther I should tell you that the corpse has been examined by the Police Surgeon, and all suggestion of foul play can be ruled out. The inquest will be held tomorrow at six in the evening, but it will be a mere formality. Emily Baines has already given ample evidence of the poor fellow's state of mind, and what she says is confirmed by the neighbours. His melancholic tendency was well displayed during Sydney's illness, for example.'

'In what way?'

'He was quite distraught.'

'Canon Thorby, that is not true. I was there on the day Sydney went to hospital. Wesley Baines was perfectly calm – concerned, surprised to find the doctor taking such a serious view – but quite calm. And later on he . . . prayed.'

'Miss Mayfield, if you were there, you must know otherwise. Mrs Baines said he was so much upset that he couldn't help to get together what was wanted, had to be sent to carry the boy downstairs and then tried to insist upon getting into the car and going with them. Then, while his wife was absent, he ignored the kind offers of neighbours to give him meals; Mrs Baines said she knew she must come home on the Saturday to save him from starving to death. Is that the behaviour of a normal, well-balanced person?'

'It's all been twisted,' she said stonily. 'I was there. Mrs Baines was the distraught one; the doctor sent me up to help her get things ready. As for the food, I think I was the first person to offer the man a meal, and he refused it, politely, reasonably; he said he was accustomed to fending for himself while his wife was out nursing.'

'Twisted,' said Canon Thorby; 'that is the operative

word. You see, even those Apostles whom we call the Synoptists give varying accounts of the same event. So much depends upon what one wishes to see. I've been thinking today, at every moment when my mind has not been otherwise engaged, about what you said this morning. I want to ask you something, which goes, I think, to the very heart of the matter. *You* saw the marks of Ethel's beating, didn't you? Now, if old Phoebe Rigby has one-thousandth of the power which you seem to attribute to her, why did she *allow* Ethel to go to school bearing those marks — marks she could show to anyone and say, "Look what my granny did to me!" How can you explain that?'

'In two ways. First, the old woman knows that she holds over Ethel some supremely dreadful threat, something that Ethel fears far more than physical ill-usage. That is why, on both my visits, Ethel has taken pains to side with her grandmother and deceive me. The first time it was an all-good-friends-here act, the second it was an I-provoked-her-and-deserve-all-I-got one. Secondly, witches never claimed, never had, more than limited powers. What they inflicted they could cure. A natural mark made by an actual stick, wielded by a human hand, is a very different matter. The things work at different levels. Sydney's illness — and, I think, Mrs Baines's shingles — were on Granny Rigby's level. When everything is known, if it ever is, you'll find that Mrs Baines came home on that Saturday not to feed Wesley but to strike a bargain with Mrs Rigby. And I believe . . . I'm almost sure that that bargain included keeping Sydney in Walwyk. Ethel is — though she cunningly denies it – much attached to Sydney. I think that is the final threat. Why should she, on my first visit, the moment we were alone, ask was Sydney all right? Why shouldn't he be? I know it's all vague and it all sounds crazy, but I'm sure it's there, and something should be done about it. I won't have Ethel ill-treated, and I won't have Wesley Baines branded as a suicide when I know he was nothing of the sort.'

'Can you prevent it?'

'I can try. I shall go to the inquest and say what I think.'

He stood up, his empty plate in his hand.

'I'm going to eat some fruit now. Surely you could eat a few strawberries; they're at their best, gathered less than an hour ago.'

'I just can't swallow.'

He said mildly, 'That – if we were studying your state of mind – could be considered proof of a hysterical state. Did you know that? It is a fact. But I won t use it it against you.'

He came back to the table.

'You know,' he said, 'I have for you the greatest respect and liking. You have already improved my school out of all knowledge; you have talent, intelligence, breeding and integrity, all of which I admire very much. But I'm going to be quite honest with you. I may say – incidentally – that standing up and making a scene at Baines's inquest will not affect the verdict one iota. What it *will* do will be to give the Sunday papers a headline: "Schoolteacher Exposes Black Magic Scandal in Essex Village." I shall then give you a cheque for a year's salary, and you will never enter our school again. I should be very sorry, very sympathetic, but I cannot employ, as a teacher, anyone who has been exposed to ridicule and the suspicion of insanity.'

She said coldly, 'I'm prepared to take the consequences of my actions.'

He then astonished her by saying most heartily:

'You really are the most admirable character! My only sorrow is that it is all to be wasted in such an *impossible* cause. Nobody is going to believe you. Oh, some bright reporter will lend you his ear and invite you to tell him a highly coloured and melodramatic story, and by next week he'll have forgotten your name, being so busy with some film star's fifth divorce. You see, you haven't a shred of evidence; even the little wax doll would have been something, wouldn't it? Nor will one voice be raised to confirm yours. It all seems such a pity.'

He had been eating his strawberries by holding them by their green hulls and dipping them, first into the thick cream and then into the sugar, and lifting them to his mouth. He now dabbled his fingers in his finger bowl, wiped them and lifted his napkin to his lips.

Pilate washing his hands, the voice in her mind said.

She said aloud, 'You know, you can't be sure of that, Canon Thorby. Once, somewhere, and I greatly regret that I have forgotten *where*, I read something. "He who is prepared to fight alone will always have an army at his back." Other people may have noticed things, had suspicions, feared ridicule. And given a lead . . .'

He laughed. 'Do you know, I was on the brink of saying, I hope you are right. You see *I'm* on the verge of schizophrenia. I never could resist the little David facing up to Goliath. And you haven't even got a sling. I must ask you one more question and then I'll take you home. Tell me truthfully. Do you think that I am involved in all this nonsense?'

'If I had thought that, I shouldn't have been so silly as to come running to you and tell you all I suspected this morning, should I? Besides, you have an alibi; it was in the paper; you were in Wandford last evening, one of the judges at the Open Air Dancing. I saw the advertisement. So you couldn't have been at Puddler Pond with the rest of the coven.'

'With the what? I didn't quite catch the last word.'

'Coven,' she said. 'A gathering of witches. They have four main ones, Candlemas, Midsummer Eve, Lammas and All Hallowse'en.'

'How singularly well informed you seem to be upon the subject. One might almost . . .' His sombre expression lightened for a second, his eyes almost twinkling. 'This is no time for joking,' he rebuked himself. 'Well, it's some slight comfort to know that you don't think I am implicated. And that's about the only comfort in the whole sorry affair. I'm deeply sorry that what seemed a very happy and unique relationship should have been brought to an end thus, but I am at the same time bound to say that I think you must do as your conscience dictates. Come along, I'll take you home.'

She said in a weak, tearful voice, 'I'm sorry, too.'

'Now, please, don't cry any more. I can't bear it. I'm Only human. I happened to like Wesley Baines; I'm sorry for Emily and the boy. But I'm supposed to go on, functioning like a machine. Run to old Thorby; he'll see to it. I try. But there are times. So, please, do what you like, make Walwyk the laughing-stock of the popular press, bring coachloads of sensation hunters to gape at us, but don't, I beg you, cry any more, because I simply can't bear it.'

'I won't,' she said, mastering herself. 'Canon Thorby, about tomorrow. Am I to regard myself as dismissed now? If so, I should like your permission to go into the school and leave it as I should like it to be found.'

'Your dismissal is entirely dependent upon your action tomorrow. Until you broadcast your nonsense, there is no change in the situation. And if, having thought things over, you allow wiser thoughts to prevail, as I very much hope you will do, you may depend upon me never to mention or even think of this business again.'

He smiled as he made this promise, and again, when, at her door, he took leave of her. But he also put out his hand and when she had placed her own in it, held it for a perceptible space, as though he were taking leave of her for ever.

13

BY FIVE O'CLOCK ON THE FOLLOWING AFTERNOON she had only one more job – and that a mere formality – before she could walk out of the school, satisfied that everything was in order. The one remaining task was to tidy her own desk, and as she was, by nature, a neat, somewhat pernicketty person, this meant little save the removal of her few pieces of personal property.

The desk stood high and was the only old-fashioned piece of furniture in the whole school. It had a sloping lid which could be propped open by the adjustment of a wooden wedge. Miss Mayfield seated herself on the high chair, lifted the desk lid, swung the wedge into position and removed her own copies of *The Oxford Book of Verse*, Trevelyan's *Social History of England* and *Jane Eyre*. Two Biros, one red and one bright blue, which she used for marking, she decided to leave to her successor, but the half-empty box of Kleenex she would take away and also the bottle of aspirin. She had the bottle in her hand and was bringing her head out from under the slope of the desk lid when the little wedge either slipped or collapsed, and the lid came down and struck her an incredibly painful blow across the bridge of her hose. Quite dazed with pain, she sat for a second watching the blood spatter down on her hands, on the edge of the desk and on the things she held in her lap. Then the room darkened and tilted sideways.

She recognized the hospital smell. They'd built it well away from the other buildings, but as Rose had often said, the hospital odour was more powerful even than that of Africa itself. She lay for a moment breathing it in, and then tried to open her eyes. The effort hurt and resulted in a mere slit of a view, just enough to inform her that she had wakened to daylight.

I've never known my eyes to be affected before! I've caught something from another patient! She thought, with a physical revulsion, of the variety of eye diseases prevalent in Entuba.

'Rose,' she said sharply. 'Rose.'

A crisp, professionally cheerful voice said:

'Ah, so you're back with us. And you're quite all right. Not a thing in the world to worry about.'

A new voice. Surely this last bout of illness hadn't been so long and so troublesome that they'd been obliged to bring in an extra nurse.

Aloud she said peevishly:

'Oh, isn't there? Then why can't I open my eyes?'

'They're slightly swollen. They'll be quite all right in a day or two.'

Ah, she knew what had happened; they'd neglected her mosquito netting.

'I'd like to see Miss Tilbury. Now. At once.'

'I'm afraid you won't be allowed a visitor today. You must be very quiet, just for a day or two.'

'Miss Tilbury isn't a visitor.' Or, wait . . . had they moved her? Rose had said something about having to leave Entuba, something about sending her home by plane. Last night, was it? A doctor had come up all the way from Nairobi and said she'd never fully recover in Entuba. She'd cried. Perhaps that was what had made her eyes so swollen and sore. If that were all, of course she could open them.

There was the narrow strip of daylight, some white bars – hospital bed, of course – and a glimpse of some complicated tubing and metal bars.

'Is this England?'

'Why, yes. This is Wandford Hospital. Don't worry. You're bound to be a little confused. You've had a slight concussion.'

'The plane,' she said knowingly. That was it. Rose had kept her promise to put her on a plane, and it had crashed.

Injuries? She lay without speaking, moving one limb after another, turning a little this way and that upon the bed. One arm felt odd – constricted and in a curious position, in some way connected with the contraption of rubber tubing and metal rods – and her forehead and face as well as her eyes were very painful. That was all. A wonderful escape – cuts and bruises, an arm broken and a slight concussion.

'Were many other people hurt, or killed?'

'Nobody but you.'

That was really miraculous. Something to thank God for.

To begin with, she was content to allow the things which puzzled her to remain unexplained. Concussion naturally left you a little muddled in your mind. But through the comfortable fog of not knowing much about anything, every now and then she'd catch a glimpse, as though the fog had lifted and she had found herself in a place where nothing, no landmark, was familiar.

She discovered that her real injury was not where she had imagined it to be, over her eyes and forehead. She had a scalp wound which even the cheerful nurse described as 'quite nasty'; all her hair on the left side of her head was shorn away, and sixteen stitches had been put in.

Then she discovered that she was more 'confused' than she had realized. Waking, she was conscious of the scent of roses, and there indeed, near her bed, was a great sheaf of them, dark crimson, white and apricot-coloured. When the nurse entered next time, Miss Mayfield asked:

'Did someone send me those lovely roses?'

'Indeed they did.'

'Who?'

There was a card propped against the vase. The nurse lifted it and read:

'Get well soon. H.T.' She turned it over. 'Canon Thorby. The Rectory, Walwyk.'

'Well, that is very kind of him,' said Miss Mayfield, visualizing an old gentleman whose private charity was sending flowers to patients in hospitals where they were unknown. 'Very kind indeed.'

'Oh, he's always most attentive when we have a patient from his village.'

'That's understandable. But to send flowers to someone he has never seen . . .'

The nurse looked as though she were about to say something, thought better of it and merely replaced the card. But when, later in that same day, there arrived a bed jacket, pale blue and pink, pretty enough for a bride, with a scribbled note, 'Best wishes for a speedy recovery and lots of love, Sally Benson,' Miss Mayfield began to worry.

'It can't be for me. There must be some mistake. I don't know anyone of that name.'

'There's no mistake. It's plainly addressed to you, at this Private Ward number. Put it on; it'll cheer you up.'

'But it isn't mine. Unless there's a society or something for providing pretty bedwear for people in hospital. I never heard of Sally Benson, and I can't see how she can have heard of me. Unless . . .' Light dawned. Rose, of course. Rose still maintained contact with an astonishing number of friends and relatives, most of them both generous and well to do. The moment she heard that Deb was in hospital, she'd press them into service. On the other hand, it was odd that she had had no word from Rose herself.

'Yes, I'll wear it. I think I know how I came by it.' She allowed herself to be helped into the pretty thing and then asked, diffidently and off-handedly because she was ashamed of the amount of 'confusion' the question betrayed:

'By the way, how long is it that I've been here now?'

'Ten days.'

'It can't be as long as that, surely.'

'Yes. You came in on the twenty-fifth of June, and this is the fifth of July.'

She had something of the feeling that a swiftly descending lift can inflict.

'Would you mind saying that again?'

The nurse repeated her words.

'Then where in the world have I been for five months? I left Africa in January.'

'I'm terribly sorry,' the nurse said, 'number seven is ringing his bell.'

As a rule, the Matron came round once a day and asked brightly if everything was all right, nodded and smiled, and vanished. Sometimes she made a remark about the weather and said, 'I hope you'll soon be out on the terrace.' But that evening she came in and sat down; she spoke about the weather – which was thundery – and said she hoped there wouldn't be a storm, because it would ruin the delphiniums; and then she said:

'Miss Mayfield, nurses and doctors are all concerned with patients' physical well-being, and the Almoner is all tied up with their financial problems, so this falls to me. I understand that you are still slightly confused about the immediate past, the time just before your accident.'

'Was it before? That is what bothers me. You see, I perfectly well remember falling ill in Entuba. I kept on having attacks of fever which, in the end, resulted in what they called a nervous breakdown – I used to cry a great deal; but really that was only because I felt so useless. Everybody there was so busy that to be useless . . . the very worst thing. So I was to come home, by air. About that, I admit, I remember absolutely nothing. The last thing that I am clear about is my friend Rose Tilbury sitting on the side of my bed and holding my hand and telling me what the doctor from Nairobi had said and saying that I must come back to England, and I began to cry. And then I'm here. And the dates don't fit. This is July, and I've only been here ten days; but I left Africa . . . at least Rose told me I was to leave at once, in January. So there's a gap, isn't there?'

'You haven't any recollection of Walwyk at all?'

'Walwyk. Somebody there, Canon Thorby, sent me those roses.'

'You've been living in Walwyk, teaching in the school there.' She leaned forward in her chair with the air of one who has pressed a switch and expects it to set a machine in motion. They had told her 'temporary lapse of memory' and said things like 'put her in the picture.'

Miss Mayfield stared with a blank astonished face.

'You remember nothing of that? Or of your accident?'

'Accident? My accident? I thought the plane had come down.'

'No. You were in the school, Walwyk school, after all the children had gone, and the lid of your desk fell. It must have knocked you senseless, and you fell and hit the side of your head against the edge of the little platform upon which the desk stood. But for the fact that the piano-tuner came in and found you, and ran straight to the telephone and called Dr Macdonald, you could very easily have bled to death.'

She looked back, and there she was, lying in bed, with Rose holding her hand and telling her she must return to England, and she began to cry.

'I haven't any memory of Walwyk at all. *What year is this?*'

'Nineteen fifty-nine.'

'And July. I left Entuba – at least, so I suppose – in January, 1956. I've lost three years.'

'Not lost,' the Matron 'said consolingly. 'Mislaid for the moment.' She rose and opened the door, and stooped and lifted something. 'Look, this came this afternoon, but after Nurse had told Sister about your slight . . . confusion over the bed jacket, we thought we'd hold it back until I'd had a little talk with you and put you in the picture.'

She held out a little blue-and-white wireless set, neat and pretty as a jewel box.

'It's from your pupils, Miss Mayfield. One of them must have written the message. It says "To dear Miss Mayfield, the nicest teacher we ever had." Those years weren't lost, were they? I'm quite sure that when that knock on the head has healed, it'll all come back.'

You never realized until you lost part of it, as few people ever did, how much the past was entwined with the present. The whole of life was, indeed, a building up of a structure, solid, unchangeable, at the summit of which you stood. One thing led to another; cause led to result; the structure mounted with you. To have three years cut out of it – lost, mislaid, forgotten, call it what you would – gave you a fearful sense of insecurity and made all that you could remember seem unreal. Even Rose, though so clearly remembered, was part of the unreality. A friendship of such long standing, based upon mutual respect and affection, could not have been ended by their parting; so presumably from this place called Walwyk she had written to Rose, and Rose had replied to her. But what had they said to one another? Could she now write to Rose in such a fashion that she would not worry her?

She made several attempts, brooding with halted pen for a long time and producing sentences like 'I have had a very slight accident, only a fall in the school, but it has left me rather weak and shaky and disinclined to write a long letter. This is just to let you know and assure you that I think of you often.' Because she knew she was writing cautiously and evasively, the words, when she read them through, sounded false, and she was afraid that Rose would leap to the conclusion that her accident was more serious than she implied. So she wrote an alternative, an imaginative description of her accident, embellished with light-hearted details. And that didn't have the right ring either.

One day, when the Matron made her visit, Miss Mayfield said:

'I should like some of my clothes. For when I am allowed up. And I wonder if whoever sends the clothes could bring in any letters that belong to me – old letters. I think they might prod my memory and help me to fill in the background.'

The Matron said she considered that a very sensible idea and she would attend to it. The clothes arrived, and with them three or four envelopes, all unsealed and bearing twopenny stamps; a list of newly published educational books; a coupon worth fourpence if you bought a certain detergent; an appeal for funds to take old people to the seaside for the day. Nothing personal at all. It was a bitter disappointment, and Miss Mayfield wept over it. She began again to write to Rose, and a very horrible thought struck her; during this lost interval of three years, Rose might even have died! She wept again, and the nurse said, with patience obviously forced:

'You've really nothing to cry about, you know. Now, if you were the poor woman in number seven . . .'

Miss Mayfield endeavoured to explain her predicament about writing to Rose; the nurse said:

'Yes, I can see that is a bit awkward. But in any case I think you should write. A nice chatty little letter can't do any harm.'

A nice chatty little letter!

In the end that was what she did write, however, and she sealed and addressed and stamped it, and sent it off into the void.

Everybody told her that worry was the worst thing; and she tried not to worry. Everybody said that one morning she would wake up and find her memory restored. Every morning she woke up and was aware of having two lives, one which ended in a hospital bed in Entuba and one which began in a hospital bed in Wandford. Out of the gap which divided them there came echoes of another life: flowers and fruit from some people called Frisby, eggs and cream from some people called Maverick.

One day she had another inspiration.

'If anyone else from Walwyk comes to the hospital, will you ask that they should come and visit me, please? I am allowed visitors now, am I not? I think that if I *saw* somebody, my memory might begin to work again.'

Two days later a sheaf of gladioli arrived, with the Canon's card attached to it.

'Oh, you forgot to ask about my having a visitor,' said Miss Mayfield, on the verge of tears once more.

'I did not! I left the message at the porter's lodge. I'll see what happened. He may have forgotten, but I didn't.'

She reported that the flowers had been delivered from a Wandford shop. During her next visit Matron mentioned casually that she believed Canon Thorby had gone abroad; he'd been absent from the hospital managers' meeting.

Time passed. They took away the bandages. Then the stitches were removed. Her cut hair began to grow in little wispy curls like a child's.

'There's a hairdresser who will come in,' Matron said cheerfully. 'Would you like an appointment? You could have it cut short all over. I think it would suit you.'

Really, they couldn't have been kinder; and every kindness evoked tears, which were unwelcome in hospital.

Physically, she was well again. She could look after herself, spent a great deal of time on the terrace over-looking the garden in which Matron took such pride, ate moderately well and, with the aid of a small pink pill, slept through the night. One day she was taken to a room on the other side of the building, and a brain specialist, with a specialist's apt double-barrelled name, spent a long time testing all her reflexes, asking questions and fixing a thing called an encephalograph to her head. He reported that he was completely satisfied that no injury had been done to her brain at all. But he did mention 'a hysterical block'. And that resulted in some sessions with a psychiatrist who started off on the assumption that the past three years held some experience which she *wished* to forget.

That called up such appalling possibilities that she refuted it with all her might.

'One cannot forget at will. Everybody has seen or heard or lived through hundreds of things which they would forget most willingly, but they can't.'

'These things are not so simple. It is very difficult to explain to the layman. Things such as you are thinking of are the concern of the superficial, conscious mind. It is when the deeper, subconscious mind comes up against something that it cannot accept that the obliterative process begins.'

He asked her many very personal, even embarrassing questions. He invited her to tell him about her sex life.

'I have none,' she said simply. He said that was non-sense; everyone did. He said it was impossible for him to help her unless she was willing to help him.

'But I am doing my best. So far as I know – that is, as far as I remember, the only time . . . Oh, it was very childish. At my first school. There was a little boy named Alan; I thought he was extremely handsome. I think he was, and popular. I was very flattered if he spoke to me and one day he did tell me about his dog. He went on to his prep school and I never saw him again. But I always thought that if I did get married and had a son, I would name him Alan. But nobody ever thought of marrying me, so nothing came of that.'

'You had a dog at Walwyk?'

'I shouldn't think it very likely. You see, I taught in a school. You couldn't leave a dog alone all day.'

'You enjoyed your work?'

'My twenty years in Africa I most certainly did. About more recent times, I can't, of course, speak. I like children. The Walwyk children seem to have liked me.' She told him about the little wireless set, and blushing because it seemed rather an immodest thing to do, repeated the message which the children had sent with it. 'In fact,' she said, 'everybody has been very kind – up to a point. What does rather worry me is that nobody at all has come to see me.'

'Is that one of the things you cry about?'

'Not directly. I cry because I can't remember. You know how it is when you forget a name, or a book title. It's like having an itch that you can't scratch. And I have that feeling about a whole section of my life. It's enough to make anyone cry.'

She was completely rational, and, from his point of view, completely unrewarding.

'You'll have noticed,' he said, 'that in the cases of a temporary lapse, such as you have mentioned, *trying* to remember does more harm than good. At some moment when you have ceased to try to remember, what you want flashes back into your mind. I think that if you can just be patient and divert your thoughts from yourself and your condition, you have every chance of recovering your memory.'

He made some vague resolve – never fulfilled – to go to this place Walwyk and see if the clue to the puzzle could be found there. Before his next visit to Wandford, however, Miss Mayfield had gone.

It all happened very suddenly: One evening the hospital Almoner visited Miss Mayfield and said that Canon Thorby had been in touch with her.

'But I understood that Canon Thorby was abroad.'

'I didn't go into the matter of where he was, Miss Mayfield. I merely listened to his suggestion regarding you. A very sensible and kindly one, in my opinion.'

Most of her work was concerned with the problems of the poor; mothers of new babies going home to take up, prematurely, the burden of family life; old people living alone; disabled victims of accidents, uncertain of the immediate future.

'Canon Thorby,' she said, 'has a friend – a widow, Mrs Mott-Tyler, in rather straitened circumstances, I gather – who takes paying guests in her house near Hove. Miss Thorby has stayed there, he says, on one or two occasions and been very comfortable indeed. His suggestion is that you should go there and have a good rest and a holiday.'

'And that,' said Miss Mayfield, 'is extremely kind of him. The question is, can I afford it? I know that when I left Africa, I had no resources; it is unlikely that I have saved much. . . .' She remembered, but did not mention, her determination to send Rose every penny she could spare once she was earning again. Had she done, so? 'I suppose I shall have my salary up to the time of my accident, and perhaps for the month following. . . . But then how do I know that I shall ever be able to teach again? Who would want a teacher who couldn't remember? I don't think I'm justified taking a holiday.'

'You worry unnecessarily,' said the Almoner. 'I don't think you fully realize how fortunate you are. Canon Thorby has made himself responsible for your stay in this Private Ward, and professes himself eager to pay for your stay in Hove.'

'But can *he* afford it? All the clergymen I have known have seemed to be so poor.'

'Canon Thorby is extremely well to do. And he delights to use his money to help people.'

'Have you ever seen him?' Miss Mayfield asked abruptly.

'Of course I have. Dozens of times.'

'What is he like? To look at, I mean.'

The Almoner's rather weary face took on the baffled look which such a question evokes in all but the very articulate.

'Well,' she said. 'He's tall. Rather nice-looking. Reddish hair, just going grey.'

'You see. It calls nothing to my mind. Yet it seems I must accept his charity.'

'There's no *must* about it, Miss Mayfield. The facts are that you are no longer in need of medical attention, and we are short of beds and nurses. Perhaps you have some plan of your own; some friends . . . ?'

'My only friend – if she is still alive – lives in Africa.'

'Then don't you think you would be wise to consider Canon Thorby's offer?'

And aren't you lucky to have it to consider?

'There seems to be no choice,' Miss Mayfield said; and despite herself, the words emerged querulously.

'The arrangement was that I should telephone to Mrs Mott-Tyler and she would come and fetch you by car. You could leave tomorrow, couldn't you? We really do need the room.'

For somebody with some definite, cure-or-kill condition. Loss of memory, like deafness, did not evoke sympathy.

'I suppose that Canon Thorby has explained my state to Mrs Mott-Tyler?'

'Oh yes. You see, Miss Mayfield, everybody thinks that to get back to normal life . . . Canon Thorby said that there would be various little jobs which you could do to help Mrs Mott-Tyler, and that if you were occupied you would be . . . happier.'

In short, they suspect me of self-pitying egoism, only just short of malingering. She felt her face go hot.

'Naturally, I should be glad to do anything I could. And tomorrow will suit me very well.'

The Almoner rose with a look of relief. 'I'll go and telephone, then. Hove, just now, must be very nice.'

She thought of her own 'holiday', spent in Birmingham, looking after her ageing father and mother while the sister who lived with them had the break which enabled her to carry on from year to year.

'Yes. I'm very fortunate,' Miss Mayfield said; and managed not to start crying until she was alone.

14

Mrs Mott-Tyler's large, beautiful house was called Barnhurst and stood in what, until comparatively, recent times, had been a lonely country lane; now it was joined to the town's suburbs by a road full of new houses and bungalows, and there were some in occupation, some being built, on its countryward side. A large garden and several ornamental trees ensured its privacy, however.

The straitened circumstances to which the Almoner had alluded, and of which Mrs Mott-Tyler frequently complained, were, Miss Mayfield thought, merely a matter of comparison. Mrs Mott-Tyler lived very comfortably indeed. She had, at the time of Miss Mayfield's entry to the household, three guests: two old ladies, who never left their bed sitting-rooms, and a retired General, very arthritic but determinedly mobile. The old ladies were waited upon and cared for by a woman in young middle age who had once been a nurse and with whom Mrs Mott-Tyler was upon what Miss Mayfield described to herself as scornfully intimate terms; the General had his own man, a shrivelled, shuffling little fellow called Washbrook, who saw to all his master's needs with a surly efficiency and spent the rest of his time evading any attempt to press him into other service. A feud of almost comic proportions was waged between him and Miss Ellison, the nurse, for whom he had once refused to bring back a packet of cigarettes.

'Let him wait,' she said darkly. 'One day he'll come to me with a cut or a scratch or a snivel, and he'll get short shrift.'

Both Mrs Mott-Tyler and Miss Ellison made an obvious effort to be kind to Miss Mayfield. It was obvious because neither of them was sympathetic by nature or imaginative enough to understand her problem. Much of Mrs Mott-Tyler's youth had been spent in India; she had shot the three tigers whose skins lay in the hall; she spoke nostalgically of hunting in Leicestershire, of ski-ing in Davos. She had carried into her fifties a good deal of a hard blonde beauty, an excellent constitution and much of the slangy dash of the twenties. Within ten minutes of making her acquaintance Miss Mayfield knew that she would have nothing but scorn for self-pity, and that had she been afflicted with loss of memory, she would have made a joke of it – 'So what the hell. I hope I've forgotten my debts.' But she had a certain charm, and she exerted herself to make Miss Mayfield feel welcome. On some rare occasions when there was no one else to do it, she would wait upon her herself, in a casual, slapdash way which always made Miss Mayfield feel both flattered and apologetic.

'I was supposed to be coming to help *you*,' she protested once.

'I don't know what Hal was thinking about when he said that. Doing the flowers, I suppose. I happen to like doing my own flowers.'

'And you do them much better than I ever could. But I could do errands – when I've found my way round the shops.'

'It's too far to walk, anyway. No, you just rest up and get a bit of flesh on your bones. What a pity it is you don't play bridge.'

The question of bridge had arisen almost at once. Mrs Mott-Tyler, Miss Ellison and General Fordham were all keen and expert players. They had hoped to find in Miss Mayfield a fourth. Asked if she played, Miss Mayfield said:

'I don't know. So far as I remember, I never did. But in the part of my life which I have forgotten, I may have learned all kinds of things.'

'People don't learn much after they're forty,' said Miss Ellison, and her manner of speaking made the words sound brutal.

So after Miss Mayfield's arrival, as before, they were dependent upon one or another of their neighbours. Each evening someone came in for bridge, and each evening Miss Mayfield read. There were a few books in the house – hardly any to her taste – and one day she asked Mrs Mott-Tyler if there was a public library in the town.

'I wouldn't know. There's a subscription library. And somebody gave me a subscription to it for my birthday,

God knows why. I'll see if I can rout it out, and tomorrow we'll go down and get you the latest version of *Gone with the Wind*.'

Kind enough, but it somehow made all reading sound silly. Mrs Mott-Tyler had a curious facility, for making everything outside certain sharply defined limits sound silly; she could even do it to Canon Thorby.

'Hal took, up good works as a protest against being second son. He had a brother – two, three years older – who was an absolute devil; madly extravagant, selfish to the bone, terribly good-looking and no morals whatsoever. So Hal bounced off in the opposite direction. Holy Orders; follow in Father's footsteps but take it to the limit. Vote Conservative but all go shares with the pocket money. Freddie went and got himself killed at Mons, so Hal had more to share out than he reckoned on, and had a wonderful time.'

Miss Mayfield could hear the stiffness in her voice as she said:

'Canon Thorby has been indescribably kind to me.'

'And to me, bless him. To Tom, Dick and Harry, old Uncle Tom Cobleigh and all. But it's his profession. Sweeps sweep chimneys. Hal Thorby does good. It must have been a field day when he thought of sending you to Jive with me. Both barrels and two birds.'

On the first visit to the library it was natural that Mrs Mott-Tyler should drive Miss Mayfield into town. Three days later, her book finished, she suggested walking down to change it.

'It really isn't so far; and I like walking.'

'I'll take you down this afternoon. I've got somebody coming in to see me this morning; and one of the Poor Dears is having a visit from her doctor, so Margery must be on duty.'

'There's no need for anyone, to come with me. I noticed the way as we drove; it was quite simple. And anyway I could ask.'

'Look, I don't doubt that you could find your way to Timbuktu. It's just that I promised to look after you, and you're not supposed to go walking about by yourself just yet.'

'Why not?'

'Oh, some of their nonsense. Margery understands it.' She went to the door and called and, when Miss Ellison came in, heavy-footed, said:

'This is your line of country, Margery. Explain in your own simple words why Miss Mayfield can't go out alone in her present state.'

'That isn't difficult,' Miss Ellison said, with a glance at Mrs Mott-Tyler's back as she strolled away. 'You see, there's always the danger in a case like yours that when you remember what you've forgotten, you'll forget what came after. If your memory returned and you were down there in the town, you'd have no idea how you got there or where you lived or anything.'

Dismayed, Miss Mayfield said, 'Could it happen like that? I thought that when I remembered, I should ... well, remember, and have it all clear again. I think that is what will happen, if it ever does.'

'Do you? Well, those who know don't. You see, this isn't your first lapse, is it?'

'Isn't it? Do you mean that while I was at Walwyk, all that I remember *now* – my childhood and youth, my years in Africa – were as lost to me as Walwyk now is?'

Miss Ellison took a cigarette and lighted it in her peculiarly gross, clumsy way.

'That's not for *me* to say. All we know is that you'd had what was called a breakdown before. And you'd never mentioned it. Canon Thorby had to find that out for himself.'

Miss Mayfield closed her eyes for a moment.

'Yes,' she said. 'Yes. Almost the last thing I can remember is my friend telling me that I was threatened with a breakdown, and that was why I had to come home to England.'

'There you are, then. In Walwyk you'd forgotten that. Now you've forgotten Walwyk. It's like a see-saw. And we don't want you wandering round Hove like a lost dog, do we?'

Miss Mayfield hurried from the room; she didn't wish Miss Ellison to see her in tears. Safe in her own room she cried. It was all more complicated and horrible than she had known. She had thought that her loss of memory was due to the blow on the head, but apparently it had another cause, something not very far from a form of mental illness.

Having cried herself out, she knelt by her bed and prayed for courage and for faith and for help. She wondered whether, in this Walwyk, she had ever prayed.

The simple faith which she now held linked her with Rose, with all the work at Entuba; did it, like the physical acts of eating, breathing, sleeping, run back through the lost years? Your soul, she cried to herself almost despairingly, shouldn't be susceptible to a knock on the head.

The days went on; pleasantly, for the most part. She wrote a long, carefully phrased letter to Rose Tilbury, describing her 'silly little accident' and saying that she was having a holiday in Hove. She had actually begun this letter while she was in hospital, but had hesitated from day to day to post it, half hoping that every post would bring her a letter from which she could judge what terms the friendship now stood upon. None had come. Then, after 'Miss Ellison's words about the possibility of her Walwyk life having been utterly detached from the rest of her past, she had wondered whether, since leaving Africa, she had ever written to Rose at all. So she must not now write as she felt – which was as though she had only just taken leave of her friend; this might be, for Rose, the first letter after a long, unexplained silence. So she wrote carefully, wondering whether to mention the lapse of memory, and then deciding not to in case Rose should be worried. She read a good deal and, as she grew stronger, undertook little jobs on the garden. Mrs Mott-Tyler looked after the flowers herself and did not welcome help with them, but the kitchen garden, cared for by an old man who came two days a week, offered plenty of opportunity for casual labour, and Miss Mayfield definitely enjoyed gathering vegetables for the house.

As she grew stronger, and the hope of recovering her

memory receded, she began to worry less about its loss than about her future. One day she said to Mrs Mott-Tyler:

'I can't stay here for ever.'

'You can as far as I'm concerned. Why not?'

'It wouldn't be right. I'm able-bodied. I'm not even forgetful in the ordinary sense. I taught school in Entuba, and in Walwyk, and I still know how. I think I should get in touch with the education authorities.'

'Which ones?'

'Walwyk is in Essex, isn't it? The Essex County Authority.'

'I don't suppose they ever heard of you. My God, don't look like that! I keep forgetting that you don't know. You weren't working for them; you were in Hal Thorby's private school, his pet, his hobby.'

'Oh, I see. That explains . . . I had wondered why nothing had been said or done about my salary. I had my accident in June, so that month's cheque should have come to me. And July's, too, almost certainly, since I should be on sick leave: Now I see; Canon Thorby has been using that money to meet my expenses. That makes me feel better. If I can go back to work at the beginning of next term, I shan't have been such a burden after all.'

'I shouldn't worry about that, if I were you. It'd be a bit odd, wouldn't it, going back to Walwyk, where everybody knew you and you didn't even remember their names? And if you go elsewhere you'd need a reference, which would put poor Hal on the spot.'

'He need only say that he had employed me and found me competent. On the other hand, if he wasn't averse to my returning to Walwyk, I could face the little embarrassment of having to learn names and so forth again. After all, having an accident, as I did, is nothing to be ashamed of. I think I should get in touch with Canon Thorby at once.'

'There's no hurry. I'm not sure that he's back. And when we had our long talk about you, he said that he would come down and see you as soon as he could. I should wait till then, if I were you.'

'When he talked to you, Mrs Mott-Tyler, did he say anything that gave any hint of what his attitude towards continuing to employ me might be?'

'Let's see. He said you'd had an accident and lost your memory and he was afraid it'd be a long job. He spoke as though he intended you to stay here indefinitely. That's all. I can't see what you're worrying about. You're happy here, aren't you? Oh, is it money? How silly of us not to have thought . . . Look I can let you have what you want, within reason. A fiver to go on with.'

'Oh no. Thank you very much. I don't want to go getting into any more debt. I can manage quite well.'

It was tact, not a wish to deceive, which made her conceal from Mrs Mott-Tyler the fact that she had written to Canon Thorby. She wished not to appear discontented, over-anxious or unwilling to co-operate. So she wrote thanking him heartily for all his kindness, telling him that her health was restored, her memory of Walwyk still missing and asking him what he wished her to do. She professed her willingness to return if that was his pleasure, and ended, 'I hope that while I worked for you I gave you satisfaction and that you will be able to recommend me for another post in the event of my having to make a change.'

There was a pillar box, just down the road, within sight of the gateway to Barnhurst, and she had stamps; a half-used five-shilling book of them and three loose ones, each for half a crown, were in the handbag which had apparently accompanied her into Wandford Hospital. She stuck one threepenny and one half-crown stamp on to her envelope, addressed it to the Rectory, Walwyk, and wrote 'Please forward if away' in the left-hand top corner; and without the slightest sense of guilt she set out for the pillar box one evening just before dinner. It did not even occur to her that the moment was seemingly well chosen; Mrs Mott-Tyler and General Fordham always drank together at this hour, and Miss Ellison was upstairs attending to the Poor Dears.

Miss Mayfield had almost reached the pillar box when she heard quick, thudding feet behind her and heavy breathing. She turned and came face to face with Miss Ellison, who had seen her from the bedroom window and run straight down and out, without even troubling to remove her apron or the bit of starched linen which, when the fancy took her, she pinned to her head while acting as nurse. Miss Ellison grabbed at the hand holding the letter and gasped out:

'What the hell do you think you're doing?'

'I am posting a letter,' said Miss Mayfield, with great dignity. 'What do you think you are doing, Miss Ellison, accosting me like this?'

'My duty. 'I've told you, you're not supposed to be let out alone.'

'Let go my arm, please.'

'You're coming back with me.

'I'm going to post my letter.'

Miss Ellison, without exerting herself much, gave Miss Mayfield's arm a painful jerk which brought the address of the envelope into clear view.

'So that's the game, is it? Sneaking off . . . And look at that!' She laughed in a coarse way. 'Two and ninepence on a letter to Essex, and then you say you aren't loopy.'

'Canon Thorby may still be abroad; I didn't wish to bother whoever had to send the letter on.'

'Well, you can come back now; and if Mrs Mott-Tyler wants you to write, you can, but you're posting nothing without her say-so.'

'I will not be treated as though I were a lunatic,' said Miss Mayfield fiercely. 'Let go my arm, Miss Ellison. You're hurting me.'

'If you don't walk back with me quietly, I'll wring it off,' said Miss Ellison between her teeth. 'And make one sound, just one sound to draw attention, and you'll be where you should have been months ago, *in a Home!*' She had seen two people approaching from behind Miss Mayfield. For their benefit, as they passed, she said in a different voice, 'It's too far for you; you should have asked me.' The words '*in a Home*' had hit Miss Mayfield like a blow. They chimed with a secret fear which sometimes came to her if she woke in the night: the fear that, off and on since leaving Africa, she had been mentally unstable;

PETER CURTIS

that she was, at the moment, enjoying a lucid interval. She could almost always reason herself out of that fear, reminding herself that she had had an accident; that until it occurred she had been employed as a teacher, a profession in which lunatics were unwelcome; that she didn't look like a lunatic . . . but the fear, though it would retreat for a time, remained there, ready to pounce again. It did so now, and in the grip of it she allowed herself to be led back to Barnhurst.

On this fine warm evening Mrs Mott-Tyler and the General had taken their drinks on to the terrace outside the drawing-room windows. Still holding Miss Mayfield by the arm, Miss Ellison went to the window nearest them and said, 'Stella, could you spare a moment?'

Mrs Mott-Tyler, a glass in one hand, a cigarette in the other, sauntered in, and Miss Ellison, letting go of Miss Mayfield's arm, stepped forward and closed the window.

'I saw her going off to post a letter. After all the trouble I took to explain why she can't go out alone. Look, I don't mind the old, or the cripples, but the daft I can't do with unless they do what I tell 'em to do.'

'Margery! "Daft" is no word to use. You should know that. Poor Miss Mayfield, you look quite shattered. Sit down.'

'I'm suffering from amnesia,' Miss Mayfield said. 'And that doesn't give anybody the right to twist my arm or call me loopy and prevent me posting a letter if I wish.'

'I think Miss Ellison was upset. You see, we are responsible for you. We did promise to . . . take good care of you. I'm sure no unkindness was intended.'

'None at all. But, damn it, I'd got Miss Ferrers on the pan; I had to drop everything and run. I was in no condition to choose my words.'

'You'd better get back to Miss Ferrers, then,' Mrs Mott-Tyler said smoothly.

'I still think you'd make things easier for everybody if you had a good straight talk,' Miss Ellison said on her way to the door.

'What did she mean by that?'

Mrs Mott-Tyler stubbed out her cigarette, took another from the silver box and lighted it.

'Oh, you know how professional people are,' she said in her laconic way. 'Always taking the gloomy view. According to them, half the world should be in the Infirmary and the other half in the Asylum.'

'She said I should be in a Home. I resent that very much. I had a fall, and some concussion, and have lost part of my memory, which even she admits might return to me at any moment. That doesn't make me a lunatic.'

'There is just one little thing which you haven't taken into account. I think that is what she meant by a straight talk. I don't know whether it'll help to settle you or not, but you might as well know. There's quite a bit of time which you have forgotten and which is unaccounted for.'

'The time I was in Walwyk?'

'No. Before that. You say yourself that you left Africa in January 1956. You went to teach in Walwyk in April of this year. You see? Margery has some excuse for her over-anxiety. You may, for all we know, have been in and out of mental homes all that time.'

Now indeed she could feel her mind reel.

'You are sure about that?'

'Perfectly sure.'

'It does leave a gap. But I couldn't have been in mental homes. After all, when you apply for a post, you have references.'

'Against that we must set Hal Thorby's passion for lame dogs. Employ her because nobody else would – that's his attitude. Oh, God, I've bitched this, haven't I? Somebody else should've . . . not my line at all. Don't look so devastated. It doesn't matter. You're all right *now*. It's just that we have to keep an eye . . . How did all this start, anyhow? Oh, your letter.'

'I wrote to Canon Thorby.' Holding the letter, Miss Mayfield rose and went to the writing table which stood between the windows. She lifted the silver paper knife and carefully slit the envelope in such a way that it could be sealed again.

'Read it,' she said. 'And tell me frankly, please. Is that the letter of a lunatic?'

'Reading other people's letters,' said Mrs Mott-Tyler with a gesture of distaste, 'never was my game.'

'Please.'

She was glad that she had said how happy and comfortable she had been at Barnhurst.

Mrs Mott-Tyler glanced at the letter, gave a shrug and handed it back.

'Sound as a bell. As I said, you're all right now. You may stay that way. Frankly, if I were you I wouldn't send that letter. I think it'll upset Hal. It puts him in an impossible position. He's very soft-hearted. He'll feel he's either got to say come back to Walwyk or write you a cracking good testimonial, which would hurt his conscience. Write and tell him you're better. And I'm sure the expressions of gratitude would please him. But I'd lay off the future arrangements, if I were you. After all, he is coming to see you.'

'I think I shall post it as it is. It concerns *my* future.'

'Please yourself. What a pity it is that you don't drink. A good whisky'd pull you together just now.'

The letter was posted next day. When, by the end of the week, she had received no reply, she concluded that Canon Thorby had not returned from his holiday, and settled herself to wait patiently.

Miss Ellison seemed to have repented her hasty words and went out of her way to make several friendly advances, which Miss Mayfield received coolly. She wondered at herself a little, for she could look back and remember having been more deeply offended in the past and having been able to forgive the offender; it was the single word 'loopy' which stuck in her mind like a burr. Even if I were as mad as a hatter, she told herself that was not the thing to say. However, when, about a week after the incident with the letter, Miss Ellison said she was going into town one afternoon and invited Miss Mayfield to accompany her, she accepted the invitation in order to change her book. Miss Ellison drove more carefully but less expertly than Mrs Mott-Tyler and was not nearly so lucky in finding places to park, so they had quite a walk to reach the shops, and by the time they had done their errands, the afternoon was almost gone. Miss Mayfield, carrying her book and handbag, went straight into the garden, where Mrs Mott-Tyler and the General had just started tea.

'We'd come to the conclusion that you'd stayed in town for tea,' Mrs Mott-Tyler said, pouring some water from the Thermos vacuum bottle into the pot. 'Where's Margery?'

'She said she was going upstairs. She had some parcels.'

Almost immediately, Miss Ellison appeared in the doorway that led to the back hall and stood there and beckoned. Mrs Mott-Tyler rose and went and joined her, and they stood, talking in low tones, for a moment or two. Then Mrs Mott-Tyler returned to the table, and Miss Mayfield noticed that she avoided her eye as she said:

'Miss Mayfield, come inside for a second, will you? Bring your bag.'

The three of them stood together in the back hall. It was cool after the sunny garden. Miss Mayfield was puzzled; the other two wore the appearance of waiting for the other to speak. Finally, letting out her breath in an impatient, faintly disgusted way, Mrs Mott-Tyler said:

'Would you mind opening your bag?'

More puzzled than ever, Miss Mayfield did so, exposing its meagre contents. There was a purse which, when she had opened it and looked into it in the hospital, had contained eight shillings and four pennies and which had been reduced by one and sixpence for the smallest size of tubes of toothpaste, and by two shillings when she insisted upon returning Mrs Mott-Tyler's 'treat' of morning coffee during one of their visits to the town; there was a comb and some hairpins, a powder compact of the old-fashioned kind, a fountain pen, the book of stamps, a nail file and a key ring.

'Were you wearing a coat this afternoon?'

'I took it, but it turned warm so I left it in the car. What is all this about?'

'Where is the coat?'

Miss Mayfield turned towards the row of pegs which ran along the wall by the back stairs.

'I brought it in and hung it up on my way through to the garden. Would you mind telling me . . .'

'Would you mind showing us what you have in the pockets of the coat?'

'Why should I?'

She went, with a feeling of impending disaster, to the place where the coat hung and felt in the nearer pocket; it contained a handkerchief. As she twisted the coat to reach the other pocket, she heard the faint crackle of cellophane. She moved her hand quickly and brought out a pair of nylon stockings.

'I swear,' she said, 'I didn't put them there; How did you know they were there?'

Mrs Mott-Tyler said, 'I did offer to lend you money, you know.'

Miss Ellison answered Miss Mayfield's question.

'The girl in the shop saw you take them this afternoon, while I was buying mine. Thank God she was too shocked to make a fuss, but she went and reported to Mr Blundell, and he's just been on the phone.'

'Lies, all lies,' Miss Mayfield said violently. 'I never touched the stockings until this minute. Are you accusing me of shoplifting? I don't even need stockings. I have several pairs. And I don't wear this kind or colour.'

'Kleptomania isn't governed by people's needs,' said Miss Ellison.

'I'm going straight down to that shop to face that girl with her lie. I don't know how those stockings got into the pocket of my coat, but one thing is certain: I didn't put them there. And she didn't see me touch them.'

'The shop is closed now.'

'Then I shall go in the morning.'

Mrs Mott-Tyler said uneasily, 'Your tongue again, Margery! Kleptomania isn't the word in this case. Poor Miss Mayfield, you just picked them up and forgot all about it. Don't look so distressed. I'll go myself and see Blundell; he'll understand.'

'Don't say that, either. I'd rather be a thief than a lunatic who didn't know what I was doing! I'm absolutely, positively *certain* that I never touched those stockings. I can remember every word Miss Ellison spoke to the assistant. She showed you some called Riviera Tan, and Golden Rose, and Beech Blonde, and you bought two pairs of Beech Blonde, size ten and a half, and they cost eight and eleven a pair. She suggested your buying two identical pairs, because that made you eligible for a six weeks' guarantee. She filled in a card, and you put it in your bag. If I can remember all that about a transaction that had nothing to do with me, surely I should remember what I did.'

She looked wildly from one face to the other. No help, no belief to be had from either. Mrs Mott-Tyler wore the look of one whose attention has been drawn to something vaguely unpleasant and who wishes it to be removed as soon as possible; Miss Ellison's expression was gloating and self-satisfied.

'Why you should want to make out that I am demented I don't know,' she cried; 'but that's what it is. All part of a plot!'

'They all say that,' said Miss Ellison.

Mrs Mott-Tyler said, 'It's a great deal of fuss about nothing. I blame myself. We should never have let her know. Come along, Miss Mayfield, think no more about it. Absolutely no blame can be attached to you. I'll order some fresh tea.'

Miss Mayfield was conscious of a terrible desire to scream. To open her mouth and scream at the top of her voice, what a relief that would be. But that was lunatic behaviour. Controlling herself, she said:

'I don't want any tea. I want to be alone.'

15

THE WORDS 'ALL PART OF A PLOT' HAD JERKED OUT
of her without premeditation; but later, the more she
thought about the whole affair, the clearer it became that
was what it was. A plot. Made to what end, to benefit
whom, she could not even guess, but it reached back, she
was certain, to Walwyk.

In this new clarity of mind she could see that the one
thing she should have done, as soon as she could stand up
steadily, was to have returned to the place where she was
known, where there were people whom she should recognize, places and things which would spur the memory. It
now seemed sinister that no one should have come to see
her in the hospital and taken the chance of being recognized. It was sinister, too, that she should never have
received a letter in all that time. A woman who carried a
fountain pen and a book of stamps in her handbag plainly
had some correspondents.

Alongside this suspicion about how other people had
behaved to her, there ran another, even more disturbing.

Unless Mrs Mott-Tyler had lied deliberately in saying that she had only been in Walwyk since April, there was a long stretch of time unaccounted for. During that time – and, indeed, during her time in Walwyk – she might have done almost anything. Suppose – the thought was fantastic, but it must be faced – suppose the plot which she suspected, the plot to make her seem unsound of mind, had been *mercifully* concocted, made in order to protect her. Suppose she had done something terrible.

She looked back at the account given of her accident. A desk lid fell and knocked her to the floor. Was that really credible? Wasn't it more likely that someone had struck her? She had a horrid vision of herself, a madwoman, in school, attacking a child and having to be knocked unconscious. Canon Thorby's *private* school, Mrs Mott-Tyler had said; and private schools were peculiarly vulnerable to scandal. Suppose it was all true about Canon Thorby helping lame-dogs and her having a bad mental record; then she had run amok and been struck down. It would all fit in with this being smuggled away, and watched, and treated like a lunatic.

It was an appalling thought, but she faced it. And she had courage of a kind. If I did something awful in a fit of madness, she told herself, I am prepared to pay the penalty for it now that I am in my right mind again.

She remembered the psychiatrist's words about forgetting something you wanted to forget. They fitted in now.

What it all added up to was that she must get back to

Walwyk. And to do that she must be cunning, bold and resourceful.

Money; that was the first essential.

She owned – at least, she had in her possession at the moment – only one thing which might be of value. Years and years ago Rose's godmother had died, and in course of time the jewellery which she had left to her goddaughter had arrived in Entuba. Miss Mayfield and Rose had spent a whole evening opening little leather boxes and cases lined with velvet and studying the old-fashioned pieces. In the end Rose had said:

'Let's each have one piece and sell the rest. There's so many things, we need, and I'm sure she wouldn't mind. At least, alive she would, but she knows better now. What do you fancy, Deb?'

Miss Mayfield knew that diamonds were colourless, and sparkled with all the colours of the rainbow, rubies were red, emeralds green and sapphires blue. There was a ring which was certainly none of these precious things, which looked, indeed, beside the other stones rather like a piece of costume jewellery, or something to wear on the stage. It was large and square, made of pink glass. Not valuable, she thought. So she had said, 'I'll have that.' And Rose had laughed and said, 'That's a choice to interest a psychologist; you must have all sorts of repressions, Deb. It's quite unlike you. You'll never wear it. Have the pearls.' Miss Mayfield had said, 'I should never see them, except when I looked in the glass. Why shouldn't I have something showy for once? I like that pink ring and I shall wear it every day. Always.' Rose had said, 'All right. Then I shall take the next most flaunting thing, this garnet brooch.'

Now, studying her assets, Miss Mayfield wondered whether, in a pawnbroker's, the pink ring would fetch a pound.

Next morning she abandoned all thought of going into Blundell's and challenging the salesgirl. That was all a mere side issue now. Wearing a meek and chastened air, she offered to gather the last of the peas and went into the kitchen garden. Washbrook, every morning, walked his dog, a fat old fox terrier, round the kitchen garden. She had, if he passed near her, spoken to him and his dog; and at first his attitude had been surly, as though he suspected her of wanting something of him; lately, that suspicion quietened, he had, on occasions, paused and exchanged views on the weather.

This morning, patting the dog, she said, 'Mr Washbrook, there's something I want to know. I wonder if you can help me. Is there a pawnbroker's in Hove?'

He blinked at her.

'There is in Brighton, which is more or less the same fing.'

'Do you know where it is?'

'You want to 'ock somefing?'

'I'm afraid I do. It isn't of much value, I know. But a pound would be very useful.' She pulled the ring from her finger and handed it to him.

'It ain't glass, I shouldn't fink,' he said, placing it on the top joint of his smallest finger and twisting it round. 'Too well set. Don't want to raise your 'opes unduly, but it could be a pink sapphire.'

'Sapphires are blue, Mr Washbrook,' she said gently.

'So they are pink. And white. Din't you know that?'

'No.' And she still didn't know it, because she did not believe him. How could he know?

'Pinks are rare, Coo! If this was a pink sapphire, it'd be worf 'undreds.'

'I don't really want hundreds – because I want to get it back. I really *need* about four pounds, but a pound would be a help. I thought, the gold would be worth a pound. And I don't want anybody in the house to know; so please don't mention that I asked you.'

She sounded humble and she looked helpless. Some deeply buried, almost atrophied remnant of manhood in Washbrook rose to the surface.

'Ask for a pound and you'll end wiv a tanner, that's my experience,' he said. 'Ask for a tenner and you may get five bob. Nearly a joke that is – tanner and tenner, see?' It was plain that she did not. 'A tanner is sixpence,' he explained. 'Tell you what, if you like I'll do the deal for you. They'd do a lady like you. And I don't want anybody in the house to know. If they knew I'd done a errand for *you* . . . Shall I try for a fiver?'

'I don't want it sold.'

'I 'eard you the first time. I'll be 'ere about the same time tomorrow morning wiv the dibs, if any.'

Next morning he ambled up to her and handed her a pawn ticket and five of the filthiest pound notes she had ever seen.

'I was right. Pink sapphire it was. Din't 'alf look at me suspicious, he din't. Calmed down when I only asked for a fiver.'

She took one of the notes and held it out to him.

'I'm so deeply grateful. You made it all so easy for me, Please have this.'

'There's no call for it,' he said gruffly. 'No, I know. Really, I only needed the four pounds – to tide me over – and I couldn't have got out without drawing attention. Please, Mr Washbrook.'

'All right,' he said, and pocketed the note. 'Any time you got a little errand . . . but on the sly, mind you.'

She knew that she must, as she put it, steal away like a thief in the night, and with this in view she had, on the night of the day when Washbrook took away her ring, tested the stealth with which she could open her bedroom door. She was genuinely surprised to find it locked on the outside. She had never, during her stay at Barnhurst, had reason to leave her room once she had retired to it, for she was one of the fortunate possessors of a bathroom opening from the bedroom. She had never heard the key being turned, either at night or in the morning, and finding the door locked filled her with alarm lest something in her demeanour had quickened suspicion in her guardians. Calmer thought assured her that it was probably a routine precaution; they knew she had no money, and though it pleased them to pretend that she was crazy, they must know that she was not so crazy as to walk away penniless.

On the evening after she had received the money, she sat, as usual, reading in her chair, a little apart from the bridge table. At her usual time – that is, the end of the first hand after half past ten – she rose and said goodnight, holding her finger in her book and saying:

'I shall finish this before I go to sleep. Will you be going into town tomorrow, Mrs Mott-Tyler?'

'Almost certainly,' Mrs Mott-Tyler said affably, shuffling the cards expertly. Across the table her eyes met those of Miss Ellison, and they exchanged a glance which said that the good straight talk had been very effective, the shoplifting episode even more so. Miss Mayfield had settled down.

Upstairs Miss Mayfield walked about in her bedroom, used her bathroom, put the centre light out and the one by her bedside on, and then, very quietly, opened her bedroom door, closed it behind her and crept across the landing and along the passage which led to the back stairs. Her heart thumped unevenly, but she reassured herself that even if she were now discovered, she was doing nothing *wrong*. She was not dressed to go out; she was going to stand by the garden door for a last breath of air before retiring.

Undiscovered, she reached the back hall and hid herself among the coats on the pegs by the stairs. She had been there for what seemed a long time, but was actually ten minutes, when she heard the jangle of the bell which summoned Washbrook to assist his master to bed, and then the sound of voices in the front hall as Mrs Mott-Tyler saw to the door the neighbour who had been the fourth player that evening. Washbrook, on the way from the dim region beyond the kitchen where he and his dog abode, passed close to where Miss Mayfield stood holding her breath. There was another long interval; then Washbrook descended the back stairs and retired. Soon after, Miss Ellison, moving almost silently in her soft slippers, came down the same stairs and went into the kitchen. When she emerged, she was eating something; the crunch of her teeth was audible. She locked the door which led into the garden, went through into the front hall and locked and bolted the front door and put out all lights.

Now the thing was not to be precipitate. Everyone must be asleep before she moved, lighted by matches, through the night-filled house. She counted sixty heartbeats; that would be about a minute. When she had done one such count for each finger, ten minutes would have elapsed. By such reckoning she waited an hour before striking her first match and consulting her watch. It was then just short of midnight.

She reached up and took down her warmer coat, placed on a peg earlier in the day, and slipped it on. Then, by the faint and wavering light of the match, she went into the front hall, stood still and listened. Nothing stirred. She struck another match and set to work, with fingers that were suddenly weak and wet, on the fastenings of the door, expecting every second to see the light flood on and to hear Miss Ellison say, 'What the hell do you think you are doing?' But luck was with her. She had the door open, and closed again behind her. She was out on the drive, almost free. She tiptoed on to the grass verge that ran alongside the gravel and, once safe on its muffling softness, broke into a trot.

In the street outside she turned downhill towards the town, where many lights still glittered. She had no notion of the direction in which the station lay, having been brought to Barnhurst by car; but she could ask. She missed a good opportunity halfway along the road where two people were just leaving a house and getting into a car, watched by their hostess who stood in the lighted doorway. It was too near to Barnhurst. She crossed over and slipped past as unobtrusively as possible.

After that, for a while she saw no one, but nearer the centre of the town several people were still awake and moving. She asked a respectable-looking couple who said they had only arrived that afternoon; the man said he thought the station lay in one direction, the woman was sure it was in the opposite. Miss Mayfield thanked them, stood indecisive and then, seeing a soldier, asked him. In Africa any kind of uniform postulated reliability and intelligence above the average, and she was shocked to discover that this young man was very drunk indeed, so drunk that he seemed to find something immensely comic about her. He laughed and said something about being too late. Then she encountered a series of helpful and knowledgeable people who waved their arms and jerked their heads and said left, right, straight on, then left, but not first left, second. And so at last she reached the station only to learn that the next train for London did not leave until five-forty.

She compelled herself to be calm. If, back at Barnhurst,

anyone had wakened, made a search and found her gone, the station would be the place where they would have come to look, wouldn't it? And with a car, knowing the way, they could have been here by now.

Nevertheless, the time of waiting seemed longer than any week through which she had previously lived, and it was not until she was safely in the train that she drew a really deep, satisfying breath.

16

THE KIND AND HELPFUL YOUNG MAN IN THE Information Office at Liverpool Street Station had told her that Selbury was the nearest station to Walwyk, and when, at eleven twenty-five on that sultry August morning, she saw the station's name on the first hanging sign and felt the train slow down, her heart began to thud again. In a moment she would be among scenes which *should* be familiar; she was about to test her own theory that the cure might lie in familiar surroundings.

She was a little fearful, too. Her absence would long ago have been discovered; by using a telephone they could have someone here, waiting for her. She gazed fearfully up and down the platform, and then descended the stairs, keeping ridiculously close to a thick-set man, the only other passenger to alight.

In the yard a taxi was waiting and she scuttled to it.

'Will you drive me to Walwyk?'

'Cost you thirty bob. Might be more. Can't tell till I know the mileage.'

'That will be all right,' she said, and seated herself on the edge of the seat, looking out eagerly to left, to right, seeking for something which would strike a chord in her memory. But she might never have been here in all her life before.

The man drove with assurance to the edge of the town, and there, where the roads forked, slowed down to study a signpost.

'You're not familiar with this part of the country?' she asked.

'No. I'm standing in for my brother-in-law, time he take his holiday.'

The sign-post said 'Walwyk'. It also said 'Renham' and 'Catermarsh'. Neighbouring villages; perhaps she knew them. But the names were meaningless. Still, she thought, lighting off disappointment, painted words were not like people; when she saw someone she knew, saw the bed she had slept in, the school she had taught in, then surely the miracle would happen.

The country was flat and uninteresting until they crossed a high bridge; then it became beautiful. And the next village was so extremely picturesque that even the taxi-driver said in a surprised and grudging voice:

'I never expected to see such a pretty place in these parts. Ugly country, I call this. I'm from Wiltshire myself. Now, where do we make for?'

She had never visualized that terrible question having to be asked; she was so sure that before it could arise she would have got her bearings.

'We must ask. Ask somebody where does Miss Mayfield live.'

Again she was lucky. The postman, who never reached Walwyk much before midday, was cycling along. The taxi-driver braked and called:

'Hi, mate. Which house for Miss Mayfield?'

'Round the Green, far as you can go. The one with railings and some birds cut out of bushes. You can't miss.'

'Thanks.' Moving forward again, he said, 'They always say that.'

This was one occasion when the prophecy was true. The house he described was unmistakable. Miss Mayfield stared at it avidly and was again disappointed. It recalled nothing. It was a handsome little house and gave the impression that within it some prim lady who had known better days eked out her small means by taking the village schoolmistress to live with her.

She asked the man how much she owed him, and after a moment of frowning calculation he said thirty-three and sixpence. As he turned at the end of the cul-de-sac and drove away, she opened the gate and went towards the door. On the key ring in her bag there was probably a key which fitted this door, but she had been away a long time and was not expected; it seemed more polite to ring the bell. She rang it, bracing herself to face somebody whom she ought to know. This was the crucial test.

Nobody answered the bell, and as she put her finger on it again, a pleasant, ringing voice behind her said:

'You won't get an answer, I'm afraid. I saw the cab and

hurried out to tell you before it left. Miss Mayfield is on holiday.'

She was a good-looking young woman, wearing linen slacks, a sleeveless blouse and rope-soled sandals which somehow struck a foreign note.

Complete stranger.

I don't know her.

She doesn't know me.

In the next second a whole new and horrible possibility occurred to her. Perhaps all this talk about Walwyk was part of the plot. Perhaps she had never lived there, never taught here at all.

'I am Miss Mayfield,' she said.

'How d'you do? I'm Barbara Grieve. My mother and I live next door. We're just back from Jamaica. Did you expect your woman to be here? I have seen her about, but not this morning.'

'I have a key . . . I think. But I came back unexpectedly and didn't want to give her a shock.'

'That's all right, then.' After one sharp glance, justified by the fact that someone had returned from a holiday without any luggage, Miss Grieve showed no curiosity. 'Coming back suddenly,' she said, in a kind but casual way, 'if you want bread or milk or anything, we've plenty.'

'Thank you very much,' Miss Mayfield said.

She was glad not to be observed in her uncertainty about which key to try. The door opened and she entered what, if the postman and Miss Grieve were to be believed, was her very own house.

Her first glance around roused wonder. Where in the

world did I get such lovely furniture? Then she saw, in the middle of the hall, a brown cabin trunk and a wooden crate, nailed down. Both had clean stick-on labels. She bent over them and read, in bold block letters, her own name: MISS D. MAYFIELD. Nothing else. No address.

The trunk and the crate were the only evidence that she had ever been in the house. It was as bare, as impersonal, as a hotel bedroom awaiting its next occupant; downstairs the sofa and chairs, upstairs the bed and the dressing table, were covered with dust sheets. There was nothing in any drawer or cupboard, no book on the shelves. In the kitchen the refrigerator was empty and its switch disconnected. There was nothing in the larder. Some exceptionally delicate and beautiful china cups were on the dresser. Miss Mayfield took one down and stood with it in her hands. I must have drunk out of this cup, washed and wiped it, hung it on its peg. A memory that did not respond to such a unique and beautiful thing must be gone indeed.

It was clear, from the condition of the house, the careful removal of all trace of her occupancy, that she was not expected back.

It was like returning from the dead. Worse. The revenant would at least recognize his old surroundings.

She understood about some misery being beyond tears. In the hospital she had cried a lot, openly; at Barnhurst she had several times cried in secret. Now she had no tears. She sat on the kitchen stool in a dry daze of despair for a long time. Then, at last, resignation and a sort of courage began to move again. All right. Her memory was still lost, and it was horribly plain that Canon Thorby had no intention of continuing to employ her; but she was still alive and she must be sensible and take herself in hand. She would probably feel better for some food; she'd had nothing since her dinner the previous evening, and she had then been much too excited to eat really heartily. She had seen a little shop on the other side of the Green as the taxi drove past it, and she had some money left. She would go and buy some food.

The woman in the shop actually jumped at the sight of her, and cried:

'Why, Miss Mayfield! Fancy seeing you! Nobody said . . . And, my, you do look poorly still. The sea air don't seem . . . Here, sit down, do!' She came round from behind the counter and pulled a chair with her, and then, with her hands on her hips, stood back and studied Miss Mayfield again. 'All your lovely hair, too. I always did use to admire your hair. So neat. I nearly grew mine. Still, never mind, it's growing out nicely – coming curly, too.'

Miss Mayfield managed what she hoped was a friendly smile.

'It's cooler this way. Now . . . there are a few things I need.' She named them, asking for small quantities.

'Did Berta know you was coming? Did she take your bread and milk?'

Milk didn't matter; bread did. She added a packet of dry biscuits to her order. The woman began putting all the things in a brown paper bag.

'That was a terrible thing to happen. Coming so close to poor Wesley Baines, too. Cast a right gloom on the village, that did. And so unfair, when you'd been so brave about saving them sheep. Mr Frisby talk about giving you a medal – you know his way. Still, there's no doubt you saved him a rare lot of money. To go through all that and then nearly die in your own schoolroom. It was the piano-tuner found you, you know. I reckon he saved your life.'

'I expect he did,' Miss Mayfield said warmly. For a moment she was tempted to throw pride and reserve to the winds and to say, Look, I've lost my memory, I remember nothing. Tell me everything you know.

The woman was already embarked upon her story, giving it all the drama in which her kind delight.

'That was a shock for him, too, mind, going in to tune the piano and finding you like that. Come running out, he did, white as a ghost, saying you'd been killed. That was the blood, you see. And again, in a way, you was lucky. Everybody was here that night, on account of the inquest, see? Doctor and police and all. Took you into Wandford in the police car, they did.'

'Yes, I was very fortunate.' She stood up and opened her purse. The woman was quiet while she mentally added and gave the change.

'Now, you oughta take care of yourself. You still look real poorly to me. D'you think you should carry that lot? Ella'll be back from Frisbys' any minute now; she'll pop across with them for you, and pleased to.'

'It isn't heavy, and I do rather want a cup of tea.'

'If only you'd said. I'd hev made you one in a minute. The kettle's on now; let me . . .'

'Thank you very much, but I left my own kettle on.' It

was a lie, but she must get away. All this chatter, this reference to people whom she should know, maddening, maddening. If she had to endure it for another moment she would break down and betray herself.

She was drinking milkless tea and eating cheese and biscuits in the kitchen when a large black cat leaped the wall of the yard and came in by the open door. It ran directly towards her, more like a dog than a cat, and rubbed itself against her ankles, purring more and more loudly.

'Oh, poor puss,' she said, bending to stroke it. 'Such a lovely welcome and no milk.'

She offered it a crumb of cheese, at which it sniffed scornfully. It rubbed around her again, then retreated and stood a little way off, looking at her confidently, and then demandingly. It mewed a little and walked all around her again. In the end she said aloud:

'All right, I can see I shall have no peace till I do,' and she unhooked a small jug from the dresser and went to the house next door.

A woman, obviously the mother of the girl to whom Miss Mayfield had spoken earlier in the day, with the same good looks grown brittle, answered the door. Miss Mayfield introduced herself.

'Your daughter was kind enough to say that you would lend me some milk. Very little would do. It isn't for me, it's for a cat, and a token offering would do.'

Mrs Grieve flinched a little.

'Oh, do you keep a cat? I hadn't seen it. To tell you the truth, I don't like them much. I know it's senseless. I'm tolerant of snakes. Do come in.'

She led Miss Mayfield into a long room crowded with objects – useful, decorative, merely curious – brought from overseas.

'We've only been back a week and I've heard so much about you, Miss Mayfield.' She gave a little laugh. 'You know how it is – you're the absolute reverse of all I imagined. Tackling those dreadful dogs . . .' Her gaze, shrewd but kindly, ran over Miss Mayfield's face and figure assessingly. 'I was about to have a cup of tea,' she went on. 'I like mine early. Do stay and drink a cup with me. Barbara – that's my daughter – has gone to play tennis and I always find my own company conducive to melancholy. You live alone, don't you? How do you get on?'

Miss Mayfield opened her mouth to say, But I have never lived alone, and then remembered that, at least since last April, she had done so. In the house next door.

'I manage,' she said. 'But, of course, during term I'm out all day.'

'Yes, and I daresay that when you get home, the peace and quiet is welcome. If you don't mind my saying so, you don't look a bit like a schoolmistress, either.'

'That is supposed to be a compliment,' said Miss Mayfield, smiling.

An elderly woman entered, bearing a tea-tray which she set on a low, elaborately carved table of Oriental origin, between the chairs. Mrs Grieve glanced at the tray.

'Two cups. Clever Carrie! Oh, and Carrie, would you take that little jug and put some, milk in it and put it on the hall table? There, now. How do you like your tea, Miss Mayfield? Now, tell me, what do you think of Walwyk?'

'I think it's very pretty.'

Mrs Grieve gave a short sharp sigh. 'I suppose it is. But . . .' She hesitated and then rushed on. 'I suppose I heard too much about it before I ever saw it, and then lived alongside such an enthusiast. My husband – he's been dead almost four years, poor man – always used to spend his holidays at the Rectory; he was a friend of Freddie Thorby's at school, and his parents were abroad most of the time. He used to rave about Walwyk, and always said when he retired he would build a house here. We came on one leave and ever after I knew that it wasn't *my* idea of the perfect place to end in, but he was so keen, I hadn't the heart . . . And then, just when we did retire, Hal Thorby's old aunt – who used to live in your house – died, and Hal wanted the house but not the huge garden and orchard. So my husband bought the land and built what we thought was the ideal house. Since his death I've been in a quandary. I do like the house, and one must have a base, and I know I couldn't sell it for anything like what it cost. And Barbara always has a very gay time when we are here. But frankly I loathe the place.'

'What a pity. Why?'

'I just couldn't say. George always said it was mere perversity. I don't think so. It's too small, and everybody is related to everybody else. It's like living in a goldfish bowl.' She took a sandwich and bit it thoughtfully. 'Yet I've lived in places where there were only half a dozen European families. My husband was a mining engineer and I've lived in strange places, quite happily. I'm never *happy* here.'

Miss Mayfield remarked that it was a pity; it was such a nice house; it reminded her, she said, of houses in Kenya.

'Oh, have you lived there, too?' Mrs Grieve asked eagerly. They talked about Africa for some time. Once, during this conversation. Miss Mayfield made a slip and said, 'I was saying to Rose only the other day . . .' But it was all right; Mrs Grieve could not know who Rose was, or that that comment had been made at least three years ago.

Mrs Grieve, indeed, seemed so delighted to have some-one to talk to that Miss Mayfield's words, or silence, mattered very little. Twice Miss Mayfield made a move to go, and each time was begged not to be in a hurry. Carrie came and removed the tea-tray, and almost immediately afterwards Mrs Grieve was suggesting a sundown drink.

'I'm afraid I don't drink.'

'A cool soft drink, then. I don't know how you feel, but I think it's growing hotter. I think we shall have a storm.'

'I haven't unpacked yet.'

Showing that although she complained about living in a goldfish bowl, she was not altogether immune from its behaviour, Mrs Grieve said:

'Barbara said you'd come back without luggage.'

'Most of my things,' said Miss Mayfield truthfully, 'are in a trunk which was here when I arrived.'

Mrs Grieve made one last effort to detain her.

'You know, I don't think you are fit to be alone yet. Why don't you move in with us? There's plenty of room. I should be delighted to have you.'

'That is more than kind. But honestly I'm much

stronger than I look. And I have been looking forward to sleeping in my own bed again.'

'Come and have lunch with us tomorrow, then. Or with me, I should say. Barbara will probably be out. I hate eating alone. I have an open invitation to the Rectory, but – and I know I shouldn't say this – I find poor Isabel absolutely exasperating. After half an hour I long to shake her. I suppose you're much more kindhearted and feel sorry for her?'

'Perhaps I do, in a way,' Miss Mayfield said cautiously.

The feeling which had afflicted her in the shop – that she must confess and beg for enlightenment or go mad if she didn't soon escape – came upon her again.

Heavy purple clouds had reared themselves in the western sky and everywhere lay in the heavy hush which precedes the first mutter of thunder. After Mrs Grieve's house her own seemed almost dark. She left the front door wide open, went through into the kitchen where the cat waited, and poured the milk into a saucer. While the cat lapped daintily, she went upstairs and folded the dust sheets in the bedroom, found, in the bathroom, an airing cupboard well stocked with bed linen and made up her bed.

When she came down again, she stood for a moment looking at the trunk and the crate. She knew that, having come so far and with such difficulty in order to look for some trace of her past, she was now, in a feeble fashion, reluctant to take the final step. The day had been a series of disappointments, and for a moment she doubted her strength to face yet another. Nevertheless, she went into the kitchen and found a sharp knife, a claw hammer and a solid-looking screwdriver.

From the front door she could see the garden bathed in a strange olive-green light; the topiary birds in the hedge looked as though they had been cut from black stone.

She put on the light and knelt by the trunk, sawing the stout cord with which it had been tied. The lid, thrown open, revealed a few shabby winter clothes: jerseys and cardigans, grey or navy-blue, a dark skirt, a snuff-coloured woollen dress, a camel-hair dressing gown very much worn. There were some shoes, two squashed felt hats, some stockings and underwear. There was nothing that revealed anything about Deborah Mayfield except that she was dowdy, and – to judge by the way her things were mended – economical.

Well, the crate might yield more. Books often had inscriptions, or the bookseller's name. And whoever did the packing might have thought the crate the proper place in which to put old letters, papers. I might even have been a diary keeper, for all I know, she thought, remembering how in Africa she had always intended to keep a journal and never found the time.

Opening the crate was quite a task; it had been nailed down in many places, with long nails, some of which had to be pried up before she could set the claw of the hammer between the lid and the side and lever the separate sections, up. One section came off with a ripping sound, and below she could see a folded newspaper. She pulled some of that away and saw the spines of several books. They were too closely packed to be pulled out at this moment, and brushing the back of her hand across her wet forehead, she set to work on the next section of the lid. It came up, cracking and creaking, and a voice from the doorway said:

'Miss Mayfield!'

There was one of those dizzying, sickening slides through time, with the familiar I-have-been-here-before sensation. Here in this lighted hall, with my hand on this rough wood, looking up and looking round, seeing this man framed in this doorway . . .

And it was like the fingertip on the self-starter which sets the engine in motion.

It was the thing she had prayed would happen.

She said, 'Canon Thorby!' and tried to straighten herself, but her legs had gone limp as a rag-doll's and refused to support her; instead, they shot out at odd angles, in a way she could never have voluntarily arranged them, leaving her sitting on the floor, lolling against the crate.

'Put your head on your knees,' a voice said from a thousand miles away.

Deliberately she held to that position. I'm not fainting; I'm watching a wild, crazy roundabout, whirring round far too quickly – Ethel, Granny Rigby, Emily Baines and Wesley, Ethel again, Sydney . . .

'Better now. Come, let me help you.' He lifted her, her rubbery legs trailing, and half carried her into the sitting room. 'I'm so dreadfully *sorry*,' he said, over and over again. 'I saw the lights . . . and heard the wood ripping; I couldn't *think*. You were the very *last* person . . .' He pulled a cushion out from under the dust sheet on which she lay and put it behind her head. 'And now,' he said, 'over all your protests, you're going to have some brandy.'

She was glad to see him go away for a moment. The burden of memories which she must now lift and stagger along with seemed, for the moment, too great. She remembered a very good poem she had once read, about the pains of resurrection and how the risen men might wish themselves dead again. For a breath's space she wished that she had remained with her maimed memory, ignorant.

She remembered that last interview, in his study; and the way he had taken leave of her. And she knew that she must be very careful.

'Here you are,' he said, handing her a glass. 'My poor Miss Mayfield, what a homecoming! Why on earth didn't you let us know?'

'Mrs Mott-Tyler said that you were still abroad.'

'Oh yes. My fault again. I've been meaning to get in touch with her ever since I returned. So much had piled up.' He threw the dust cover from one of the chairs and sat down. 'There seemed no urgency. The last I heard from Barnhurst was that you were happy and comfortable, but still not quite well. Anyhow,' he leaned forward and gave her his most charming smile, 'I'm delighted to see you back.'

'I longed to be back. That was the trouble. Mrs Mott-Tyler and Miss Ellison were so careful with me. They just couldn't realize that I was quite well. In the end – I might as well tell you before they do – I ran away.' She sipped at the brandy and gave a little shudder.

'I must let them know. They'll be very worried.'

'I shall, of course, write and apologize for leaving as I did. But you know how it is; after any illness there comes a time when you can't bear to be coddled any longer.'

'How long have you been in full possession of your . . . your memory?'

'That's rather a difficult question to answer.' She smiled at him. 'And who could honestly claim full possession of his memory? There was space when I couldn't remember *anything* about Walwyk. Then, of course, later I remembered a great deal. Probably not everything. One thing I do remember, though, and I should like to speak to you about it at once because it does affect the future.'

'Ah, the future.'

'That thing is this – I realize that my accident was a godsend; it just saved me from making a most calamitous fool of myself. If I'd gone to that inquest and poured out all the hysterical nonsense that I'd bothered you with . . . well, I just don't know. . . .'

He looked at her steadily, and she forced herself to return his look, keeping her gaze innocent and limpid. When he moved, leaning back in the chair, he said quite lightly:

'I'm disappointed in you, Miss Mayfield. I thought you were made of sterner stuff. With the martyr's crown practically on your head, you go and recant. Yes, I'm disappointed.'

Matching his manner, though her whole inside was shaking, she said:

'Very few martyrs had my chance. A sound clout on the

head and a long, long time to think things over; and last, but not least, sound counsel.'

'I don't propose to go into this at the moment. You look to me as though you should be in bed. I'll say that I'm happy to know that you have revised your opinions about poor old Phoebe Rigby.'

'I certainly shouldn't have come back here if I hadn't.'

That was a point to her. 'No,' he said, drawing out the word slowly. 'I don't suppose you would. In your present condition, a good dose of shingles . . .' He broke off and laughed. 'I've thought so often about that conversation and come to the conclusion that you missed your mark in life. Novelist *manquée*. With that knack of creating something sensational out of such mundane stuff, you could have made a fortune. The thing is that such a talent, running disengaged, as it were, can be dangerous.'

'I know. It was dangerous to me. It almost lost me the best job, the happiest home, the kindest friends I ever had.'

She was astonished at herself. Where was all this inspiration coming from? Now she had him in a most difficult position. He extricated himself smoothly.

'That brings the future up again; and frankly I don't think you're fit for further discussion. Have a good night's rest and make Berta bring you your breakfast in bed. Perhaps you'd like to lunch with us tomorrow.'

'Mrs Grieve has already invited me.'

His eyes twinkled.

'Already? I'm afraid you'll have a little problem there. Oh, she's a delightful creature; we've known her for years and love her dearly; but she can't bear to be alone for a moment, and she talks without ceasing. I wonder, having met you, that she hasn't installed you in her spare room.' He stood up. 'Not that that would be such a bad idea. You do look appallingly frail. And, for goodness' sake, don't go struggling with crates and things like that.'

'I was looking for my letters.' The words were out before she had tried them over; and because the act belonged to her lost-memory time and she had pretended to him that her memory had returned some while ago, she felt that it was a slip and was discomfited. To cover the slip, she said:

'I thought – in fact, I hoped – that my post was being sent on with my books. You see I haven't . . .'

'How remiss of me! I should have told you at once. . . .' He reached for his wallet and then withdrew his hand. 'No, I know; it is on my desk. A letter – not for you, but *about* you – from Miss Rose Tilbury.' His voice took on a light, teasing quality. 'I don't think you should complain of not receiving letters; apparently you don't write them. Or not often enough. Miss Tilbury wrote to me because, she said, she had had a letter from you, sent from hospital in July, and since then no news at all.'

And it was true, that having had no reply to the letter in which she had announced her accident, she had not dared to write again. Only within the last ten minutes she had been certain that Rose was still alive – or, at least, had been alive as lately as the June of this year.

'Did she say whether she had written to me?'

'Yes. Twice, I think she said.'

'I never received a letter from her, either in the hospital or at Barnhurst.'

'I expect the hospital was to blame. They're gathering dust somewhere, awaiting someone's attention, I expect. I'll make some inquiries. Anyway, I wrote your friend a reassuring letter. I told her you had made a good recovery and that we were taking care of you.'

What more had he said? She must write to Rose the first thing she did.

'Well,' he said, 'I'll look in tomorrow, probably around six, and see how you are getting on.'

When he had gone she put her head in her hands and tried to think calmly. She was in a perilous position. So perilous that if her memory and her knowledge of the situation which it brought with it had come to her even as she put the key into the door, she would have obeyed her impulse to turn and flee. It was impossible that she should be allowed to come back here and live unmolested. The moment the Canon had recovered from his surprise at seeing her, he would begin to think things over, and he would never believe that she *had* recanted. They'd get her, as they had poor Wesley Baines.

Thinking of him brought to mind his words about God working in a mysterious way; and suddenly she was lifted out of her fear and doubt and filled with a sense of destiny. She had remembered at the precise moment that she had *because* it was then too late, she had been brought back to Walwyk and committed to remaining because her sole purpose was to save Ethel Rigby. It was as simple as that.

17

'WELL,' CANON THORBY ASKED QUIZZICALLY, 'DID
you have a nice lunch?'

'A nice *long* lunch,' she said. 'You must remember,
though, that everything Mrs Grieve has to tell me about
her past life is new and therefore interesting to me. I really
had a most entertaining time.'

'You're looking a great deal better.'

'Coming home completed my cure.'

She had found the remains of the Tío Pepe. And she
had gone across the Green again and spent the last of her
money on some more cheese and butter and some flour.
She had spent much of her morning making cheese straws.
An offering in the House of Rimmon.

As soon as he was comfortably installed, she said with
a bright confidence:

'We were going to talk about the future, weren't we?
The awkward part of this would all have been over before
we met if Miss Ellison hadn't taken such a peculiarly strict
view of her instructions to look after me.' She recounted

229

the incident, making it sound trivial and slightly amusing. 'But I'll tell you exactly what I said in my letter, Canon Thorby.' She told him, ending, 'If you have the slightest doubt as to my sanity, please don't hesitate to say so. Worse things have been said, and done me no harm.'

Busy as his mind was with the main issue, he was aware of an obscure change in her manner, her voice, even her way of looking at him. Something old-maidish, easily flustered, slightly fumbling, had left her; she seemed brisker, bolder.

'Put like that, it sounds so simple; but there is a complication. Dear Miss Mayfield, I hate saying it – but I have already replaced you. You see, after your accident I couldn't leave Miss Benson to struggle on until the end of the term; I gave her what help I could, but it wasn't enough. And I heard of a young woman who was just down from Girton. Her home is in Selbury and her widowed mother was very anxious for her to find a post where she could sleep at home. She came in, every day towards the end of the term, on a scooter. She and her mother are so delighted by this arrangement that I simply haven't the heart to tell her that it no longer holds. You do see, don't you? We had no notion of when, if ever, you would be fit to take up work again.'

She forced herself to maintain her bright calm.

'I do see, perfectly. Then we come to my other point. Would you be prepared to give me a testimonial?'

'Certainly. Why not? But I should hate to have to do so. I have a far better suggestion. Miss Halstead doesn't want to live in the house. You have no home. I think you should remain here. When you feel fully restored, you can look in at the school when you wish, make yourself responsible for some undemanding classes, three or four times a week, if that would give you pleasure and interest; but let Miss Halstead carry on until Christmas at least. That would give us time to think things over. What do you say to that?'

It was a suggestion exactly in accord with her wishes, but something – and there was no name for it – whispered that too eager an acceptance would be unwise.

'I don't think I could do that, much as I appreciate such a generous proposal. It would put me so deeply in your debt; and I should feel so very useless.'

'Don't forget' – he bit the end from a cheese straw and regarded what remained with some attention – 'don't forget that you were injured on school premises, while in the school's service, and by a piece of school property. If you liked to take action against me, you could probably claim some enormous compensation – especially if you could prove impaired memory.'

'What will you think of next? In any case, I'm sure it was entirely my own fault. I couldn't have fixed the little wedge properly.'

'It was very worn. The wonder is that the accident hadn't happened before. I'm not saying this to persuade you one way or the other, Miss Mayfield. It is simple fact. I am to blame for all you have suffered. And nothing I could ever do would make up for it.'

'Are you certain that you are not saying this to ease my mind about staying and not really doing much work?'

'I think you should know me better than that. I'm a great believer in the direct approach; and I think . . .' He broke off and drank some sherry and began again. 'Look. We're both reasonable, adult people; let's be honest with ourselves. My culpability over a wedge that was likely to give way at any moment is the least of it; you could have noticed and complained and had it repaired. My real guilt lies elsewhere. First, that I did not notice all the . . . the bother brewing up in your mind. I went with you to Phoebe Rigby's when you complained about Ethel having been beaten; I dealt with the superficial situation and ignored all the deeper implications. And then, when you'd worked yourself into a state, and were worried past all bearing, and had been knocked down and trodden on and had opened your heart to me, all I could do, God forgive me, was to say, Go say all this at the inquest and you're sacked! So you went to finish all the marking, and you were collecting your belongings, and so . . . it happened. Whatever you allow me to do for you will never ease my conscience. I shall carry a burden of guilt until the day I die.'

'But, you see, you were right. I've thought about it so much. Look at the importance I put on finding the print of bare feet in the mud! You said somebody had been tempted to bathe. I took no notice. No, Deborah Mayfield couldn't be wrong! She was going to the inquest and to make a scene. You said if she did, she couldn't teach in Walwyk any more, so she went to tidy up in her finnicking way. And had an accident. If you need absolution, Canon Thorby, I can give it to you here and now. Throughout, you behaved reasonably and sensibly. I made a clown of myself, and I was hit over the head, as clowns so often are.'

'You talk about generosity! Nobody ever made a more generous speech. Be as generous in action. Stay here. Let Miss Halstead do all the hard work; she's young and tough and enthusiastic. You just live here and take care of yourself, and – allow us to take care of you.'

'There's nothing I would like better; except, of course, really to get back into harness again. But I do see your point about Miss Halstead. Till Christmas, then.'

'Till Christmas. Now, give me all the news of Stella Mott-Tyler. I haven't seen her for a long time. She was the most dazzling beauty, whose engagement to my brother was momentarily expected and somehow never came off. . . .' Gladly, Miss Mayfield began to talk on this new subject, obeying the injunction of the ancient proverb 'Say the pleasant, but not the untrue; say the true, but not the unpleasant.'

There were ten days remaining until the opening of the school term. The children had subscribed and sent her the pretty little wireless set, so it was natural enough that she should visit every one of them in their homes and tender her thanks.

Ethel Rigby was cleaning out her rabbits. Mrs Rigby had opened the door and said how nice to see Miss Mayfield, and was she quite better and what a shame it all was. Nobody could have been friendlier. She said that Ethel was with the rabbits.

'Come through,' she said.

And there was just a fraction of a second, just before Ethel had herself in hand again, when Miss Mayfield knew that to Ethel Rigby this was not just the return of a schoolteacher, restored after an accident, but something upon a different plane. A man in a laboratory, confident of the result of his experiment and then finding something fantastically different from his expectation, might have looked as Ethel Rigby did, raising her head from the hutch she was scrubbing. It was not surprise, or pleasure, or dismay. Nothing so human. Just for a moment Ethel's pretty, pale, rabbity face wore the visual expression of all the curiosity of the whole human race. And what will happen now?

Then, pale, pretty and rabbity, she listened to Miss Mayfield's words of gratitude; and she said her little piece: she hoped Miss Mayfield was better; she'd been sorry to hear about the accident.

Sydney Baines was alone in the cottage. Miss Mayfield had already heard, through Berta, that Mr Tharkell had offered Mrs Baines employment. Apparently, race-horses in training needed almost scientific attention, food weighed out to a fraction of an ounce, temperatures taken, their reactions to muscular exertion assessed. So when Miss Mayfield called at the Baines's cottage, Mrs Baines was away at her new job and Sydney was bottling plums. Doing it very handily, too.

'I came to thank you, Sydney, for your part in sending me that lovely little wireless set. It cheered me every day.'

'The boys wanted to get a red one, but the girls said blue and white.' Sydney's voice held the discontent of all minorities. He had grown during her absence and lost some of his sturdy look. She thought, Poor child, he's fatherless, and her determination hardened in her.

'The colour really doesn't matter. It's the size and handiness that I like. I shall bring it to school sometimes next term, and we can listen to talks, and music and plays.'

'Are you coming back to school, Miss?'

'Oh yes. Of course.'

'I'm glad of that. They said you never would. And we missed you.'

'Do you still help Ethel with her rabbits, Sydney?'

'Not like I did. You see, my mum is out all day, and my . . . I have to do a lot of things about here now.'

'In fact, you are the man of the house now.'

He produced a smile.

'Ethel's all right, though. My mum is often round there, sort of keeping an eye on things.'

'That's fine,' Miss Mayfield said.

She went to every house in which a child lived and, naturally, often encountered a parent. After one or two such meetings she began to suspect – and after a few more, was certain – that a subtle change had taken place in their attitude towards her. They were very friendly, more friendly, in fact, than they had been before; but every now and then, from behind the smiling, welcoming mask, something else would peep out, leer at her for a moment and then be gone before she could identify it. Invariably, though, this appearance and disappearance accompanied a mention of Wesley Baines's name.

When it first happened and somebody said, 'Sad about

Wesley Baines, weren't it?' and the look flashed out, not sad at all, but conniving and knowing, she had caught her breath, connecting the look with her conversation with Canon Thorby, believing that the speaker had by some means learned that she doubted the suicide story. But surely the Canon would never have reported that to anyone. Then somebody said, 'Let's see, now. You had your mishap right arter poor Wesley's, didn't you, Miss?' And the look was there, and gone again. They said, 'Pity about Wesley; he'll be missed.' And, 'Wesley was a right nice chap; never reckoned he'd go and do a thing like that.' Their words varied, but they all mentioned Wesley Baines sooner or later, and always with that look.

It happened with Mr Frisby, who came along to call upon her one morning. He shook her hand and greeted her effusively, and presently accepted, with an uncomplimentary expression of surprise, a glass of the Tío Pepe.

'You saved me,' he said, 'more than I care to think about, Miss Mayfield. Left to it, those damn dogs could have savaged thirty or forty – and they're fetching four shillings a pound on the hoof. And Lassie would have taken the rap. Some people, even now, don't believe there was another dog. Nobody else ever saw hair or hide of it. I'm deeply in your debt.'

'I saw the other dog. Apart from that, I did nothing, except call Lassie by name, and that had no effect.'

'It did, it did. You showed the flag. Dogs that set about sheep like that go absolutely berserk; they don't stop at one; they'll maul the lot. Your going there and calling, though it might not seem to have any effect, brought them back to their senses, made them realize they were dogs, not wild wolves. And I'd like very much to give you a real nice present. No, I mean it. Edith and I have been talking it over. We thought . . .' he hesitated, whether from diffidence or for effect, Miss Mayfield could not say – 'a nice fur coat.'

'But, Mr Frisby, that would be ridiculous. It's most kind and . . . and generous, but I did nothing. And all the time I was in hospital you sent me beautiful flowers and fruit. You more than repaid me.'

He made a face and a sound of scorn. 'I'd send such bits of nonsense to anybody I knew was ill, whether they'd done me a good turn or not. It was Edith's idea about the fur coat; she said she didn't think you had one. Of course, she may be wrong. You may have a mink tucked away somewhere. You're not one of those with everything in the shop window, are you?'

The thing looked out and leered, and, perhaps because Mr Frisby was less fundamentally shy than the villagers, it stayed long enough for her to name it – almost. It was a look which said, Come on, come off it; you're not nearly so prim as we thought; you're only human, just like the rest of us!

She longed to say, Mr Frisby, if you really wish to do me a favour, tell me why you look at me like that.

It was not a thing one could say.

'It was a kind thought, Mr Frisby. And I certainly haven't a mink tucked away. As a matter of fact, I've never even wanted a fur coat.'

'Then you must be unique. The point is, I feel in your

debt. Maverick and I have never exactly hit it off; he'd have jumped at a chance to twist me. As it was, with only one sheep killed, the rest unharmed, and your word for it that another dog was involved, I got off lightly. So whether you like it or not, you're going to have a present from E. Frisby. And it might as well be something that you want. Come on, please give it a name.'

She realized suddenly that here was a chance not to be missed. It didn't do to be proud.

'If you really feel that way – and, I repeat, there is absolutely no reason why you should – you could do me a great favour. You could lend – I say "lend" because I would do my best to repay you, but I might not be able to manage it – lend me fifty pounds. You see, I have had some unlooked-for expenses, and I'm not quite clear about my future. Canon Thorby has engaged another teacher who will be here at least until Christmas; I'm going to help a little, but I can't hope for much salary. Fifty pounds would be a great help to me just now.'

'I can see that; and it's yours. But I wanted to *give* you something. Well, you'll have it in your Christmas stocking.' He took out his wallet and selected ten five-pound notes from a wad of them.

'There, you are. Forget all about it.'

'I shan't do that. You've helped me more than you know. And I shall pay you back – very slowly, perhaps – but as soon as I can.'

They argued the point for another minute or so, and then he changed the subject by saying:

'Did you hear that Tharkell had made a job for Emily

Baines? I offered her one, too. Everybody felt sorry for her. It seemed an odd sort of match, right from the start. But there was more in Wesley than met the eye, wasn't there?'

There it was again!

'I liked what little I knew of him.'

'Just so,' Mr Frisby said.

It was Mrs Grieve who enlightened her. Kindly, garrulous, a little demanding, she could become in time a nuisance as a neighbour, Miss Mayfield realized; but there would be no time. In a few days the term would begin and school would constitute a refuge and an alibi. Moreover, Mrs Grieve's restlessness was increasing; she was beginning to talk of going to visit her brother in Cape Province.

'I just can't face winter in Walwyk. Even having the house so warm is a disadvantage; you feel the cold so terribly when you do go out. And I haven't seen Reggie for six years.'

So the friendship had flourished after the fashion of friendships aboard ships or in holiday hotels. Caution was not needed, because time itself set limits to the demands such an association might eventually make.

One day, over the teacups, Mrs Grieve said bluntly:

'I've said before, haven't I, that this place is the worst hotbed of gossip I ever knew. I really think I owe it to you to tell you what the latest is. Or have you heard and decided to ignore it?'

'Why "owe"? Is it concerned with me?'

'It definitely is. And I can't bear to see you going about

like a babe in the wood any longer. Whoever started it should be tracked down and exposed and made to apologize.'

'Is it . . . I suppose it is something to do with my state of mind?'

'Good Lord, no! It's about you and Wesley Baines.'

'Oh.'

Take it calmly, she told herself. It can do little harm. And for your purpose it is just as well that attention should be focused upon something simple and silly, over and done with.

'I'll tell you exactly what they're saying. You know me well enough to know that I don't believe a word of it, don't you? And I jumped on Isabel Thorby the other day when she spoke of it. It was that, as much as anything, that made me decide to tell you.' She lifted her thin hands with a clinking of rings and checked off the main points of what was being said. Almost as soon as Miss Mayfield arrived in the village, Mrs Baines began talking of leaving. The moment Mrs Baines went with Sydney into hospital, Miss Mayfield was asking Wesley to supper. On pretence of delivering a pair of shoes, Wesley called at Miss Mayfield's house and went in and stayed for a long time. The news of his death had been such a jolt that she'd only saved herself from falling by clutching at the banister. Wesley was known to have a weakness for women out of his class; he'd married the only moderately educated woman he'd ever met, and when he found one a notch higher, he'd fallen headlong. And since his wife refused to divorce him and his Methodist principles wouldn't allow him to live in sin, he'd gone melancholy and drowned himself.

Miss Mayfield was disgusted to the very depths of her being, shocked, hurt, ashamed. But she had a feeling – irrational, perhaps, but very strong – that this was the way she was intended to feel. In this place there was an ulterior motive behind everything. Behind, perhaps – yes, horrid as the thought was, it must be faced – behind Mrs Grieve's explanation and sympathetic anger.

'I'm grateful to you for telling me. It explains a few things that had puzzled me.'

'You take it very calmly,' Mrs Grieve said, lifting the teapot to refill the cups.

'What am I supposed to do? Foam at the mouth and run in circles?'

Mrs Grieve laughed.

'You really are the most surprising person. I verily believe that I was far more upset – on your behalf, I mean.'

'Getting upset wouldn't help. This kind of thing seems to me to be an inevitable part of life in a remote place. They don't read, to get to the cinema is an effort, so they manufacture their own folk tales, as they have been doing for hundreds of years. I don't like it, but I can bear it. If I live to be eighty, I shall probably look back and gloat over having figured in a romance, however far-fetched.'

Her sixth sense, now curiously alert, informed her that in her reception of the news about the gossip, she had in some subtle way disappointed Mrs Grieve.

Why?

*

That question was answered next day, when, in the evening, Canon Thorby came to see her.

He said, 'I have a proposition to make to you, Miss Mayfield. It's rather a delicate matter. How unselfish are you?'

'About average, dare I say?'

'The situation, is this. There's poor Barbara Grieve, who really is the most attractive and delightful girl, spending her time being dragged from place to place by her mother, who simply can't settle. Two years ago she was here between trips, and young Ralph Staples – I don't think you've met him – was obviously very much taken with her. She's been back here for about three weeks now, and they've got together again and the whole affair looks most promising, and now she's being whisked off again. I've been thinking things over, and I wondered whether *you* wouldn't accompany Mrs Grieve instead.'

'To South Africa?'

'Yes.' He settled in eagerly to point out the beauties of this, his latest scheme. 'You see, once Mrs Grieve gets to Cape Town, she'll have her brother, and a round of friends in no time at all; and you, Miss Mayfield, could go and pay a visit to *your* friends in Entuba. Don't you think that would be pleasant? And it would be doing a good turn.'

'I think that is just your way of putting it. You're trying to spoil me. And the prospect is very tempting. There are two good reasons, though, why I can't go with Mrs Grieve.'

'Mrs Grieve being one. I feared that.'

'On the contrary. Mrs Grieve and I get on very well; we have more in common than you would think. No. There is the first, the question of money.'

'Oh, please. You must know by this time that when I make a suggestion of this kind, I'm more than ready to look after all that side of it. Tell me your other reason – and it had better be a good one, because I really do think that the complete rest, the sea trip and seeing your friends would be the very best thing in the world for you just at this moment.'

'My other reason is that if I left Walwyk just at this moment, it would look as though I had been driven out.'

'I don't quite follow.'

'Perhaps you haven't heard the peculiarly nasty rumours that are circulating about me.'

His eyes narrowed, and she knew that he had.

'I hoped not to be obliged to mention that. It is, surely – and you must see it – a reason for going away and letting the whole horrid thing die down.'

'No. It's a reason for staying here.'

'I didn't imagine,' he said, with a touch of spleen in his voice, 'that you could be so contrary. Really, I'm quite displeased.'

'I'm sorry. And I do realize that if you are displeased enough, you can forbid me the school and banish me from this house. Then I should just get a job in Selbury and buy a scooter like Miss Halstead's and come here every evening and ride round and round the Green, just to prove that I wasn't ashamed to show my face.'

To her surprise, he broke into hearty laughter. He

laughed until he coughed and had to take out his handkerchief and wipe his eyes.

Dear Miss Mayfield. The thought of you on a scooter, vindicating your reputation . . . Really, you'll be the death of me yet! And talking about "forbid" and "banish". As though I would. When I said I was displeased, it was because I was disappointed. It seemed such a good scheme, beneficial all round. But if you feel so strongly about it, there's no more to be said. You're sure that you wouldn't like some time to think it over?'

'I'm positive.'

There was silence for a moment. Then he said:

'Now, just to show you how altruistic I was being, I'll tell you this. Yesterday I had a long letter from Mrs Halstead; her daughter, she said, was too shy to write. A vacancy has arisen in Selbury Grammar School. Miss Halstead would like to apply for it; Mrs Halstead would like her daughter to apply for it. Scooting, which is pleasant in summer, is, as Mrs Halstead points out, a very different thing in winter, and Miss Halstead has always been one to take cold easily. There were two pages of this, and the point when reached – well, you can guess.'

Miss Mayfield, who had faced with fortitude but little pleasure the prospect of playing second fiddle in her own school, said joyfully:

'Miss Halstead doesn't want to come back?'

He nodded. 'And since you frown upon my plan, I shall take considerable pleasure in telephoning Mrs Halstead this evening and telling her that so far as I am concerned, Miss Halstead can go to . . . Selbury Grammar School.

Shall I, at the same time, make an offer for the scooter?'

Conscientiously, Miss Mayfield joined in his laughter. But when she had seen him out and closed the door, she stood for a moment leaning her back against it, and her face was grave and bleak. She had won another round. But how many more to go?

18

TERM BEGAN ON A GOLDEN SEPTEMBER MORNING. Knowing what was being said about her. Miss Mayfield found facing her class for the first time something of an ordeal, and was secretly relieved that Juliet Reeve was no longer in school. She had passed her examination satisfactorily, a fact for which Miss Mayfield could take no credit at all. So far as the children were concerned, however, the rumour might never have been born. Miss Benson did refer to it, saying:

'Not to worry. If it wasn't that, it'd be something else. We stand to be shot at. They always maintained that Mrs Westleton was Canon Thorby's mistress, and as for me, I'm not only loose but frequently drunk and disorderly as well.' She gave a snort of laughter. 'It's astounding that they entrust their precious offspring to our care, don't you think?'

Miss Benson had had a birthday during the summer holiday and now owned a new two-seater convertible, red as a fire engine.

*

When the term was three weeks old, Miss Benson, opening the piano, said:

'I don't think you'll have Sydney Baines today, Miss Mayfield. And I shall have something to say to his mum when next I see her.'

Miss Mayfield's heart gave a little jump.

'Why?'

'Well, on Friday Mr Tharkell drove her and Sydney to Selbury. They were off to spend the weekend with her sister in Cambridge. And he promised to pick her up last night at eight; that's the last train in from Cambridge on Sunday. Sunday morning one of his horses went down with the staggers or the glanders or something, so he rang up Uncle Eric and asked whether he'd oblige by "just running in" and fetching her. Uncle Eric was otherwise engaged, so he shoved it on to me; I was going to be in Selbury anyway, and it wouldn't hurt me for once to come away early and do a good turn. So I went and I waited, and the train came in, no Baines. I made some inquiries and learned that it was just possible, if you were mad enough, to get a later one which went round by Ely and got in at ten to eleven. Like the muggins I am, I waited, thinking what a fix she'd be in if she had missed the good train and had to take the slow. I hadn't got a coat, and it turned bloody cold, and I smoked all my cigarettes – you know what Selbury is like on Sunday. And the ten to eleven came in, and still no Baines. Mucked up my whole evening.'

*

And that, so far as Walwyk was concerned, was Mrs Baines's and Sydney's epitaph.

Village gossip, turning like vultures from the well-picked-over carcass of Miss Mayfield's association with Wesley Baines, began to chew over his new morsel: Mrs Baines's curious disappearance.

What a way to leave Mr Tharkell, who'd kind of made a job for her. Ah, but even if she owed him a month's notice, she had the right of it there, for he said himself that she had a month's wages due on the Monday. Right bothered, he was. He'd always had a soft spot for her, ever since she'd nursed him through the jaundice. Rung up the police, he had. Go on, not the police. Yes, the police; said she was missing. Know what the police said? Unless she'd committed some crime, it was no affair of theirs; she was a grown woman, free to come and go as she wished. Did Mr Tharkell have any reason to think anything had happened to her, like murder or such? Then there was nothing they could do.

But there was the house, full of furniture and all the little gadgets poor Wesley had made. And clothes! Mr Tharkell said that when he drove her to the station, she'd had just a small suitcase and Sydney had a holdall, just what people would take going for the weekend. Sydney wore his best suit and carried his mackintosh; Mrs Baines had the black coat and skirt she'd had for Wesley's funeral and an overcoat.

What about the rent? Due, like everybody else's, on September the thirtieth. After that, would the Canon take possession and let Dick Hayer and Clara

Woodley have it? Time they got married. . . .

The cottage acquired, almost immediately, the sad look of a deserted house. Somebody lobbed a stone through the window of Wesley's workroom, and no doubt others would have followed but that Canon Thorby opened his Scripture lesson next day with a homily upon respect for other people's property and pointed out that if another stone went through the Baines's or any other window, there would be no trip to London for the Cup Final this season. No other stone was thrown.

Mrs Baines had been gone for a week when Ethel Rigby, lingering after everyone else had gone home, said:

'Miss, can I speak to you?'

'What is it, Ethel?'

It had not escaped Miss Mayfield's watchful eye that Ethel had cheered up since Sydney's departure, and even now, though what she said was not particularly heartening, she spoke with something almost jaunty in her voice and manner.

'I thought I'd better tell you quick. My gran says I'm not to be Mary Queen of Scots.'

Due to Miss Mayfield's illness and absence, the scenes from history had not been enacted at the summer fête, and were to be part of the Christmas entertainment.

'Oh, Ethel,' Miss Mayfield said in genuine dismay, 'I am sorry. You were so exactly right. It was the one piece of casting that pleased me more than any of the others. And now with Juliet gone, and Christine, I'm very short of tall girls. Couldn't you persuade her to change her mind?'

'No.'

'Do you think I could?'

'No. And, Miss, I'd rather you didn't try.'

'Did she give you any reason?'

'Yes.'

Miss Mayfield waited, for the reason, but Ethel remained silent.

'Don't you think I'm entitled to know the reason? I'm the one who is placed in an awkward position.'

'I can tell you what she said.' There was the faintest possible emphasis on the last word. 'She said she don't hold with dressing up and play-acting.'

'But that isn't the real reason. There is another.'

Ethel gave a nod. 'Between her and me.'

'And you can't tell me what it is? You know, Ethel, any-thing you said to me would be in the strictest confidence. You can trust me. There's something . . . not quite right between you and your grandmother, isn't there? I've suspected it all along.'

'I know that. So does she.'

'Don't you think, if we talked it over, we might find a way out?'

'It's something no amount of talk could alter. It would make it worse. *I*,' said Ethel with a kind of stoic pride, 'never said anything. Sydney went blabbing. Then that time she give me the hiding, you saw for yourself. All I'm saying now is that I can't be Mary Queen of Scots.'

'And all I've said is that I'm sorry. But that isn't the important thing. I'm fond of you, Ethel. I want you to be happy.'

'I shall be quite all right *now*. I don't much mind not being in the scenes.'

'I mind *for* you.'

'You don't have to fret about me. I can manage now.'

Just then the door to the cloakroom opened, and there was Mrs Rigby, wearing an old-fashioned straw hat, black, trimmed with pink and blue cornflowers.

'Excuse me, Miss. I watched all the others come out, and no Ethel . . . So I took the liberty.'

Before Miss Mayfield could speak, Ethel said in a whiny voice:

'It's the sums. I was kept in.' She jerked her head towards the blackboard, upon which there were some sums.

What presence of mind; what an ability to sum up a situation!

'Could she do her keeping-in tomorrow, Miss? You see, we had an appointment with Mrs Head the dressmaker. Ethel's winter dress.'

'If I'd known you were waiting, Mrs Rigby . . .'

'I expect Ethel forgot.'

'I was all muddled up with the sums.'

'I reckon you could keep her in till Christmas and she still couldn't count,' Mrs Rigby said pleasantly. 'Even her rabbits, she'll count ten one day and twelve the next.'

Miss Mayfield saw Ethel stiffen when the rabbits were mentioned. But she said with a land of peevishness:

'It was twelve; and that's too many now there's no one to help with the food. I think I shall sell the lot.'

Mrs Rigby gave a little laugh, 'You silly girl. What will

you say next? You know you think the world of them rabbits.'

'You mustn't keep poor Mrs Head waiting any longer,' Miss Mayfield said.

When she reached home she found that the post had brought her a letter which Berta had taken from the mat and put upon the gate-legged table. The address was typewritten, and the long buff envelope bore in the top left-hand corner the printed words 'Certain Future Assurance Company'.

Like everyone else in the British Isles, she had from time to time received admonitory communications from various assurance companies, bidding her prepare for a comfortable old age, to insure against fire and flood, to make certain, in the event of her sudden demise, that her dependants would not be doomed to starvation. She almost did not open this latest arrival. She had picked it up and carried it in her hand into the kitchen, where she put it down. She made her tea and carried it into the sitting room. When she was about to go to bed, she remembered that on many occasions recently she had intended to leave a note for Berta asking her not to make such strong morning tea. It had become steadily blacker and blacker and was beginning to affect her digestion. Last term she would have found it easy enough to speak about it; now always in all her dealings with Berta was her awareness of the girl's part – possibly unintentional – in fostering the rumour of her affection for Wesley Baines, and that had affected their relationship, so that now it was much easier to leave a note.

So she took a knife and slit the envelope, intending to use its clean inner side for her purpose. The note to Berta was not to be written that evening, for out of the envelope came a sheet of paper closely written all over in Mrs Baines's characteristic characterless hand.

No date. No address.

Dear Miss Mayfield,

If it had been safe I would have come and seen you before I left, but I thought it over and decided best not. You were kind when I was in trouble and I'm sorry I spoke as I did when you brought the papers about the scholarship for Sydney. I hadn't got things straightened out then. Now I have. It would all take too long to write, so what I want to say to you now is, *be careful*. I don't know how much you know, or if you realize what you are up against. Your accident should have warned you. And you know what happened to Wesley.

You can't save Ethel, if that is what you're thinking of. All you can do is look out for yourself, like I have.

I hope you won't go showing this to anyone. I should know and it'd be the worse for you. I've broken with them, on account of the filth and the wrong ideas; but I always was a quick learner, and believe me, I know it all. They're all in it and there's nobody you can trust, so be warned by me and mind your own business, or better still get out of the place.

Yours sincerely,

Emily Frances Baines

Detached from its background it could have been a letter from someone slightly demented; as it was, it fell slickly into place, another little piece of the puzzle. With a quite ludicrous uplift of the heart, Miss Mayfield thought, I was right about *her*. She changed sides to save Sydney; she brought the intelligence and teachability which had enabled her to pass her professional examinations to bear upon the learning of the Black Arts. She had been disgusted by the 'filth'. She wasn't the convert they thought they had made.

In reverse, Emily Baines was rather like some of the Africans Miss Mayfield had known. Brought to the Mission by the yearning for education or the need for medical attention, they would learn the hymns, say the prayers, be baptized, take Christian names. Then, faced with a drought or some other disaster, they would relapse and go running to the witch doctor. But that didn't cancel out what they had learned.

Emily Baines, a somewhat unwilling convert to the dark creed in the first place, had relapsed and deserted, but she had taken with her what she had learned. 'I should know and it'd be the worse for you.'

Holding the neatly written sheet, she pursued the analogy. It was the letter of a Kikuyu, forced to take the Mau Mau oath and aware of its potency, who yet felt that he owed a little allegiance to some European who had been kind. She said it. 'You were kind when I was in trouble.'

She looked again at the envelope. Her name and address were typed clearly, but not expertly or evenly. A two-finger job.

Wesley Baines could have held a policy issued by this company, and Mrs Baines might have gone to the London office, and she could have said, 'Can I borrow an envelope and use your typewriter for a minute?' Or she might be employed by the firm in some capacity.

In either case, she could be reached through this address.

Miss Mayfield sat down and wrote a carefully worded letter:

'I was very pleased to hear from you,' she wrote, 'and I hope that everything will go well for you and Sydney in your new surroundings. Believe me, I shall be very cautious. You could help me in what I am *determined* to do without harm to yourself. Could we meet, in a place of your choosing, very soon?'

She posted the letter in Selbury. After a time, it was returned to her by the postal authorities. Someone had written, 'Unknown at this address.'

19

THE TERM MOVED ON. EACH DAY WAS A LITTLE shorter than the one before, and as the evenings darkened, Miss Mayfield would look ahead at what she had to do and inwardly she would quail.

It was with a feeling of recognizing a disaster long expected that she saw, one morning halfway through October, Ethel's place empty when the school assembled. She had actually asked: 'Does anyone know anything about Ethel?' when every face swivelled to the door behind her – the door to the cloakroom. Turning quickly, Miss Mayfield saw Mrs Rigby, standing exactly where she had stood when she had come to take Ethel to the dressmaker's, but in a very different state of mind and body. She looked genuinely distraught, her face very pale and her eyes wild. Having caught Miss Mayfield's attention, she stepped back into the cloakroom, making a sign that she wished to be followed. When Miss Mayfield joined her, she said hoarsely:

'Shut the door. I don't want it spread abroad yet. I

hoped she'd come to school. I hoped she'd be here. Now I don't know what to do.'

She leaned against the wall and held her hand to her breast. The prim voice and manner of one who has been in 'good service' had deserted her, together with the composure which had made her such a slippery adversary.

'You don't know where Ethel is?' asked Miss Mayfield.

'She've stayed out a night once before and come to school. So I hoped . . .'

'Had you been unkind to her again?'

'May I drop dead if I laid a finger on her, *or* said a harsh word. I'd got sausages – her favourite – cooking for her tea, and she went off after the rabbit food and never come back.'

'Did you look last night? Surely . . .'

'Miss, I took a torch and I called and I called, and I hunted over every inch where she could've been. Hours I searched. Then, as I say, I reckoned she'd done like she done before.'

'We must organize a search at once. You should go to the Post Office – no, the Rectory is nearer now – and telephone the police.'

'The police!' Mrs Rigby's grey pallor deepened. 'But, Miss, they'd hev her in the "Missing Persons" in the *News of the World*. We can't go putting Ethel in there! She'll turn up.' Something was reasserting itself. 'Oh yes, she'll turn up. We would look silly calling in the police just over a bit of bad temper.'

'We'd look sillier if something happened to her and

they hadn't been informed. She's only fourteen, you know.'

The shock of finding that Ethel was not in school was beginning to wear off, and it was clear that Mrs Rigby was regretting the impulse that had brought her there.

'I'll go and see what Canon Thorby advises,' she said, with a reversal to her prim manner.

'That would be wise,' Miss Mayfield said. 'Let me know as soon as you hear anything.'

'I will, Miss. I will.'

Within ten minutes Miss Benson came through from the Junior room with some obvious excuse.

'Did I just see Granny Rigby on the premises?'

Miss Mayfield nodded. 'She came to see if Ethel had come to school. She walked out last evening.'

'That's exactly how her mother went. It's a bit early for Ethel to be starting that game.'

'There could be other explanations,' Miss Mayfield said in a cool voice.

'Such as?'

'From what Mrs Rigby said, a fit of temper.'

'Was the old girl much upset?'

Miss Mayfield almost said, Yes, particularly when I suggested asking aid from the police! But she remembered her new rule, Trust nobody.

'She seemed very much upset.'

'I told you she was a devoted old thing, didn't I?'

'You did. The point is that in Alchester I'd had one or two experiences with parents who were not devoted. And that made me so suspicious. I know better now.'

She told herself that she was becoming as unscrupulous a liar as Granny Rigby herself.

At twelve o'clock Canon Thorby came into school; he carried several letters in his hand.

'I gathered you'd be anxious about Ethel,' he said. 'We don't *know*, of course, but her grandmother has now a shrewd idea of where she might be. The summer before last they both went to stay in Great Yarmouth with somebody very remotely connected with them, a great-uncle's step-daughter, or some such, who keeps a small boarding house there. Ethel and this young woman got along extraordinarily well, and Ethel wanted to go again this year. Mrs Rigby has written a letter to the young woman, whose name, believe it or not, is Bedfellow, and as I have to go in to Selbury, I'm taking it to post there. We've asked Miss Bedfellow to telephone the Rectory as soon as she gets the letter. So we shall know tomorrow morning.'

It seemed to Miss Mayfield that some quicker way of gathering the information could be found, but she was never going to criticize their arrangements again.

'I hope she is there,' she said.

'So do we all. She had thirty shillings in her possession. She had sold some rabbits. Is there anything you need from Selbury? I'm open to take small commissions.'

Next morning, as the school assembled, Baxter brought a note: 'Just to let you know that Ethel is safe and sound with Miss Bedfellow. Heard five minutes ago.'

Like everything else, it was smooth and plausible.

Unlike many other things, it was susceptible to proof. During the dinner hour that day Miss Mayfield said to Miss Benson:

'I suppose, being a car owner, you wouldn't know anything about the bus service from Renham to Selbury.'

'Only that it's carefully arranged not to link with trains. Every now and then there's a grumbling letter in the Selbury *Free Press* about it. I believe they run two a day. Why?'

'Well, there's a parcel at the Selbury Post Office that they think belongs to me. The wrapping is torn, part of the address is missing, and the contents are – I quote – "damp and protruding". The Postmaster wishes me to go and examine it. The point is, I can guess what it contains. The woman I used to live with – she teaches Domestic Science – is convinced that on my own I shall starve to death, so she often sends me parcels of what her classes have made. She chooses the most impossible things and packs them insecurely. I thought that by Saturday it would be past salvaging.'

'I'll run you in,' Miss Benson said eagerly. 'I can get to Selbury now in fourteen minutes.'

Miss Mayfield gave an exaggerated shudder.

'That was kindly meant, I know. I happen to be a very nervous passenger. I'll wait till Saturday.'

She turned away and began dishing up dinners.

'I swear,' Miss Benson said, 'I'll stick to forty all the way.'

'Honestly, I wasn't trying to cadge a lift. It never occurred to me.'

'Not to me, either. As a matter of fact, I want to go to Selbury. I went in on Saturday and forgot the most important thing of all – a new lipstick. And I have a date tomorrow evening. I really need that lipstick.'

In the end Miss Benson was begging to be allowed to drive her into Selbury.

Miss Mayfield kept her eye on the speedometer, and every time the wobbling needle went about forty, she said, 'Please.' Only once did she drop her role of nervous, slightly unwilling passenger, and that was when Miss Benson said:

'D'you know, I have a theory about Ethel Rigby, something nobody else has thought of, and if I said it, they'd just laugh and say, "But they're only kids." The average person is very Ignorant and sentimental about the young. Trained people know differently. Ethel was dotty about Sidney Baines, and I mean dotty.'

'Then why should she go to Yarmouth? I'm sorry. I don't see . . .'

'I'll bet you Sydney knew where they were going and let it out.'

Almost afraid to think lest telepathy should be as efficient as some people claimed, Miss Mayfield thought, But Mrs Baines wrote to me from London.

Aloud she said, 'That is possible. Yes, very possible. And no one else ever thought of that.'

'I'm a bit of a psychologist. Ethel and Sydney did more than gather rabbit food.'

'He was only twelve,' Miss Mayfield protested.

'Did you never read your Aldous Huxley?'

'We're touching seventy. *Please!*' Miss Mayfield said.

'There's the Post Office. I'll park on the Square and go to the chemist's and turn round and pick you up.'

'I wonder would you *very* much mind getting something for me as well? I've made a list, and here,' she fumbled a little, 'here is a prescription, and some money.'

The prescription was old, a remedy for the indigestion which living with Janet Lovelace had provoked, and the last time she had used it, it had taken fifteen minutes to prepare. Everything else on her list was as simple, old-maidish and troublesome as she could make it. Half an ounce of powdered orrisroot, for example. 'It may seem old-fashioned,' she explained, 'but it is a better moth deterrent than any of these new things. The same with the sweet spirits of nitre; half a teaspoonful in a glass of hot water, with two lumps of sugar, breaks up a cold more quickly than anything I know.'

They'll think I've gone crackers, Miss Benson thought.

Harmless and bumbling Miss Mayfield made her way into the Post Office, went with a sudden briskness to the row of telephone booths and shut herself in and asked for the Yarmouth Telephone Exchange.

A male voice answered, and immediately she was harmless and bumbling again. She was a silly old lady who had been told that a Miss Bedfellow took paying guests in Yarmouth, but she'd forgotten the address. Could they help? Did they have a street directory? She was so sorry to be a bother.

The male voice said quite kindly that what she needed was Inquiries. Inquiries was female, with a brisk voice which said that it had an idea that Miss Bedfellow was on the telephone; it was a name one noticed, wasn't it? Yes, Inquiries was quite right. It read out, in a clear distinct way, both the address and the telephone number.

Miss Mayfield said some hasty words of thanks, found some money, gave Miss Bedfellow's number and waited, feeling the sweat break out on her neck.

Another female voice, calm, unhurried, said, 'Sea Mist Boarding House. Miss Bedfellow speaking.'

'Would it be possible for me to speak to Miss Ethel Rigby?'

'I'm sorry. What name did you say?'

She repeated it.

'There's no one of that name . . . Oh *Ethel Rigby*. Oh, I know. You can find her at Walwyk, W-a-l-w-y-k. It's in Essex. Curlew Lane, Walwyk. Whatever made you think she was here? It's two years ago.'

God, please, God, help me to give a reasonable answer, or she'll go and write a letter or something, and I shall be betrayed.

It slid into her mind, complete with names and everything.

'Yes, two years. How time flies!' she said. 'I'm Mrs Crawford, of Gorleston. My daughter made Ethel's acquaintance during that summer holiday, and as we're arranging a party . . . I'm afraid Essex is rather far, isn't it? Just for a party, I mean. Thank you. Goodbye.'

*

She left the booth and went through a performance which an observer would have found eccentric. She took a letter from her bag and went to the counter and asked a question about airmail charges to Barranquilla. All the time that the clerk was consulting the rules, she was dabbing her letter on the wet sponge provided for the convenience of people who did not care to lick stamps. When the writing was blurred and the paper limp and moist, she received, absent-mindedly, the information she had asked for and went to the door.

It was some time before Miss Benson arrived.

'It's your own fault you had to wait,' she exclaimed. 'That prescription! What's in it? Rhinoceros horn? Well, where's your parcel?'

'In the dustbin. There was a jar of something which had broken and soaked everything. I did salvage the letter, but I don't suppose I shall be able to read it.'

'It'll be more legible when it's dry,' Miss Benson said comfortingly. Really, poor old girl, she did look upset; a parcel probably meant a lot in her meagre life.

'Is there anywhere else you'd like to go now we are in this giddy metropolis?'

What I'd like – at least, what I think I ought to do – is to go to the Police Station. What should Miss Benson say if I said that? What excuse could I give? She's no fool; she might connect my two errands. No, I must leave it until Saturday.

'No, nowhere else, thank you.'

'Then I'll take you to the Club and buy you a drink. To make up for losing your parcel.'

'I don't drink.'

'Look,' Miss Benson said, 'if I may say so, that's a silly sort of thing to say. So off-putting. And you only mean that you don't drink alcohol, which leaves quite a range of things you can drink. *Lovely* tomato juice; and then it looks as though you're just taking care of your waistline. Not that you have to worry; you've got a lovely figure.'

'Me?'

'You. And a lovely complexion, too. And now that your hair's short and curly . . .' She broke off and grinned. 'I guess I'm speaking out of turn, but you could do a lot more with yourself if you took a little trouble.'

Miss Mayfield made one of those inarticulate sounds, expressive of attention, in which people indulge when their attention is elsewhere. Miss Benson chose to take it as an invitation to proceed with her lecture.

'That lipstick, for instance. I know it. Eve Eden's Natural Pink. We used to use it at school and think what devils we were! The point is, if you use a lipstick, you might as well use a real one. And if you haven't a moral objection to a smear of powder, why jib at a spot of rouge? Have I offended you? Honestly, it's only because you are such a dear, and it seems a pity you don't make the best of yourself. Ma Westleton, now, she could rub her face in Bath brick for all I'd care. Actually, she was always on at me – where did I get my hair cut, what powder did I use. I used to give her a bum steer every time.'

'A what?' asked Miss Mayfield, thinking that even in her present distracted state of mind she could not have heard what she thought.

'Sorry. It's an American expression, meaning wrong direction, hint or advice. I got quite a kick out of seeing her look sillier than usual. All for the Canon's benefit, of course. But you, that's different. . . . Here we are.'

She swung the car expertly into the forecourt of a house which stood back from the road and which announced itself to be the Selbury Town and Country Club. She parked alongside three other cars.

'There'll be nobody here. We're early.'

Inside the Club, which was all dark panelling and thick carpets and sporting prints, she pushed open a door, and Miss Mayfield, following, found herself in a ladies' cloakroom.

'Now, just for fun,' Miss Benson said, 'let me try my hand on you. Look, everything straight from the shop, in case you're fussy. Far more hygienic than if you went for a facial, however high-class . . . Just sit down and let me play around for a bit. If you don't like it, you can wash it all off again.'

There was something almost macabre about sitting there, now and again glancing into the looking-glass and seeing her whole appearance change, while behind that mask which was her face the thoughts went on. Ethel Rigby was not in Yarmouth with Miss Bedfellow. Where, then? Where?

'Perfectly clean comb, look!' said Miss Benson, who seemed to have gathered – where from Miss Mayfield could not imagine – that her headmistress was a fanatic about cleanliness.

She damped the comb, ran it through Miss Mayfield's

hair, remembering – and somehow that cheered Miss Mayfield more than the transformation in her appearance – the scar.

'I must be careful; it was this side, wasn't it? That was a thing! You know I tried to come and see you, twice. The first time they said no visitors, and the second time they said you'd just left. I often wondered if you thought I'd been a bit casual about the whole thing. Did you?'

All the while her slim brown fingers were making little curls and nipping them into place.

'Oh no. They were so strict. I never saw anyone the whole time I was in Wandford.'

'But Canon Thorby told Uncle Eric he'd—'

She broke off, and in the glass their eyes met and held for an interminable moment.

'Oh, well, I may have it wrong. Uncle Eric is inclined to waffle on, and I don't always listen. There. How's that? Though I say it myself, Elizabeth Arden herself couldn't have done better in the time.'

Miss Mayfield forced herself to show interest and enthusiasm.

'I don't look a bit like myself,' she said, paying Miss Benson's handiwork the highest compliment within her power to give.

'Come on, then,' Miss Benson said; and carrying her new face carefully, Miss Mayfield followed her back into the hall and thence, up a few stairs, into the bar, where the first person they saw was Mr Freeman, who usually whiled away the time between leaving his office and returning to his lonely home by drinking two glasses of sherry and picking up what gossip he could in the Club.

He jumped to his feet at once, greeted Miss Benson with delight and, in his turn, paid her handiwork the compliment of not recognizing her companion. When Miss Benson, in her offhand way, effected the introduction, he was so much surprised, and so shocked by his surprise, that he was almost babbling.

'I know Miss Mayfield, of course, of course. Good evening. I was so taken aback for a moment. I was given to understand that you had left these parts. What a very pleasant surprise. Now, what will you drink?'

'Tomato juice,' said Miss Mayfield obediently.

'Ah, yes. I remember perfectly. We drank coffee together, didn't we? And you, my dear? The usual dry Martini? Such a pity, you know. An appreciation of sherry will die with my generation, and nobody will realize what the world has lost.'

The Selbury Town and Country Club did not employ a bar-waiter; members fetched their own drinks, and as Mr Freeman went with sprightly step to the bar, Miss Benson said, out of the corner of her mouth:

'Look out for him, Miss Mayfield. He's an old wolf if ever there was one. I will say, to his credit, he sticks to his age group, which some don't.'

'I paid you my promised visit,' Mr Freeman said, setting down the glasses and then taking the chair next to Miss Mayfield's. 'I had occasion to go to Renham – a little matter of business – and as it was a fine day, and Saturday, yes, the first Saturday in August if I remember rightly, I drove on, hoping to claim that cup of coffee.

They were packing your belongings. I was very much disappointed.'

'I'm sorry,' she said. 'I hope you'll make the effort again.'

He looked at her a trifle blankly.

'You are still living in Walwyk, Miss Mayfield?'

'Of course she is,' Miss Benson broke in. 'Oh, I know what happened. You got hold of that idiotic story that was going the rounds. All the brats heard it, too, and wept buckets.'

'I met with a slight accident, Mr Freeman, and suffered a temporary loss of memory. I suppose, with typical exaggeration, they told you that I should spend the rest of my life in a padded cell.'

It was so near to what he had been told by the young woman and Canon Thorby's chauffeur, who was nailing down the crate of books, that Mr Freeman felt, and looked, quite uncomfortable. Even Miss Benson seemed affected by it, fiddled with her glass and then lighted a cigarette with more fuss and force than usual.

'An accident?' Mr Freeman repeated. 'Dear me, I am sorry to hear that. You look – if I may say so – a great deal better than when I saw you last. I hope that is an indication of a complete recovery. What happened?'

Miss Mayfield told him briefly. Miss Benson added:

'Typical, that is. The best streamlined models for the young; for the teachers something out of *Jane Eyre* or *Nicholas Nickleby*. It was just the same with the piano. We struggled on with the first one ever made, I swear, until about three years ago, when some stub-fingered little cretin

269

decided he wanted to learn to play. Then we got the Broadwood.'

'Ah, well,' Mr Freeman said, 'youth must be served!' And he looked at Miss Mayfield quite tenderly, because she, too, had lost the raucous, awkward, demanding, inestimably precious thing called youth, and she, too, had survived its loss. This evening she was looking positively attractive; he'd known that she could. All she needed now was some pretty clothes. He found himself thinking of an undyed squirrel coat, soft, silver-grey. He'd read, or been told, that squirrel was not a hard-wearing fur, but what did that matter? He had plenty of money.

Good God! he said to himself, what am I thinking? At my time of life! And, of course, I should have to look very carefully into this nervous-breakdown rumour; no smoke without fire, you know; and they were definitely packing her things and could give me no address. Fishy, that.

And then he remembered the conversation they had held in the office, the trend and content of it, and the memories it had evoked of his own distant past. Something mysterious there. His curiosity, keen as a truffle-hound's nose, began to quiver. If only something would remove the Benson girl.

He was in luck. Hardly had the thought passed through his mind when the door opened and three young people came in, a girl and two men.

'Hullo, there!' Miss Benson cried. She stood up, said, 'Excuse me, won't you,' and went and joined them at the bar.

'And how are things at Walwyk?' asked Mr Freeman,

settling down cosily. 'If I remember rightly, on the day of our first meeting – to which, if I may say so, I look back with considerable pleasure — you were somewhat concerned about one of your pupils.'

It was an enormous temptation to cry, Oh, and I still am! The relief, the inexpressible relief, that it would be to tell someone the whole truth, about the accident, about Barhurst, the letters that never reached their destination, the tightrope of deception that she must walk every day. But she remembered her decision to trust no one in future. She remembered the words in Mrs Baines's letter: 'They're all in it, and there's nobody you can trust.' Just because Mr Freeman had nice manners and lived at a little distance from Walwyk, that didn't make him trustworthy. Indeed – and with one of the dreadful plunges into dark possibilities to which her mind had lately been prone – she thought, This whole thing *might* be a deep-laid plot. For just as she could trust nobody, surely They must have doubts about her trustworthiness, her complete change of attitude. They might very well have said to Miss Benson, Take her into Selbury on any excuse that offers; take her to the Club and sit down by Mr Freeman and then leave them; he'll soon have the truth out of her.

She said, 'I'm happy to tell you that she has left the old grandmother about whom I was uneasy and gone to live with someone else; in Yarmouth, I believe.'

'I'm glad, if that is a load off your mind,' he said, and with such earnest kindness that her heart smote her for suspecting him. But I must suspect everybody, just for a little longer. To make up for that, she smiled at him, and he noticed again that delightful little crescent in her upper lip.

'I wonder,' he said, 'whether you – and Miss Benson, of course – would have dinner with me. The routine food here is not very exciting, but' – he looked at his watch – 'we're in good time. We could order anything you liked.'

'That's very kind of you. This evening I am in Miss Benson's hands. She drove me in. I had to go to the Post Office to see about a parcel. She may wish to get back.'

'I hope,' he said, with just a degree of sourness in his voice, 'that she will leave promptly, or dine before she drives you. I'm afraid that is her fourth Martini.'

'She's probably used to them.'

'For one who doesn't drink herself, you are very tolerant.'

'Teachers and alcohol,' she said, 'remind me of a story. I expect you have heard it. About the teacher, a man, who was applying for a post?'

'I don't think I have.'

So she told him the story which Janet Lovelace had once told her. About the young man who, before the interview, was warned that one member of the appointment committee was a passionate abstainer. Suddenly, among the questions, this member shot out, 'Mr Smith, does the name Haig mean anything to you?' 'Oh, yes; he was a Field Marshal in the First World War.' Asked about Gordon, he replied that he was a General, killed at Khartoum; and of Booth, he founded the Salvation Army. Determined to trick him, the member of the committee finally said, 'And what is Vat 69?' The young man thought for a bit, and said,

'I'm afraid I don't really know. Could it be the Pope's telephone number?'

Mr Freeman, whom, by some miracle, this story had hitherto passed by, was delighted by it and laughed out loud. Part of his delight was occasioned by the unexpectedness of such a story coming from this source, and his delight was in no way diminished when Miss Mayfield added:

'Of course, I missed the point entirely when it was told to me, because I didn't know the names *were* drinks.'

That, for some reason, struck him as one of the most endearing things he had ever heard any woman say.

'You say that you are in Miss Benson's hands this evening. Unless you feel obliged to do so, I don't see why you must return with her. I should be delighted to drive you home.'

She longed to be home, to be alone, to be able to abandon this effort to seem normal and lighthearted. She told him again that he was very kind and that she appreciated it, and added:

'Actually, I'm rather anxious to get back. I left several small jobs unfinished. But, of course, if Miss Benson doesn't want to leave yet, then I shall shamelessly take advantage of your offer, both of the dinner and the drive home.'

'Splendid,' he said. And at that moment Miss Benson turned and came towards them.

'I'm sorry,' she said, 'but I must go. Aunt Edith has bridge this evening.'

'Miss Mayfield had just agreed . . .' Mr Freeman began.

'Not quite,' she said, with a smile. 'I really would very much prefer it to be another evening, when I hadn't the thought of things undone nagging at my mind. Then I could really enjoy myself.'

'Then will you suggest a date?'

'I'd like it to be after half-term.'

'And when is that?'

'The weekend of the thirty-first.'

By then, she thought, I shall have done what I have to do. And if I am still alive, I shall not be in the state of mind to suspect a pleasant old gentleman of being a spy. In fact, if I ever do keep my date with him, I'll tell him the whole story.

'The weekend of . . . All Hallowse'en,' he said slowly. And suddenly he looked at her sharply, dropping his gallant cock-bird manner. 'That's rather far ahead. Are you sure you couldn't spare just one evening before that?'

I'll warn her, he thought.

'You see, I'm going to London for half-term. I'm going to . . . to buy myself a new dress.'

Well, in London she would be safely out of the way. And how touching that she should wish to have a new dress. If only she would choose something soft, in blue. . . .

'As soon after half-term as possible, then. How about Tuesday?'

'That would be delightful.'

'I'll come and pick you up. At half-past six, shall we say?'

Very odd, it was, to be making arrangements for a day she might never see, a day which might very well be – she reckoned rapidly – yes, her funeral day; after an inquest, with a kindly verdict of suicide while of unsound mind, with – this time – quite a lot of evidence about the mind's unsoundness. They got away with Wesley Baines; they may get away with me. Am I preparing, for this pleasant person, a situation of some embarrassment, perhaps even a small pang of regret. Or is he in it? This is terrible. If this goes on much longer, I *shall* be out of my mind.

'Half-past six, on Tuesday, the third. I shall look forward to that,' she said.

While they had been making their arrangements, one of the young men had turned from the bar and handed Miss Benson a drink.

'That's your one for the road, honey,' he said. She had taken it, patted his arm and said, 'Thanks, Davy,' and stood drinking while Miss Mayfield and Mr Freeman made their date, watching them with amused, half-closed eyes. Mr Freeman, having attained his primary object, turned to her and said, a little doubtfully:

'If you must go now . . . don't you think perhaps a sandwich . . . It wouldn't take a minute.'

'Blotting paper, you mean? Are you insinuating that Miss Mayfield and I will end in a ditch? Really! Mr Freeman, you've hurt my feelings past all repair. If only you were a tailor, instead of a wine merchant, you might have a bit of chalk on you; you could draw me a line and invite me to take a walk. And if we were real teachers, instead of a couple of amateurs, we'd have enough chalk in our fingernails. . . . I'm out with my headmistress, I'd have you to know. And she likes to be driven at exactly forty miles an hour. And so she shall be. That is why we have to go *now*.'

It was Miss Benson talking, but there was a slight difference, a hint of truculence. The remark about tailors and wine merchants wasn't exactly polite, and what did she mean by a couple of amateurs? She might be teaching for pin money, but she was properly trained; and Miss Mayfield had been teaching all her life. A little . . . ever so slightly drunk.

Mr Freeman came out with them to the car park and opened and closed the car door for Miss Mayfield.

'I've even remembered the lights!' Miss Benson called out to him. And she backed the car, neatly and precisely, negotiated the gateway and turned into the street.

Then she said, 'You've hit the old boy for six! But be careful, he's a dreadful flirt, with more scalps at his belt than any man in Essex – always excepting our own dear Canon, of course.'

'Canon Thorby never struck me as being flirtatious.'

'No,' Miss Benson agreed. 'There is a difference. He makes no effort. Women just fall for him. And there's only one woman in his life, sister Isabel. Oh, I don't mean anything Byronic. It's just that since she came back from the dead . . .'

'Since she did *what*?' Miss Mayfield asked sharply.

'Came back from the dead,' said Miss Benson with a little giggle. 'Long before my time, of course, and I must admit I never heard the full story; they're cagey about it, naturally. And I don't suppose she was really dead – in a clinical sense, I mean – but as good as. Aunt Edith says she still *is* and that old Phoebe Rigby didn't do a good job on her.'

'Mrs Rigby? What had she to do with it?'

'When Isabel Thorby was — shall we say — moribund, Mrs Thorby, who was alive then and a bit of a crank, insisted on calling in Phoebe Rigby, who brewed some nettle tea or something horrid and got her breathing again.'

'What a fascinating story. And rather . . . rather uncanny, don't you think? There is something far away about Miss Thorby. At least, I thought so the day I went there to lunch.'

'She gives me the creeps. But then so does he, in a way.'

'Canon Thorby?'

'Who else?'

'In what way? Why?'

'I dunno. There's no reason for these things. Look how some people are about spiders. All I know is I don't even like him coming into my classroom. He offered me the headship, you know, when Ma Westleton resigned; and I thought. He'll be in and out with his *amo, amas, amat*, and his quadratic equations. So I said firmly that I'd been trained for Juniors and preferred to stick with them.'

'That was fortunate for me.'

'I'll tell you another thing, too. So silly I never told anyone. Three or four times a year I just have to put in an appearance at church — Christmas, Easter, and so on. And every time, to take . . . from him . . . It makes me gag, literally. I've done my best to get over it, but I can't.'

Be careful, Miss Mayfield admonished herself. This, too — this slightly intoxicated confidential talk — may be a trap.

'What a pity. He's so kind and generous.'

'And handsome, intelligent, not without a sense of humour, morally sound, charming and with that famous well-tubbed look. I know. I know. But there's no help for it. Once, when I was eleven, home for the holidays, Aunt Edith had a Christmas party, and they were all fooling about, kissing under the mistletoe – you know the form. *He* kissed *me*. Pure goodness of heart it was, too; I was gawky and plain, with a brace on my teeth – no kissing subject, I assure you. D'you know what I did? Fell down, flat out, in a faint, for the one and only time in my life, so far. They had to give me brandy.' She roared with laughter, too loud and too long. And the car shot forward at a frightening pace. 'This'll kill you. Everybody thought I was overcome with *emotion*, and when, later on, Aunt Edith braced up to give me her bumbling little bird-and-bee talk, she warned me that I was evidently *very* highly sexed, and must be careful. Me!'

'I'd no idea that you felt that way about the Canon.'

'I conceal it as well as I can. It suits me to be here. I live for nothing, and damn well. Even my petrol comes out of Uncle Eric's pump, and all my car expenses are taken care of by the business. Some income-tax fiddle or other. So I can save like mad. I'm saving up to get married, but, for God's sake, don't breathe a word to anyone. . . .' She spent the rest of the journey telling Miss Mayfield about the man of her choice; how wonderful he was, and how poor, and how many years it would be before he would earn anything like a reasonable salary. Her voice, her whole manner, changed when she spoke of him.

'I've kept it quiet. They'd want to have him down here and *inspect* him, and, poor dear, he wouldn't fit in at all. And if I went around with a "Reserved" label on me, I should have a pretty thin time. And if I don't have fun now, it's damned certain I never shall. . . .'

It all had the effect of making Miss Mayfield feel rather ashamed. She thought, She has bared her heart to me, and I have given nothing in return. I have, in fact, only one thing to offer as a confidence this evening, and that is that Ethel Rigby is not in Yarmouth. And that I dare not say.

As she got out of the car she said:

'Thank you very much. For taking me; and for a very enjoyable time as well.'

'I talk too much,' Miss Benson said. 'But then I very seldom have anybody I can talk to, really. Look, take these. Little present. They'll be useful on your date.' She pushed into Miss Mayfield's hand the things she had gone to the chemist's to buy and had opened and used in the cloakroom of the Club.

'I shouldn't, really. You're much too kind. But I will use them, I promise you. On special occasions.'

You see, she said to herself as she opened her door and closed it and was at last alone, this thing is poison. It creeps in and contaminates every relationship. I'm almost sure that that is a nice girl, that Mr Freeman is a nice man, but I daren't act on that belief. What with that, and this nagging worry about Ethel, I wish the next eighteen days could be over. . . .

20

'I'M REALLY QUITE CONCERNED ABOUT YOU,' CANON Thorby said. 'You don't look a bit well. I hope you're going to get away for half-term.'

'I am indeed. I'm going to London.' She forced her tired face into an expression of animation. He was right enough about her looks. The last days, worrying about Ethel and planning the immediate future, had been extremely trying. The nights, when imagination slipped its leash and seemed to enjoy presenting her with scenes of horror, had been even worse, until she had resorted to some little pink pills, a legacy of her illness; they made her sleep, but left her heavy-headed in the morning.

'That will be a change, and a change, they say, is as good as a rest. Now, if you want a really pleasant, comfortable place to stay, I can recommend one.'

'Thank you very much; but my friend – the one with whom I lived in Alchester – is joining me, and we are both staying with an aunt of hers. In Chiswick.'

'Baxter will take you to the train on Thursday

afternoon, and meet you on Monday evening. Unless, of course, you would like to prolong your break a day or two. That could easily be arranged. I am concerned about you; you look so frail.'

'I know exactly what is wrong with me, Canon Thorby. I need glasses. I had my eyes tested last Saturday and was told that I was suffering a severe eyestrain, and that eyes in such condition would take the strength from any other part of the body. Did you know that? I didn't. Mr Saunders told me of a case of chronic indigestion which had been cured by a pair of spectacles.'

'If only you'd asked me! Saunders is *not* the best man. What a pity!'

Anyway, she had diverted his attention and explained her exhausted look. No adage was truer than the old nursery one about the tangled web. Still, hers was almost completed now, for this was the week of half-term; and this year October the thirty-first fell upon a Saturday. She would have Friday to do all the things she had to do in the way of preparation; Saturday would see action. Beyond Saturday she would not look. Except to reflect that if things went wrong, she would not be under the necessity of providing herself with a pair of plain-lensed glasses for the Canon's benefit.

Find Emily *Baines, find* Emily *Baines*, the train began to chant as it pulled out of Selbury station; then it quickened and changed rhythm, Find *Emily* Baines, find *Emily* Baines.

At the Liverpool Street Hotel she was given, as timid,

inexperienced-looking travellers always were, a room on the station side, which was a blessing, because it helped her to believe that it was the noise, not her own anxiety, which kept her awake.

The office of the Certain Future Assurance Company, at the address stamped on their enyelopes, was on the first floor of an office block in Holborn. Miss Mayfield rode up in the lift because she could see no stairs, and was ejected on to a carpeted landing the size of a hearthrug. There was a door straight ahead of her which was labelled 'Bivco Engineering', one to the right which announced that it gave upon the premises of A. Schmidt, Practical Furrier, and to the left were the words she was looking for. Opening the door, she stepped into a cage of glass and mahogany in which, behind a desk, sat a good-looking, rather hard-faced blonde woman about thirty years old.

They exchanged perfunctory good mornings, and then it was Miss Mayfield's turn to state her business, which she found easier to do than she had expected, because of the privacy. She had been imagining a large open room full of people who would raise their heads and listen.

She had, in the lift, taken from her handbag the envelope in which Mrs Baines's letter had arrived. She now held it so that the blonde could see it.

'I'm extremely sorry to be driven to bother you like this,' she said, sounding humble and pathetic. 'My sister sent me this letter, and she must have written it here. I think she did it purposely, because, you see, she's not supposed to write to me *at all*. Father is very angry with her and said that we were not to correspond. But I mustn't bother you with all that. . . . The point is that she did write to me, and I wrote to her, at this address, but the letter came back, and I'm terribly worried about her.'

'What was the name?'

'My sister's? Baines. Emily Baines.'

'There's no one here of that name.'

'No, I was afraid not. But she must have been here. She's just lost her husband – that is what makes the whole thing so very sad – and I wondered if she'd been here about his insurance, or whether perhaps she was looking for a job. This address was my only hope. You can imagine how I feel.'

'Dear me, yes.' In her thirty years the blonde had experienced many relationships with many people, but she had never had a sister, and suddenly she realized how much she had missed. A sister was one who would stick to you through thick and thin, daring even a father's rage; and how dreadful this poor little creature's father must be was evidenced by her shrinking figure, her shy manner, her halting way of speech.

'What is the date of the postmark?' she asked, and when Miss Mayfield told her, she indicated a leather-covered banquette against one wall of the cage and said, 'Sit down. I may be a minute or two.' She opened another of the cage walls and vanished.

Miss Mayfield occupied her time of waiting by speculating on the chances of Emily Baines's having changed her name. It wasn't very likely. For one thing, there was no reason why she should; for another, she would be almost certain to apply for a post in some way connected with her profession and would need to show her qualifications.

Oh, well, she said to herself, I *can* manage without her help, but it would have made things so much easier for me.

The blonde returned, carrying a slip of paper.

'I found it,' she announced, with some triumph. 'She did apply here, on that date, for a post as nurse-receptionist to one of our doctors. But it meant Saturday-morning work, and she has a child – is that right?'

'Yes, that's right,' said Miss Mayfield breathlessly. 'A little boy.'

'She said she'd think it over and let Mr Steggles, the Personnel Manager, know; and next day she did. She said she'd found something that would leave Saturday free. Mr Steggles was struck with her, because she telephoned. Most people who say so never do. She was at this address then, but, of course, that's a little while ago.'

Miss Mayfield read, '44 Macebury Street, SW4.'

'Thank you so very much. Even if she has moved, they may know her new address. You have been more than kind.'

The blonde said – and meant it – that it had been a pleasure, and that she did hope she'd find her sister.

Macebury Street had a familiar look. It was akin to the one in which Miss Mayfield and Janet had had their flatlet in Alchester; a street fighting a rear-guard action, not against fish and chips, but against the throwing of the paper into the gutter; a street clinging desperately to some remnant of respectability. Exactly the place, Miss

Mayfield thought, halting by number 44, that Emily Baines, in sudden and penurious exile, would look for – and be lucky to find.

Like its neighbours, the house was tall and narrow, once the home of a prosperous Victorian family whose servants inhabited the basement and attics. Its pale stucco had peeled and blackened, no paint had been near its woodwork for many years, but the knocker and the doorknob had been polished recently, and the curtains, though much mended, were clean.

A melancholy woman, in seedy black, the quintessence of all widowhood, answered the bell.

'Mrs Baines. Yes, she's in. Go right up as far as you can, and hers is the first door on the left.'

The hall smelt of years of cooking, of hundreds of damp coats that had hung on the angry-looking hall stand, of hundreds of anxious conversations held on the call-box type of telephone. It also smelt of floor polish.

Miss Mayfield climbed a flight of handsome stairs, one less handsome, and then a set that was steep and narrow. Out of breath, partly from the exertion, partly from excitement, she knocked on the first door on the left, and Emily Baines's voice called, 'Come in.'

Miss Mayfield opened the door upon a fair-sized room, sensibly, if shabbily, furnished. There was a table and two upright chairs near the window, a sagging but comfortable-looking wicker chair near the gas-fire, and one of those settees which could be converted into a bed. Thrown down on this was a blue cloak with a red lining. On the far side of the room was a three-panel screen, at this moment set in such a position that the gas-stove and kitchen cupboard, ordinarily concealed, were exposed to view. Mrs Baines, in a blue dress which matched the cloak, but with a gay apron tied over it, stood at the stove, stirring something in a saucepan. Without turning, she said:

'It's on the table, Mrs Morgan.'

On the table some pound notes lay folded by a small blue jug, which held three tawny-yellow chrysanthemums.

'It's not Mrs Morgan,' Miss Mayfield said.

Mrs Baines whirled around, still holding the spoon, from which some drops of custard fell to the floor.

'Miss Mayfield!' Her voice was hoarse with shock, and Miss Mayfield rebuked herself for lack of consideration. Before she could apologize, Mrs Baines said:

'Who else is with you?'

'Nobody. I'm all alone. I'm sorry I startled you. I didn't think. I just happened to be in London – it's half-term, you know – and I thought I'd look you up.'

'How in the world did you find me?'

Briefly, Miss Mayfield explained.

'I thought I'd been so clever. A plain envelope with a London postmark might get opened, I thought. But insurance and circulars, everybody gets them. . . .' She turned back to the stove, placed the spoon back in the saucepan, and turned off the gas with a little plop. She set the screen carefully in place, hiding the stove. When she faced the room and Miss Mayfield again, she had recovered her composure.

'Do sit down,' she said, pulling forward the armchair. 'I'm sorry you caught me in such a mess.' She eyed the blue cloak and a basket of groceries on the floor by the settee with disapproval. 'My hours are a bit awkward. Six to eleven I work in the mornings; shop on my way back and make a meal against when Sydney comes home; then back on duty from two till six. That way, I'm here in the evenings and at the weekend, so he isn't roaming the streets.'

'It sounds an excellent arrangement. How is Sydney?'

'Oh, he's fine. He's at school – about fifteen minutes on the bus. Only a modern secondary; but I saw the Headmaster, and he seemed sensible. He said he'd keep his eye on Sydney, and if he was as good as I seemed to think, he'd see he wasn't held back. Most likely he'll go on to the technical; he's handy, Sydney is.'

She spoke brightly, she smiled; only her elusive, flickering glance betrayed an inner lack of ease.

'I'm so glad that things worked out well for you. I did often wonder.'

'We were very lucky. Finding this place to live, for instance; within walking distance for me. I'm at St Philip's. Did you come by the recreation ground? Big red building on the corner. Shockingly understaffed, of course. They were glad to take me, I may tell you. So you're in London for the weekend?'

'I came to find you. Mrs Baines, I want your help. At least,' she added hastily, seeing that wild flicker of the eyes, 'I just want to ask you a few questions.'

Mrs Baines's expression set and hardened.

'Look, if it's about Walwyk, you're wasting your time. I don't want to talk about it, or think about it, or remember it. I got out. For me, it's all finished and done with. If you had any sense, you'd do the same.'

'I can't,' Miss Mayfield said simply. 'You see, there's Ethel. She's disappeared. I'm terribly worried about her. I think they've hidden her somewhere. I did wonder whether you could give me any idea where she could be.'

'I know nothing about it,' Mrs Baines said flatly. 'And if I did, I shouldn't tell you. I've done with it. I've cut that part of my life clean way.'

'It must have been very horrible, for you to feel so violently about it.'

Mrs Baines ignored the bait.

'It's all over and done with,' she said.

'It's for Ethel's sake, Mrs Baines. A poor helpless child. If you would just . . .'

In a strangely even, controlled voice, Mrs Baines said:

'Miss Mayfield, if Ethel Rigby stood in the road and a bus was coming, I wouldn't move my hand to pull her on the pavement. Fretting about her was the start of things going wrong for me. Through her, I lost my husband and my self-respect. The one I'll never get back, the other'll take me years.'

'Don't you think,' Miss Mayfield said diffidently, 'that perhaps to help me might go quite a long way towards the recovery of your self-respect – that is, of course, if you really feel you have lost it.'

'I tried to help you. When I wrote to you. What good did that do? You're after me like a bloodhound, and you wouldn't be warned. You go right on, busybodying about, and one day it'll be a "Poor Miss Mayfield, she must have

288

had a weak heart; too much kneeling!" And they'll say, "What a nice way to die – in church, at your prayers." Well, I've warned you.'

And helped me, too, if you did but know. I was never sure that they would *dare* use the church. . . .

Mrs Baines moved her arm and looked at her watch.

'I mustn't waste any more of your time,' Miss Mayfield said. She rose reluctantly, looking at Mrs Baines's neat head and thinking of all the knowledge she must have hidden away there. For a moment she was on the verge of anger; then she remembered that there were some men who had been prisoners of war who could never be brought to mention their experiences. If Granny Rigby's cult ran in any way true to form, Miss Mayfield could imagine how very distasteful a brush with it must have been to a woman of Mrs Baines's nature.

'There's just one thing,' Mrs Baines said in quite a different voice, pleading, uncertain. 'You wouldn't tell anybody where I am, would you? Decent places to live are so hard to find. I wouldn't want to have to move again.'

'You know I wouldn't. I hope everything will go well for you and Sydney, always. Remember me to him, won't you? I was very fond of Sydney. And now that I have found you, perhaps next time I come to London I might look you up again?'

'That would be nice,' Mrs Baines said, without much enthusiasm.

They were both standing now, looking one another straight in the face and for once Mrs Baines's eyes did not waver. Their glances met and held in what, in almost any other circumstances, would have been an embarrassingly lengthy stare. And somewhere, deep down below all the defensive layers of Mrs Baines's stubbornness and rejection, something stirred, struggled and broke to the surface.

'Leave it alone,' she said in a quiet voice. 'You've no notion what you're up against. It's so . . .' She broke off with a shudder.

'It pleases me that you should care what happens to me,' Miss Mayfield said. 'And I'm grateful. Please don't worry. I *think* I shall be all right.'

21

SATURDAY WAS A BRIGHT, COLD DAY IN LONDON, but as the train carried Miss Mayfield eastwards, it ran into rain; the slate-coloured clouds hung almost as low as the billows of smoke that came from the engine, and the raindrops slashed at the windows. She had chosen a slow train, one that stopped at every station, and it was almost dark when she alighted at the one immediately preceding Selbury. It was a sizeable village, just large enough to have a taxi waiting on the chance of picking up a customer.

'I want to go to Renham,' she told the driver.

'Renham. Ooh, you done wrong, then, to get out here. You shoulda kept in the train far as Selbury. Still, whass done is done. Renham, now, would that be beyond the river, or this side? Because, to tell you the truth, I don't much fancy that road in this rain. Might run into floods.'

'Renham is this side of the river.'

To have driven in a taxi to Walwyk on this day would have been tantamount to entering with a brass band and banners.

She had chosen her destination carefully, marking it down on one of her trips to Selbury from Walwyk. It was an empty house and had been empty for some time, though it bore no sign that it was for sale. It stood just back from the road and was separated from it by a high wall, in which was set a gate, too narrow to admit a vehicle. In the space between the house and the wall, two tall fir trees grew. It seemed made for her purpose; even the most kindly and chivalrous driver must drop her at the gate and leave her to make her way to the door, and she would be spared the embarrassment of being watched knocking on the door of an unoccupied house.

When she had been on the lookout for such a place and had found one so ideal, she had had the same feeling that she had when Canon Thorby announced that half-term would be at the end of October. For a moment she had felt *guided*, destined. She had put that thought away; it was a sign of eccentricity to see significance in every tiny thing; it might also seem arrogant. Nevertheless, the feeling had recurred and become more powerful, especially after her visit to Mrs Baines. The kindness of two women had gained her two things she wanted, and the first of these – the assurance that Ethel Rigby was alive – was enough to make certain that when, at the last minute, she was frightened and tempted to turn back, as she knew she would be, a sense of duty would come to her aid.

'This is Renham,' she said leaning forward. 'The house I want is just on the other side, past the public house. It has some tall dark trees in front.'

When they reached the spot, the man said:

'You'll get wet. Ain't there a drive-in where I could set you down by the door?'

'Only the farm entrance, to the side: It isn't any nearer, and it's very muddy. This will do very well, thank you.'

She paid and thanked him and hurried to the gate, which, not having been opened for many months, resisted her pushing and then creaked. But the taxi had already reversed and driven away.

Safe behind the wall, she put her suitcase on the ground and opened it. On top of everything else was one of her new purchases, a torch which worked in two ways: it had a button which, when pressed, produced light and which, when released, quenched the light, and another button which, when pressed, stayed down. The torch itself had a square flat bottom, so that it could stand without support, and the head of it could be swivelled round, like a desk lamp. Next to it lay a mackintosh bag containing something square and heavy – and, from the way in which Miss Mayfield handled it, delicate and precious. The bag had a zip at the top. She unfastened it and put her shabby black handbag in on top of what already lay there, hesitated for a moment, then took a woollen cardigan, pushed that in on top of the handbag and fastened the zipper.

Now for the disguise. And here again, surely, she had been guided, for on the Friday afternoon, on the arid London pavements, she had never even thought about rain. What she was looking for was some garment which in shape and colour was entirely unlike anything she possessed, something which, should anyone by some ill chance catch a sight of her, would not call Miss Mayfield to mind. And it must be cheap, because one of her purchases had been very expensive indeed. It had taken all Mr Frisby's loan and most of her own money as well.

She was walking along Oxford Street, and whereas every other woman window-shopping was searching for 'something that looks like *me*', she was looking for something that looked unlike herself when she found a window full of garments called Singing in the Rain. They were made of some plastic material, coats and hats to match, the coats very full, gathered into a yoke, the hats bonnet-shaped, with strings which could be tied in a bow under the chin. Some were in plain colours, yellow, scarlet, green and blue; some were in tartans of − surely − no recognized clan. But you could buy a whole outfit for only thirty shillings.

And for once, for the only time in her life, Miss Mayfield was prepared to buy something with no lasting potential. She went in and bought a Singing in the Rain − one of the tartans, green and tan and yellow.

She now pulled the tent-shaped coat over her black one, ripped off her dowdy hat and squashed it into the suitcase, and put the tartan bonnet on her head, tying the strings firmly. She then closed the suitcase and pushed it between the trunk of one of the fir trees and the wall. Shall I live to reclaim it? That is the kind of thought I *must not* indulge in!

She tucked the mackintosh bag under her left arm, took the torch in her right hand, opened the creaking gate and set off for Walwyk.

Within a few minutes she was conscious of a feeling of respectful gratitude to the designer of Singing in the Rain outfits. The rain which fell upon her shoulders ran into the pleats and gathers at the yoke and were shed at the hem, which at all points was at least eight inches from her legs. You could, in fact, have stood still in one of these garments and preserved a space the size of a small table upon which no rain could fall. In the same way, the outjutting brim of the bonnet kept the rain from getting into your eyes. In moderate comfort, considering the weather, she walked towards the bridge.

The man who drove the taxi had been right. The road was under water, brown, muddy and swirling; there it lay, an encroachment of the river upon the dry land, with the high-pitched bridge rearing up out of the water like an island. In the centre of the road, on the part which any vehicle would use, the water must be above axle level.

She pressed the switch of her torch, as she had been pressing it every now and again since leaving the empty house, and swinging the beam from side to side, assessed the situation. Knee high. Maybe rather more.

But the road on each side was slightly banked. Above the brown swirl, she could just see the extreme tips of the withered weeds, the little bushes which had marked the road's boundary. Holding well to the left, she pushed on, and the cold water lapped no higher than her ankles. She reached the bridge, crossed it and, on the far side, found herself wading through mud as thick and viscous as porridge. She used her torch, but on this side the road boundaries had vanished, and there was nothing to do but plunge ahead. Thick, sucking mud, halfway to the knee, and then to the hem of the new mackintosh, and then to the knee.

Her breath began to fail. I'm not going to get there. I'm going to get stuck here, in this mud. Stick-in-the-mud, a denigratory term, so lightly used; and how few of those who used it ever knew what it meant. It meant lifting one leg out of a vice, with an effort and a strain which took your whole strength and being, and then putting it forward a few inches – how long was a normal step? – feeling it engulfed again. And having done it once, do it a second time, and a third.

Bedded in the sticky mire up to the knees, she bowed herself forward and gasped. Something to lean upon, just for one minute while she mastered her breath. A rail, a stick, a post, anything . . .

It came, the support she needed, but in the strangest form. Miss Benson's cheerful, careless voice, saying – such a long time ago, before all this started, at a time when she could take such a remark at its face value—

'You see, we have good grass-growing weather. Cattle need pasture, and for that you need rain. Most of East Anglia is dry, compared with the rest of England. But just in this corner we seem to get what rain we need.'

What rain we need, Miss Mayfield thought, pulling her leg out of the sucking mire and, with difficulty, moving it forward six inches and plunging it in again. And suddenly the very weather was part of the enemy, to be faced, scorned, tramped down. The thought made her move more sturdily, and after a few more difficult steps the mud and the water grew more shallow. She was on the high-road again, between the beech woods. And the rain was easing off.

Well before she reached the first house, she turned from the road, taking to the fields on Maverick's side of the road. She had walked this way three times before, marking the course in her mind: here a gate between two fields, here a stile, in another place a ditch crossed by a plank and in yet another a ditch one must step across. Towards the end of her detour she passed quite close to the edge of the wood where Puddler Pond lay, and farther on she was near enough to have seen, had it been daylight, the back of her own house. As it was, she could see the lights in the houses on the Green; and she wondered in how many of them people were looking forward to this evening's celebration, and with what feelings.

She now bore towards the village and emerged at last in the lane where the school and the church stood.

She had hunted down Mrs Baines in order to ask where the All Hallowse'en coven was held, and Mrs Baines had refused to tell her. Then she had said, 'That'll be the end of you. It'll look neat and simple. Poor Miss Mayfield, weak heart, too much kneeling.' And that kind of death could only overtake one in church. Actually, she had suspected the church all along, but she needed to be sure.

She moved towards it cautiously. In the shadow of one of the enormous yews she stopped and stood and held her breath and listened. She crept on as far as the porch, and there listened again. When she lifted and turned the heavy iron handle, it made a noise which set her heart jumping and perspiration leaking from every pore. After that, still holding the handle, she waited for what seemed a long time. Nothing happened, there was no sound, and at last she plucked up courage and pushed the door open, inch by slow inch.

She had one of those curious thoughts, not exactly irrelevant, but mistimed and misplaced. I didn't need to bring my woolly cardigan! The church, which on a sunny afternoon in spring had struck with such a deathly chill and which, even last Sunday, had been only just comfortably warm, tonight was like a hothouse. The heat struck as it would from the open door of an oven. In the hot darkness she waited again, and then at last, plucking up her courage, pressed the knob on the torch, directing the beam towards the ground. Off again, and in darkness she covered the space she had measured with her eye, stood, waited and listened; on again, another small journey planned and in darkness undertaken, and finally she had reached her objective, the little room in the base of the tower.

She had made sure, long ago, when her suspicion first centred on the church, that in the base of the tower, below the heavy timbers that made the ceiling of the little room, there were none of the narrow, round-headed windows. Whoever had built the tower for a place of defence had chosen to shoot down upon his enemies. Therefore, she could now have a light; not *safely*, for nothing was safe, but without undue risk. She set the torch on the floor behind the door, which she dared not close because she must listen sharply in case anyone came. In its limited light she opened the mackintosh bag and took out the cine-camera which had cost so much money, and which a pleasant, pimply young man had yesterday taught her to handle. He had been amused by her demand for a 'quiet' one. Never before in his experience had any buyer of a camera been concerned about the noise it made, but this funny little creature – an unlikely customer, in any case – had acted as though she were buying a musical instrument, saying, 'Let me *hear* that again.' And her final choice of a model, the most expensive of all he had to show her, had been dictated not by its virtues as a camera, but by the fact that after several tests, as she had said, 'This one makes less noise.' And in a way that was true, as it would be true of an expensive car.

Against the all-pervading roar of the London traffic, the difference in volume between one succession of little clicks and another might seem extremely unimportant, but Miss Mayfield knew that in Walwyk it might mean the difference between success and failure.

Sure now that the camera was in working order, she folded the bag in which she had carried it and the unnecessary cardigan and stuffed them into the front of her coat. She turned the torch beam on to the worn stone stairs that clung to the wall and vanished through the opening in the ceiling; then she switched it off and climbed the stairs, moving like some deformed animal, using her feet and elbows, holding the camera clear of the stone with one hand, the torch with the other. On the thick dust, on the bat droppings, on the massed regurgitations of generations of owls, she settled herself to wait. Just before moving the switch which plunged her into darkness, she had looked at her watch. It was twenty to nine. And after that there was no more time.

22

THE THING THAT MOST AMAZED HER WAS HER OWN
amazement. After all, she had suspected and then been
certain that such things went on; she had been prepared to
say so in public, and to say that Wesley Baines had not
killed himself. Moreover, she had done a good deal of
reading on the subject, reading which had sometimes
evoked horror and disgust and sometimes amusement,
because there were details which were ludicrous in their
naïveté. Nevertheless, throughout the early proceedings
her most overwhelming emotion was amazement. Then it
is true, she thought. And, Can I really be seeing what I am
seeing? So might someone who had read about the Sphinx,
or the Colosseum, feel when confronted with the real life-
size object.

They assembled stealthily; there was a rustle and a
whisper, a feeling of motion and occupation in the
empty place, and then, quite suddenly, the homely,
pleasant smell of roast pork. And Miss Mayfield,
who had read of 'feastings', was for a moment surprised,

and then full of wonder at her own surprise.

She dared not, at first, descend from her hiding place. Someone might arrive who had reason to enter the little room at the base of the tower. And she knew that she must wait for the noise to begin.

It began, and increased steadily, as it does at any party when the first caution, reserve and shyness wear off. She could, in fact, have been listening to any party, except the voices were louder, the laughter a little less inhibited. She realized that she must now leave this place of comparative safety. The moment had come.

She came down the worn stairs in the way small children sometimes do, in a sitting position, lowering herself cautiously from one to another in the darkness. As the stairs turned, she could see the lighted outline of the half-open door; the noise was much louder now, and the roast-pork odour stronger. The door, she was glad to see, stood in the position in which she had left it, far enough open to give her a clear view and yet offer some protection. If anyone had entered the little room, he had left no sign. She crept to the door and looked into the church.

It was then that her first amazement struck her. That she should be so surprised, so shocked. After all, in Africa she had seen plenty of naked bodies. . . .

You could think some very long thoughts in almost no time at all, and in the half-second it took her to raise the camera, she had time to think that black skin was in itself, in some strange way, a kind of raiment; no black-skinned people could look as naked as these Walwykians did. And she thought, too, that there was some profound truth in the Bible story – now generally considered to be allegorical – about the nakedness and the fig leaves. Man's great step forward out of the animal world was not made at the moment when he heaved himself up on to his back legs – apes could do that. No, man's Rubicon had been crossed when he first covered his nakedness, probably with leaves, as the Bible said. And she thought, too, that there was a difference between a naked stranger and a naked person whom one knew. . . .

And why think about it at all? she asked herself, setting the camera to work. The very heat of the church might have informed her.

The pictures wouldn't be good. The church was lighted by candles; there were a lot of them, but they gave off almost as much smoke as light. And in the centre of the trestle table upon which the meat and drinks were spread, there was a bowl which smoked like a volcano.

It was a drug. Whoever breathed it long enough could no longer rely upon his senses.

But this – her fingers tightened on the camera – this is a machine which cannot think or feel or be affected by any drug. It can only record. It is recording now! And that was, oddly enough, a very horrid thought when you looked at the fat round haunches of the Postmistress, ordinarily corseted into the decent solid roundness of a tree trunk, or when you looked – at the pendulous breasts, like empty paper bags, of Phoebe Rigby. When you looked . . .

I'm not *really* looking. I'm just part of this machine, the part that holds it steady, keeps it aimed in the right direction. All that part of me which is capable of being shocked – or amused – is back home, in bed. Let it be so.

But she was looking for Ethel. And Ethel was not there among the naked revellers.

Concern for Ethel began to swell and spread in her mind, like those little objects called – what was it? – Japanese Flowers, which would open when placed in a glass of water. All along, it has been Ethel.

I don't mind about the others. They're volunteers. They joined. They chose this. Let them caper about, guzzling and drinking. . . .

But where is Ethel?

Presently. That was the voice in her mind again. This is only a beginning. A warming up. I don't think I'll waste any more film on it.

She moved away, behind the door, and indulged in some more swift, profound thoughts. Table manners. There again, you had the conflict between the animal and the human being. To eat was to live, and the primitive instinct was to fall upon food, tear it with claws and teeth, gobble it down. Up the long ladder of the centuries the creature whose destiny was to be man, made in God's image, the creature who was to be Shakespeare, Beethoven, Einstein, had dragged himself. He had reached the point where, with a plate of food in front of him, he would unfold his table napkin, make conversation, pass the salt.

Out there, they had discarded all such niceties, together with their clothes. They had ripped at the meat with their hands, crammed it into their mouths, laughed, talked, kissed one another with full mouths, with grease-gleaming lips.

Presently the quality of the noise changed, warning her to take up her station again. Once more, despite all that she had read, she was amazed, and shocked, and revolted. The books said 'sexual orgies', and 'debauchery' and 'perversion', but to her these had been mere arrangements of certain letters which formed certain words. They had no more prepared her for what, on this All Hallowe'en, was following the feasting and the drinking in Walwyk church than the words 'red' and 'scented' would prepare a person for the beauty of the rose he had never seen. Even to look upon this scene was to be soiled. To call it bestial was to insult every animal in creation, for this was deliberate obscenity.

Grotesque, insane, she thought, forcing herself to hold the camera steady and listening to its gentle clicking.

Don't think about it, she told herself. Let the camera do its work. Abstract your mind. Notice that Harold Thorby has no part or lot in this; repent the fact that since your accident you have held him suspect. Notice that in no case are both husband and wife involved. Up at Puddler Pond on Midsummer Eve, Wesley Baines must have broken one of the inviolable rules. Eric Frisby is here, but not Edith; Freda Tharkell, but not John. Miss Benson is not here; you could have trusted her. The Mavericks are innocent. Berta Creek is here, and Baxter, and Juliet Reeve – oh dear, so young, so pretty and so clever, tragic beyond all words. Worse, far worse, than I ever dreamed. . . .

In a moment she would be crying. I must take a more academic view, she thought. Is it the drug which renders them capable of such sustained and varied performance?

One has always known about prostitutes . . . but theirs is the passive role. What aphrodisiac can make men . . . And if one were not seeing it with one's own eyes, could one believe that old Granny Rigby . . . ?

I've had enough of this, she thought sickly. It could, in any case, be only a prelude. She tried to recall the figures the kind young man in the shop had given her; so many feet of film which ran for so many minutes. Did he mean in the taking or in the screening? Best to be on the safe side anyway.

She lowered the camera, wondering as she did so whether the rutting mob out there would mind, would be ashamed to know that their . . . antics had been recorded. Or would they have the courage of their convictions, and say, This is our ritual. We don't criticize yours. Nobody compelled you to watch!

She was oddly, almost comically, aware for the first time of the ambiguity of her own position. They had so far done no harm to anyone but themselves. They were adulterers and fornicators, but the worst you could say about them, really, was that they were nudists who practised a form of free love. And she was Peeping Tom, whose motives could be very suspect. Ethel, her chief concern, wasn't even here. *But she will come,* the voice in her mind assured her. *This, too, is a preliminary.*

That brought to her mind an awareness of her own physical exhaustion. Moving very softly, she went to the stairs and sat down.

After an incredible space of time the nature of the noise without changed again. Prominent in it was the sound of shod feet on the stone floor. She stole back to her position and was, once again, surprised. All signs of the feasting had been removed; the revellers were clothed again. They and the church presented the ordinary Sunday-morning scene. Even as she looked, they all went down on their knees, not quite in the manner of churchgoers, though; they knelt with their hands and heads lowered to the floor and their rumps in the air. She remembered suddenly another word she had read, 'parody'.

The door through which, every Sunday, Canon Thorby emerged from his vestry opened, and two figures stepped into the church. One was Ethel Rigby, clad from neck to heels in a scarlet cloak embroidered all over with cabalistic symbols in black and white. A circlet of red flowers rested on her head, and below it her fawn-coloured hair streamed softly down. She had a wide-eyed, tranced look. Sleep-walking? Doped? Drunk? Beaten into a state where the last possible resistance lay in a deliberating absenting of the self? Even as she asked these questions in her mind, another, far more vital question occurred to Miss Mayfield, and suddenly she was shaking as though stricken with palsy, sweating at every pore.

What am I going to do?

You silly, silly, blundering, bumbling daft old fool! There's no excuse for you. You knew. You'd read about it. How could you be so plumb crazy as to think that you could save this girl? How, in God's name? With a cine-camera? You guessed, you suspected, you knew. You were going to save Ethel. And you took no sensible, practical measure at all.

The shattering realization of her madness and inefficiency coincided with her recognition of the other figure. Seven feet tall – but that was an illusion lent by the high silver headdress, the long white-silver girt robe. Very tall, very proud, dominant. And she had never seen Isabel Thorby except as limp and drooping, negative and retreating. But it was Isabel Thorby who held Ethel's hand and brought her forward and said in Latin:

'I bring the bride.'

And in the corrupt dog Latin that had come down to them by word of mouth through who knew how many ages, they replied solemnly:

'May she find favour in his sight.'

Miss Thorby said:

'Behold the bride,' and as she spoke, she twitched away the cloak. Ethel's nakedness had a classic beauty because of her unawareness. Smooth and white and slim as a statue, and as unknowing.

Holding her hand, Miss Thorby led her to the altar, and Ethel lay down, her hands clasped behind her head, one knee raised.

'We are met,' Miss Thorby said.

'We are met. We await his coming.'

Then, in solemn parody of the action which her brother performed on this spot each Sunday, Miss Thorby took the wafer and the silver Communion cup. The wafer she laid upon Ethel's body, just below the breasts; the cup she set in the arch of her lifted knee.

If it stops at this, Miss Mayfield thought, there is still no great harm done. It's blasphemous and wrong and silly,

but she doesn't know it's happening, and if it stops here . . .
Miss Thorby lifted the wafer.

'This is the flesh of the Usurper. Let it be food for dogs!'

From somewhere, Mr Frisby's good cattle dog Lassie came forward, moving as a dog does when moving against its will, head low and tail tucked down. It sniffed at the offering, hesitated and backed away.

'Even the dog spurns it,' Miss Thorby cried triumphantly. She dropped it and ground it under her heel.

Then she lifted the cup and, saying, 'Here is his blood,' offered it to Granny Rigby, who did with it something so degrading that Miss Mayfield shut her eyes and released her finger's pressure on the camera, hoping that she had been in time. Not even for purposes of evidence did she want a picture of that!

And now Miss Thorby was praying – if you could call it that. She said that all was ready; that all those present had given proof of their faith and devotion. She mentioned the bride again, going into details about Ethel's tender virginity as the madam of a brothel might speak enticingly to a reluctant customer about the newest recruit to her trade. She ended, 'Great Master, we await you.' Everyone repeated the words.

Then they rose. Miss Thorby reached over Ethel's supine body and produced a bowl. She held it in her right hand and dipped into it with her left, and each member of the congregation, forming into line, approached her and was touched, by her left hand, in the palm of each of their hands, on the forehead, each cheek, chin and throat. Seven little dabs made with the swiftness of a snake bite. When they had been anointed and had passed on, they rubbed their hands together, rubbed their necks and faces, turned and pressed their palms to their neighbours', rubbed one another's faces and necks. Now and then, when the light caught it, Miss Mayfield could see the greasy gleam of the unguent. She remembered what she had read about preparations of deadly nightshade which could lead to frenzy and hallucination.

They were now in a circle, moving round and chanting, at first quietly, and then more and more excitedly. They began to leap and to scream. Miss Thorby took Ethel by the hand, jerked her upright and into the ring, which was moving anticlockwise. Miss Mayfield remembered another of the words which had not meant very much. 'Widdershins'.

All at once Miss Thorby cried, 'Stop!' and like automatons they stood still.

'There is a barrier. Are we all of one mind? Has any been unfaithful?'

This was no part of the ritual, for she spoke in English and with some agitation.

Miss Mayfield thought, washed over with a wave of fear, Can it be my presence that is preventing whatever it is they wait for? If they can smell me out, then this isn't just nasty nonsense. She knew again the fear she had felt at Puddler Pond – the fear of the manifestation of evil, which had turned out to be a frightened flock of sheep. She remembered her feelings about the cat.

Dear God, she prayed from her heart, forgive me. I'm

a very weak adherent; I keep over-estimating the power of the enemy, which is a form of treachery.

'It is the font,' Miss Thorby said. 'I sense resistance from that direction. Used and blessed and not emptied since, I suspect.' She spoke as a housewife might of a saucepan put away unwashed, and she said 'blessed' as any normal person might say 'thrice-accursed'.

The font stood at the tower end of the church, within a few feet of the doorway where Miss Mayfield was. So nearly right. Her mind wavered again. They had power. She remembered that Lucifer, Ahriman, the Devil, name him how you would, had, before his fall, been an angel, powerful enough to be jealous of God. And it was possible – it was logical, in fact – to see in all this parody, this business of the wafer and the sacramental wine, a continuance of the age-old defiance. Like rebels tearing down a flag and stamping and spitting on it.

They surged towards the font.

I must hide the camera. I'm going to be caught. I've been a fool and must pay the price of my folly. But I'll try first. I'll say I wanted to join. It might even work. Minorities always welcome a convert. I'll lie and lie. But I must hide this camera.

The stairs – they ran up, hugging the wall, built into it. Below and behind the lowest one was a dark, cavernlike space. She pushed the camera into it as far as it would go, and then went and stood by the door, waiting to be pounced on, accused.

But they were all engrossed with the font.

'It is as I thought. The mark is there. And he is waiting. Defile it, quickly.'

They made their circle around the font; they spat into it; they used it as old Mrs Rigby had used the Communion cup.

And once that is done, thought Miss Mayfield, they will detect the real focus of resistance, the spy in their midst.

Ethel moved with the rest. She did not chant, or leap, or scream. Her arms hung limp and white, her hands in the hot-pawed clutch of her neighbours. She passed Miss Mayfield twice and was almost opposite the tower door on her third round when something happened. All movement, all sound stopped. Then, as suddenly, as silently, as corn falling to the scythe, they all, except Ethel, fell flat to the ground. And through the hot-house air of the church there swept a chill, as though a wind from the ice fields of the Arctic had blown in.

With her hair bristling, and goose-pimpled all over, utterly bemused and frightened almost to death, Miss Mayfield could think only one thing. Save Ethel!

She was out, she had Ethel by her shoulders; the red wreath tilted and fell off. And there they were back in the tower room; and she was pushing the door into place and fixing the iron bar which hung from a ring set in the wall on one side of the doorway, and which, when lifted, fell into an iron socket fixed on the other side. And even as she dropped it into place, she thought, If what I think is out there, a stout door and an iron bar will be no protection at all.

Afterwards she disliked to think about what she feared.

She was, in a fashion, the victim of her faith. She acknowledged a Power which had parted the Red Sea, brought the walls of Jericho tumbling down, rent the veil of the Temple, rolled the stone from the mouth of the tomb. The almost inevitable concomitant of such belief was to acknowledge another power, responsible for all the bad things, all the lies and cruelties and injustices in the world, a power which might make a stout iron bar break like a rotten stick.

Standing there, like a mother partridge defending one chick, she waited for it to happen.

For several minutes, nothing happened at all. And when, at last, those outside made a move, it was marvellously reassuring. They yelped and howled, they flung themselves against the door, flesh and blood against sound timber and cold iron. And she remembered a phrase, one of Rose's sayings, 'God has no hand, but man's to work with.' It was equally true of the Devil. Everything else – black magic, white magic, miracles, answered prayers – they were left-overs, dregs, the vestigial remains of primitive man's bewildered recognition of things beyond his control.

If they had any power other than their own, they wouldn't throw themselves against that door, she thought, and turned to Ethel.

She said, 'You're all right now.' She said, 'Ethel, look at me.' She said, 'Ethel, you know me – Miss Mayfield.' Ethel stood, unresponsive as a doll, icy-cold to the touch.

Miss Mayfield unhooked her skirt and stepped out of it. She dropped it over Ethel's head and hooked it around her waist. She took her spare cardigan and pushed one of the flaccid white arms into a sleeve and then the other; it was exactly like dressing a dummy in a shop window. She buttoned the cardigan, and then put over it the plastic Singing in the Rain coat, thinking that if Ethel's frigid form ever engendered any warmth, it would at least be kept in. At intervals as she worked, she talked to Ethel, bidding her wake up, begging her to speak, to look. She even shook her once, very gently. But Ethel was beyond the reach of ordinary sound or touch.

Outside, the howling, the inarticulate expression of rage and frustration went on until Miss Thorby's voice cut through it. Miss Mayfield did not catch the actual word, but it must have been a call for silence. What now, Miss Mayfield wondered, and again she moved between Ethel and the door.

Nothing happened; the silence stretched out achingly, so that presently one's own breathing, one's own thudding heartbeat, seemed to affront it. They couldn't have gone home. . . .

Then in the quietude there was a sound, so small that at no other time, in no other place, could she have heard it – the soft susurration of Ethel's hair brushing the plastic. Miss Mayfield swung round and was in time to see the last movement of the hair, swaying as Ethel tilted her head into a listening attitude.

Never in all her life had Miss Mayfield seen such complete concentration. Ethel was listening with the whole of herself, down to her very heels. Once, slowly and comprehendingly, she nodded her head; once she smiled. Miss

Mayfield, who could hear nothing, again had that feeling of being opposed to something which she could not measure. And again she threw herself against it with the only weapon she had.

'You're not to listen, Ethel! Whatever it is, it's wrong. You're to listen to me, Ethel, not to them! Not to them!'

Ethel gave no sign of hearing the actual human voice so close to her ear; she did not move her eyes or betray by look or gesture that Miss Mayfield's urgent words were even an interruption of her listening. When she moved, it was with the precision of a perfect machine, and so suddenly that Miss Mayfield, who was looking at her, was nevertheless taken completely by surprise. She snatched up the torch which Miss Mayfield had switched on and placed on the floor once the need for concealment had passed; and as her hand closed on it, Miss Mayfield thought, They need darkness. She had only just time to duck her head as Ethel brought the torch down with all the force she could command.

The blow missed her head by the fraction of an inch and fell on her shoulder, sending a paralysing thrust of pain down to her fingertips and across her breast.

And that's my right arm gone! Now she is stronger than I am. She'll overmaster me and open the door. She'll be raped and I shall be killed!

The force with which she had struck had disturbed Ethel's balance, and as she teetered, stupidly, motivelessly, Miss Mayfield shot out her left hand, grabbed the torch and struck – against Ethel's fawn-coloured head – the first violent blow she had ever dealt anybody in her life. Ethel crumpled down into a little heap on the floor.

Oh, God, I've killed her. I never meant to hit so hard. What got into me? I must be mad. God, don't let her be dead. It would be such a triumph for Them!

That prayer, anyway, was answered. For when she had set down the torch and redirected the beam, she could see that Ethel was breathing as steadily as a sleeper; and her pulse, though a little slow, was strong and even.

She had hardly satisfied herself that Ethel was not dead, not even bleeding, when Miss Thorby cried:

'Ethel!' In some obscure fashion she must have become aware of a break in the contact. 'Ethel! Do you hear me? Answer me!'

Miss Mayfield looked at Ethel, half expecting her to rise and make an automatic response, but Ethel lay as though asleep.

When Miss Thorby next spoke, there was a hint of hysteria in her voice. 'Answer me, answer me. Are you afraid of her? She can't hurt you if you do what I say. Ethel, Ethel, Ethel!'

The high-pitched, almost yelping cry seemed to cut into the little circular room, to rebound from its walls and then die away. There was a moment's silence.

Then, still sharply but with more control, Miss Thorby called, 'Miss Mayfield!'

Well, there was nothing uncanny about that. Miss Thorby might have seen her; she would certainly guess.

'I don't care whether you answer me or not; I just want to make certain that you can hear me.'

'I hear you perfectly well,' Miss Mayfield said.

'We know you're mad. Deep down, you must know yourself that you're mad. Come out now and give yourself up and I promise you shall be treated kindly. If you don't, it'll be the public lunatic asylum. Do you know what that will mean?'

By and large, Miss Thorby seemed to have a good deal of first-hand knowledge about lunatic asylums. In a voice growing steadily more shrill, more distraught, and in phrases that became more and more incoherent, she poured out threats and promises, interspersed always with the accusation of madness. 'You've done this kind of thing before. You've been locked up. . . .' In the spate of words pouring from Miss Thorby's lips there were truths as well as lies. She even mentioned the name of the place where Miss Mayfield had stayed during her breakdown on her return from Africa. Their investigations had been very thorough.

The screaming tirade, with its mingling of fact and fantasy, combined with the steadily increasing agony in her shoulder, beat upon Miss Mayfield's mind until she was almost overwhelmed. She backed away to the foot of the staircase and sat down, covered her left ear with her hand, bitterly regretting the impossibility of covering the other. She could still hear, however; and slowly the idea that she might indeed *be* mad began to take possession of her mind. Hadn't she, earlier in the evening – after asking herself. What am I going to do? – admitted the craziness of her behaviour? Would anybody who was not mad, knowing so much, venture out single-handed to snatch a victim

PETER CURTIS

from such a pack of wolves? Even her distrust of Canon
Thorby, of Miss Benson, of Mr Freeman, now rose up to
challenge her sanity; not to trust anyone was a symptom of
some forms of madness. So was the idea that all alone you
could overcome anything, an overblown sense of your
own importance and power – paranoia. . . .

'Then if you won't come out of your own accord, you
must be made to come out, made to come out. Do you hear
me? You have one more chance. Come out and we'll do
our best for you. Stay there and you will be forced to come
out, and you'll go straight into the asylum.' There was a
slight pause. 'Then you have only yourself to thank for
what happens now. And Ethel's blood will be on your
hands.'

After that, there was a silence which lasted until Ethel
began to cry.

23

ETHEL CRIED IN THE LOST, WRETCHED WAY OF someone waking from a hideous nightmare. Miss Mayfield went down on her knees beside her and one-handedly, awkwardly, lifted her head into her lap and held her and patted her and assured her, over and over again, that everything was all right now.

For several minutes Ethel snuffled and sobbed and burrowed into the warmth and solidity of another human body without caring about its identity, but presently she lifted her head, looked at Miss Mayfield and said, with immense astonishment:

'Miss Mayfield!'

'That's right. Here I am. And here you are. And everything is all right now.'

'How did *you* find me?'

'With a little guesswork and a little luck, Ethel. Here you are. . . .' She fumbled out and handed over her handkerchief in a way she had done dozens of times before. In a crisis, they *never* had a handkerchief, poor children, and being loaned one, they either returned it immediately all blubbered and wet or failed to return it at all. Ethel was plainly one of the non-returners. She wiped her eyes and blew her nose and tucked the handkerchief into the cardigan sleeve. Then she reared herself up and looked round.

'Are we in prison?'

The question cheered Miss Mayfield disproportionately. Whatever her experiences had been, Ethel's wits were unimpaired; there was something very much like the popular idea of a prison cell about the bare stone-walled room.

'No. We're in the church tower,' she said cheerfully. 'And – the door is barred. We're quite safe. We just have to wait here till morning.'

'Church,' Ethel said. 'But that . . . I swore they'd never get me there. They did, then. After all I went through, and Sydney, and my dear little owd rabbits!' She spoke with despair and began to cry again.

A trifle uncertain of where she stood, Miss Mayfield said:

'Nothing happened, Ethel. Nothing at all. They got you here, but I was waiting. I just took you away and brought you in here.'

Ethel put her hand to her head. Looked down at herself.

'These ain't my clothes! And where's my shoes? Miss! You're just saying things to make me feel better. They did get me. They did! They did! After all.'

'They did not get you,' Miss Mayfield said firmly. 'You must believe me, Ethel. I'm telling you the truth. I got you first.' About the clothes, she realized, she must be truthful in order that Ethel should believe what else she said. 'I gave you my skirt and a spare cardigan I had because when I snatched you away, you were wearing nothing but a wreath of flowers, and even that fell off. I didn't want you to catch cold.'

'I'm dead ashamed,' Ethel said. 'Dead ashamed.'

'There's absolutely no reason to be.' She put herself in Ethel's place. 'Actually, you were wearing a long cloak, and just as *that* was snatched away, I snatched *you* away. You see? I don't think anybody but me ever saw you without clothes, and you mustn't mind about me. I've seen dozens of girls without their clothes on. In my art classes, and then later on when I helped in a hospital . . . It's absolutely nothing to me, Ethel. Just forget it.'

'Thass like you to say that,' Ethel said. 'You always was the kindest . . . we all said you was the kindest teacher. . . .'

Tears threatened again. Blinking, groping for her handkerchief, Ethel ducked her head and pressed against Miss Mayfield's injured shoulder. She was aware of the flinch and the recoil, and straightened up, resuming that unchildlike self-control which was – Miss Mayfield realized – the very core of her character.

'You're hurt,' she said. 'They've done something to you again.'

'No. I was clumsy in the dark and hurt my shoulder. They can do nothing to me.'

'Don't you be too sure! My gran'd do you a damage as soon as look at you. The things she done to me . . . but then you do know some, though you let her fool you.'

'You helped her to, Ethel. All this might have been avoided if only you'd trusted me.'

'I didn't dare. There was Sydney; and then there was my dear little owd rabbits. . . .' A strong convulsive shudder ran through her. 'And that done it. I said to her, "There, now, I'm through with you." And I walked out.'

'I can't tell you how worried I was. Where were you, Ethel?'

'Up at the Rectory. The funny thing is . . . Miss, did you ever hev a dream and afterwards you could remember some parts and not others? Well, thass how it was. I walked down Curlew Lane, thinking I'd cut through Mr Tharkell's and back on to the road, and there was Miss Thorby. Of course, I was howling my head off; I was fond of them rabbits, but I didn't want her stopping and asking what I was howling about, so I bent down and made out I was getting their feeding stuff; and that was a daft thing to do, because it set me off worse than ever. So she did stop and she did ask, and before I knew where I was, I was telling her everything. Then there's a bit thass all blurry. Next I knew, I was up at the Rectory. She said my gran'd never find me there. Nor she never . . . at least, not *found*.' Ethel broke off and scowled. 'Miss Thorby and me spent a lot of time playing daft games.'

'What kind of games?'

'Seeing which of us could look into a bit of looking-glass longest without blinking. Or sometimes it'd be a puddle of ink. Or even staring one another out. I sort of got tired and went to sleep mostly and then everything'd go blurry again. I was always in a muddle with the time, too; it'd be tea-time in the middle of the morning.'

'You were hypnotized, Ethel. Miss Thorby is a hypnotist.'

'What! You mean like that owd man that could make the girl sing? I saw the picture. Ah, then! Now I see. Thass how they got me here and out of my clothes. You see, Miss, the very last thing I ever said to Miss Thorby was that I never would. That was the day she was seeing if the belt fitted. The minute I see it, I knew how I'd been had; as bad as if I'd stayed with my gran. I said to her they'd never get me . . . and the next thing here I was with you, and they had as good as got me.'

'Oh no. Remember what I told you.' Listening to Ethel had the merit of diverting her attention both from the perilous situation and from the pain in her shoulder. Besides, the story was not yet complete.

'What did you mean about the belt, Ethel? Had you ever seen it before?'

'Once. That was what started all the trouble. At least, I shouldn't say that, perhaps. But for that, I might now . . . I was about ten, see. Yes, four years ago. I'd got a bad tooth and I woke up with it aching. So I went down, and there was my gran making a wreath of her best geraniums, flowers you mustn't hardly breathe on, leave alone cut. I thought she'd gone daft. I say to her, "Gran, whatever are you doing?" And she towd me, it was a wreath for a girl to wear in a sort of game. But it was secret. I weren't to mention it to anybody, and if I didn't and if I was a good girl, one time I should be the girl to wear the wreath. Then she sent me off to bed with a bit of wool in my tooth with clove oil on it and some of her brew to send me to sleep.'

For a second something that was almost a mischievous smile curved Ethel's pale lips.

'You know how kids are. Nosey as ferrets! I never drunk the brew. When my gran looked in I foxed, and when she went out I followed. There's a crooked owd gravestone by one of the windows out there. I clawed up on it and looked in. That was Berta Creek that year. . . . Berta Creek and Frank Revatt, got up to look like the Devil. I seen it all.'

Miss Mayfield only just restrained herself from saying, Oh, you poor child! Some things were better left unsaid; they underlined what should be skipped.

Ethel went on, with sturdy good sense, 'I ain't simple. I'd kept my rabbits; I'd seen dogs; but that was different, and I made up my mind, there and then, I wasn't going to hev no truck with such goings on. Funny thing was, though I knew the belt the minute I see it, I'd never thought of Miss Thorby. . . .'

'You've been a very brave, very determined girl, Ethel.'

'I didn't hev no choice. Prancing about there with nothing on, and then *that* with whoever they fix on to do it. And there's another thing, too. Once that happen, you *belong*. You can't help yourself. You just go on and on. Take my gran. In her way, she's fond of me; lot kinder about letting me hev my way and so on than Audrey's mum, f'rinstance; but over this one thing – why, she'd watch me cut into little bits. She'd do the . . .'

Ethel broke off and, turning her head from side to side, sniffed the air.

'Miss, do you smell burning? I do!'

Miss Mayfield stood up and, unable to turn her head, faced about. The square in the loft floor at the head of the stairs seemed to be very faintly illuminated, and as she watched, a skein of grey smoke looped down, hung for a moment and was sucked back.

I should have known, she said to herself. Of course they wouldn't give up so easily. Miss Thorby had said, 'Then you have only yourself to thank for what happens now. And Ethel's blood will be on your hands.'

'I'll go up and see how much hold it has taken. I might be able to stamp it out. You can come just to the top of the stairs, Ethel, and hold the torch.'

'I shall come with you. If it's stamping . . .' She then used a word which Miss Mayfield, who had never heard it before, could only guess was an oath. 'Got no shoes. Here, I'll take this and give it a bash!' She snatched the mackintosh bag from which Miss Mayfield had taken the spare cardigan.

They climbed the stairs; Miss Mayfield, feeling weak and unsteady, clutched at the wall with her left hand. At the top, Ethel pushed alongside her and gave the verdict.

'Too big for stamping on. I see what they done. Poked sticks and things through that slit up there and then chucked in a light. Paraffin rag, I shouldn't wonder. I can smell it. Now what're we going to do?'

'I don't know, Ethel. I just don't know.'

This was defeat. Despair and misery and self-reproach rose like a wave and swamped her. Dear God, you can't let it end like this. She's borne so much and been so brave.

I know I'm a fool, but I . . . I did try! Please, God, help me now. I'd die, most willingly, if it would save Ethel.

'We must go down. You first,' she said.

Ethel went nimbly down the stairs. Miss Mayfield followed, more slowly. Her right arm was now on the side of the wall and she had no support. She felt sick and dizzy and afraid of falling. Ethel, having reached the floor, turned and directed the beam of the torch upon the stairs, and as the elongated cone of light swung round, it shone upon the bell rope.

'One tweak,' Canon Thorby had said, 'and every able-bodied adult would come running to deal with the fire or the flood.'

'The bell,' she said. 'We must ring the bell.'

'One tweak' had been an understatement.

'You take hold of the tassel in both your hands, Ethel, and I'll put my good one over yours. Now, together, *pull!*'

The rope gave a little, but no sound resulted. Raising and exerting her sound left arm increased tenfold the agony in her injured one. Sweat sprang out on her forehead and about her lips, and she had to set her teeth in order not to cry aloud.

'If you'd leave it to me,' Ethel said, 'I'd do better on my own. I could sort of jump at it.'

Miss Mayfield backed away and sat down on the stairs and cupped her right elbow in her left hand. Relieved of the weight of her arm, the broken bone responded by a slight decrease in pain.

Ethel jumped at it literally. Ignoring the tassel, she took

hold of the rope as high up as she could reach and then jumped, so that the rope bore, for a second, her whole weight.

'Shifted it,' she said; and repeated the performance. And suddenly, with a noise which in the enclosed space seemed to shake the very stones of the floor, the bell spoke.

'Easy once you've got it going,' Ethel cried, her voice lost in the vibrating boom. Hauling away, she threw Miss Mayfield a smile of triumph and – yes – pure pleasure.

She's a child still, Miss Mayfield thought, and children are, thank God, very resilient. If she can get out of here alive and escape their toils, she'll be all right yet.

Ethel no longer needed to jump. The great bell swung of its own momentum, helped by her regular plucks at the rope. The noise of it, like the very spirit of the violated church made vocal, cried its outrage into the November night, so that as far away over the marshes as Renham people stirred uneasily in their sleep.

24

In Walwyk, honest couples like the Mavericks, the Haywards and the Drivers woke up together and said:

'The bell! Curlew Lane again.' Men began to pull on their clothes and reach for their boots, grumbling, cursing the County Council for not doing something about the river which flooded so easily, saying that the rain must have been heavier than they reckoned.

In the Maverick bedroom, Mr Maverick, stamping into his Wellingtons, was aware, and slightly ashamed, of a secret feeling of pleasure. Last time the cottages in Curlew Lane were in danger, he had effected a rescue with a horse and tumbril. This year he had a Land-Rover. He'd bought it after a good harvest and had always said that anywhere a horse and tumbril could go, a Land-Rover could go. Here was his chance to prove it.

'Just as good and ten times as quick,' he said to his wife. 'I shall be up at the church picking up the chaps by the time it'd take to harness old Punch.'

'I still don't think,' Mrs Maverick said, 'that it's flood this time. Might be fire. If it is . . . Tom, Tom, promise you'll be careful.'

'Am I ever anything but?'

In other households the innocent partner, heavy with the effects of some of Granny Rigby's brew, slept on unheeding, while the other crept into the cold side of the bed and lay rigid. Presently some of them would creep out again, to save face, to pretend.

Canon Thorby had no need to grope for trousers or to fumble with shoelaces. He was wide awake and fully dressed, for he never went to bed on these occasions until Isabel was safe indoors again. He was not drunk, nor was he completely sober; long ago he had found that brandy was the most effective buffer between him and what remained of his conscience.

When the first reverberating noise of the bell boomed through the night's quietude, he sprang to the alert like a sentry. This time something *had* happened. Something he had awaited with dread for thirty-seven years.

In that space of time he had proved quite conclusively that a man could come to terms and live in moderate comfort with a situation which, when first understood, had seemed intolerable. It was, in fact, something of the position of a humane anti-vivisectionist who discovers that the one person he loves is suffering from a disease which demands constant resort to a serum produced by some unspeakably cruel process. There was precisely the same compulsion to ignore everything except the well-being of the loved one.

Isabel was his loved one. The almost pathological attachment ran back to the days of his earliest childhood, when Isabel, indomitable as a tigress, had stood between him and the torments which Freddie delighted to devise for anyone smaller and weaker than himself. Only two years his senior, Isabel had been his champion, his mother. His real mother had expended all her maternalism on Freddie and Isabel, and his father was already deeply engrossed in a genealogical study of every family in Walwyk, as recorded in the Parish Registers, counting it a very happy day when he could say, 'Do you realize that when Ralph Fletcher married Matilda Hayward, he was marrying his grandmother's aunt? Fantastic as that may sound, when you consider the dates . . .'

Only Isabel had cared about Harold, and in return Harold cared only for Isabel, so beautiful, so clever and so kind.

In the year nineteen twenty-two, when Harold was serving his curateship in a Stepney parish, Isabel had gone to North Africa on a 'dig' somewhere near Carthage. And she had come home in a state for which no twentieth-century physician had a term, though the realistic Victorians called it a decline. Not speaking, refusing to eat, she had lain in her bed, waiting for, longing for, death. Even he, who had always been so close to her and who had come home for the purpose from his Stepney parish, had failed to make any contact with her. On his second day home she had taken an overdose of sleeping tablets, and died.

They'd wasted a whole day, thinking her asleep; and when in the evening the doctor came, he was reproachful. 'If only you'd sent for me sooner . . .' The parents were distressed, his mother particularly; but for him the whole light had gone out of the world. Then, while in the study the doctor and his father were circulating cautiously around the question of the exact wording of the death certificate, his mother had said:

'They say Phoebe Rigby . . . Drive me to Curlew Lane.'

'But . . .' he said.

'Don't argue. We've wasted too much time already.'

They'd gone out to his car, a little bull-nosed Morris two-seater. In Curlew Lane, outside an ordinary-looking cottage, his mother had said:

'Stop. Turn round anywhere as best you can.'

By the time he had negotiated a turn in the narrow, sloping lane, his mother and a neat, prim-looking little woman were waiting.

'Drive Mrs Rigby to the house and take her to Isabel's room. I'll walk.'

He'd had some vague idea that Mrs Rigby was the layer-out for the village, and the feeling of haste about the business added some faint last touch of horror. He'd led her to the door of the room where Isabel lay and said, 'Please ring if you want anything.' She'd given him a peculiar look and gone in and shut the door.

He had gone to his own room and stood for a moment fighting his tears; then he had got back into the car and gone to meet his mother, who never, in all the years he could remember, had ever walked farther than from her own garden door to the church.

When they drew up before the Rectory door, his mother had said:

'Sit still for a moment. Don't speak.' She herself sat, silent and rigid, staring straight out through the windscreen. He sat and thought about life without Isabel, and realized with full force, for the first time, that he had given to his sister all the love he had to bestow on any woman. His bereavement was absolute.

Presently his mother sighed, and stirred. They went into the house. Mrs Rigby, pale and exhausted, was coming down the stairs.

'She's all right now, ma'am. I'm going into the kitchen to fetch her a little broth.'

The doctor, naturally, had denied the miracle; rather would he accuse himself of a too hasty verdict. The Reverend Thorby had also held staunchly that it was all rubbish; it was, in fact, through the medium of his jibing tongue that whisper of the affair had ever reached the outside world. Mrs Thorby spoke of the matter only once – to Harold's knowledge – and that was some years after, just before her own death.

She said, 'You must be tolerant, Harold. The world is older than Christianity. Look after Isabel, but don't interfere.'

Well, he had been tolerant, and he had never interfered. There had been times when the strain of his ambivalent position had almost broken him, but even the strain had eased with the years; he could tell himself that Hinduism, Buddhism, Mohammedanism and Christianity could be coexistent; that no creed had the monopoly of virtue. About the details of Isabel's cult he was deliberately ignorant. It was never discussed, and in his own mind it was sealed away, a Bluebeard's chamber about which he was not even curious. His main concern was to keep it secret. It was little Miss Mayfield – deliberately chosen for her harmlessness – who had opened the door and compelled him to look within, and his immediate reaction had been not horror, but dread lest anyone else should catch a glimpse. His village was very dear to him; its care and embellishment, the well-being of its inhabitants represented his unconscious attempt to atone. But above fear of scandal for Walwyk ranked fear for Isabel's good name. On the evening of the day after Wesley Baines's death, he had gone to Isabel and said:

'It's quite hopeless. I've tried threats and persuasions, but she is determined. I have told her that you are away and you must *be* away. Presently I shall drive you to Wandford, and you must go down to Stella Mott-Tyler. If the worst comes to the worst, she will swear that you have been there for a week.'

Isabel had shown no alarm, no concern. She had given way to his insistence on condition that he let Phoebe Rigby know about Miss Mayfield's plans. 'That is the kind of thing which Phoebe takes care of supremely well,' she had said.

Phoebe had, presumably, done the work; he had attended to the camouflage. Then, on that thunder-darkened evening,

Miss Mayfield, whom he had thought disposed of for good – and he had taken pleasure in seeing to it that she was most *comfortably* disposed of – had come back. Isabel had remained unconcerned.

'She knows on which side her bread is buttered; she'll never put a foot wrong again. It's best she should be here where we can keep an eye on her.'

He'd had a feeling that at that moment an invisible turning point had been passed. But he put that away among all the other never-to-be-considered things.

When the bell rang out, it was not of fire or flood that he thought; it was of Isabel, and the little schoolteacher who should be spending half-term in London.

As he ran across the garden, he noticed that although the body of the church was in darkness, there was light in the tower; the arrow slits in its upper portion gleamed yellow. He touched the switch by the door as he entered, and the place was filled with light. He had no notion of what he expected to see – that was one of the things he never thought about – but nothing could have surprised him more than to see the empty, orderly church, looking just as usual.

Miss Thorby had allowed her company a moment or two for their expression of hatred and frustration in the wolf howl and the futile assault on the door; then she had given the sign to disband. Like all underground movements, the witches of Walwyk were skilled in the rapid removal of all evidence of their existence. The candlesticks, the bowl, Miss Thorby's headdress and silver belt had been taken away by preappointed hands. The crowd had dispersed, and in the church only the members of the inner circle of all, the 'necessary seven', remained.

To them Miss Thorby had issued her orders which had resulted in the kindling of the fire. One day, she was sure, she would by faith and devotion attain the power to be free of such dependence upon material things; there would come a day when she could say, 'Let there be fire!' and there it would be.

The fire was made; the five members were dismissed. Granny Rigby and Miss Thorby were alone in the church.

Granny Rigby said rather uncertainly:

'It's just to frighten them, like. You don't mean to *burn* Ethel!'

'Precious as Ethel is to you, she is more precious to me,' Miss Thorby said curtly. 'When they come out, take Ethel. Leave the woman to me.'

'You think they will come out?'

'From fire everyone flees.'

Once, long ago, their roles had been reversed; then Phoebe Rigby, the initiated one, had issued orders and been curt to Isabel Thorby, the novice; but gradually pupil had outstripped teacher. At one level, Phoebe Rigby operated very well, but she lacked the mystic quality, the hypnotic power, which was Isabel Thorby's. Often, as the balance of power tilted, Phoebe Rigby had looked at Isabel and thought, But for me you'd be buried now; I wish I'd let you be!

'It's got a good hold now. I can smell it,' Granny Rigby said uneasily. 'Smoke can kill you, too. That Ethel, she's pigheaded. . . .' She made to go to the door, bang upon it and call to Ethel, but Miss Thorby said:

'Wait.'

And then the bell cried out.

'Thass Ethel!' the old woman cried with a comical mixture of dismay and pride. 'Trust Ethel, never at a loss!' Then dismay gained ground. 'What now? In five minutes they'll be here.'

'You must go home,' said Miss Thorby calmly. 'You have no reason for being here. I shall lock the church. By the time they find the other key there'll be no evidence left. I shall say that the heat set the bell ringing. I shall be here waiting, having run straight out – in my nightgown.'

It was a plan of which, in any other circumstances, Granny Rigby would have approved, taken as proof of great cool-headedness and inventiveness; but part of the evidence which was to be destroyed was Ethel!

'You can't do that. Thass leaving Ethel to burn!'

'Come along. There'll be another Ethel.'

Mrs Rigby flung herself at the door and, against the booming of the bell – just as Ethel, on the other side of the door, turned to Miss Mayfield with her pleased triumphant smile – she screamed:

'Ethel, come out! You'll burn to death. You don't hev to do nothing you don't want. I promise. Ethel. I promise on the Bible. Miss Mayfield, can you hear me? Bring her out. You're going to burn . . . burn to death. . . .'

Miss Thorby stepped close to Mrs Rigby and said into her ear:

'You're wasting time. They can't even hear you. Come.'

She laid her hand on the old woman's wrist. And at the touch the suppressed hatred and jealousy of many years boiled up and overflowed. Only a few days back, this coldhearted bitch had taken Ethel, and *never bothered to let her know, let her hunt all through the night and then, in the morning, go and make a fool of herself in front of the schoolteacher.* That in itself was unforgivable; and now she was leaving Ethel to burn.

Mrs Rigby gave Miss Thorby a hearty push. Miss Thorby thought of only one thing: if Phoebe was found in the locked church, it would infinitely complicate the explanations. She reached out and took a firmer hold, trying to get the old woman by the shoulders and march her out ahead of her. Mrs Rigby resisted, struck at her, and in a second the church, which had witnessed so many curious scenes, witnessed one more – two elderly women engaged in an all-in wrestling match.

There was no doubt of the issue. Miss Thorby was younger, much taller and slightly heavier, but Mrs Rigby had led an active life, scrubbing her floor, polishing her furniture, washing, digging in the garden. She had the concealed, sinewy strength of a donkey. And there was hatred in her, whereas Miss Thorby was activated only by expediency. In the second before Canon Thorby switched on the light, Mrs Rigby gave one great heave and flung Miss Thorby away from her. She reeled backwards and, falling, struck her head against the font.

The light went on. Canon Thorby said, 'Isabel!' and Granny Rigby answered him.

'Thass Ethel. She's in there, with the schoolteacher,

and the loft is afire. Ethel, you gotta come out.'

He might not have heard her. He went straight to the foot of the font where Isabel lay. He lifted her, and the limp lolling of her head told him all he needed to know.

He felt no sorrow at all. No one can suffer the same amputation twice. His grief for a dead sister was thirty-seven years old, and the grass was green over it. Relief, yes! This was the end. No. Not quite the end. He must, for the last time, make sure that her good name was not involved. A fire in the church tower – a stumble in the dark; yes, it would all fall into place, it could all be explained, if only . . .

He went to the tower door and without ceremony shoved Granny Rigby aside.

'You must come out immediately,' he called in the confident voice of one whose authority has never been seriously challenged. 'Miss Mayfield, I don't know what has been going on here, but I am here now. You are safe to come out.' There was a perceptible pause, and then he added, 'Do you want to be responsible for that child's death?'

'Thass the Canon,' said Ethel jubilantly. 'We're all right now. He never had nothing to do with *them*.'

'Wait,' Miss Mayfield said, fighting against the wave of dizziness, the near dementia of pain, and smoke and noise, and the necessity to choose beween two evils. She looked up and saw that near the head of the stairs there was a licking flame, a beam end that sagged.

'Wait,' she said again. 'Just one more minute. Someone else may. And, oh . . .'

She tottered across to the hiding place under the stairs, leaned down, let the wave of vertigo wash over her, and retrieved the camera.

They might kill her, but they wouldn't kill Ethel; she was too valuable.

'Hide this, Ethel, in your cardigan. There are pictures in it of everything that happened here this evening. Proof. If anything happens to me, take it to the police. They'll look after you. Don't let anybody else have it, whatever you do. And don't give in. Go on being the brave good girl you have always been. Now, open the door.'

And so, in the end, we walk out of the trap into the arms of our enemies. Well, better people than I have been defeated, too. The Christians walked into the arena singing, but the lions ate them just the same.

She tried to walk out proudly, but it took Ethel's arm, slipped under her sound one, to keep her upright and to get her to move. The opening of the door made a fresh draught which set the fire overhead roaring like a furnace; as they stepped out, the first timber fell, bringing with it a great firework display of sparks and volumes of stinking smoke. She and Ethel might have been spewed up from the very mouth of Hell.

Then several things happened at once. Granny Rigby ran forward, crying 'Ethel!' just as though she were an ordinary old woman greeting a beloved granddaughter after a long separation. And Ethel, letting go of Miss Mayfield's arm, shifted the torch into her right hand and said:

'Keep right away from me or I'll let you hev it.'

And there was a clatter of hobnailed boots in the porch. Tom Hayward had arrived. Miss Mayfield recognized him.

The first of the honest men. For whom the bell had rung. I must speak to him, appeal for protection.

She took a step forward into thick, sucking mud. She fought against it, as she had fought all those hours ago, but this was deeper, more clinging. She went down and down. . . .

Sinking in it, drowning, no longer able to see or move, she could still hear. It was like the time when she had had a tooth out under gas; completely anaesthetized, she had heard everything, even the noise of the tooth root being ripped from the jaw.

She heard Canon Thorby say:

'Ha, Hayward. First, as usual. I'm afraid there's little to be done. We must all get out. I'll see to my sister. Will you help Miss Mayfield?'

She heard – and it was the last thing she did hear for a space – the ends of the broken bones in her shoulder grate together as Tom Hayward lifted her. Pain screamed through her. And even Tom Hayward's strength could not lift her out of the mud. She sank . . . and drowned.

25

SOMEBODY MUST HAVE PULLED HER HEAD FREE AT last, for she could hear again. What she heard made little sense at first.

'. . . let you know and leave the girl with you,' a man's voice said. A woman's – calm, very soothing – replied:

'We should see what the damage is. You might worsen it, jolting all the way to Selbury. After all, I did my first aid. There's no blood.'

The next voice – and it was recognizable; it was Ethel's – spoke with gruesome delight.

'That was Miss Thorby was bleeding! Coo, you should hev seen . . .'

The man's voice said, 'Shut up. You've made enough of yourself for one night.'

Now I must open my eyes, begin to think and plan again.

She was in the Land-Rover about which Bobby Maverick had talked so much at the beginning of the autumn term. It stood under a glaring bright light in some open space with buildings – yes, the Maverick's farm yard.

'It's all right,' Mrs Maverick said. 'Everything's just all right now. I'm just seeing whether it's best for Tom to try to get through to Selbury now or wait till morning.'

'My shoulder,' Miss Mayfield said, 'the right.'

Hands that were gentle, but not fumbling, probed the hurt, and presently Mrs Maverick said:

'Well, thank God for that. It's only your collarbone. And them I do know about. All my brothers broke theirs one time or another, and Tom's done his in twice. Could you put your good arm round my neck and lean on me? That'd be better than lifting. It's only a step.'

It was almost a step too much; the big warm kitchen, when they reached it, swung like a merry-go-round.

'I'm all right,' Miss Mayfield said. 'But I feel better . . . with my eyes shut.'

Mrs Maverick's unhurried voice went on issuing orders.

'Hand me those scissors. . . . Tom, get that child my slippers; they're beside the bed. . . . You, Ethel, open that cupboard – there're two hot-water bottles. Fill them out of the kettle that's on the stove. . . . Tom, show the child the spare room. . . .'

All the time her hands were busy, bandaging both Miss Mayfield's shoulders. Why both? Not that it mattered. There was the same relief that had come when she cupped her elbow in her hand. She forced herself to the surface for long enough to say:

'That feels better already. Thank you.'

'It'll do till the doctor comes. Tom, there's a bottle of

codeine in the bathroom cabinet. And fetch the whisky. Gracious, child, what a yawn. You can go and pop into my bed. It's next to the one you put the bottles in. Or would you be hungry?'

'I'm always hungry,' Ethel said.

'Look in the larder, then; that door there. There're sausage rolls, I know, and . . . see what you can find. Thanks, Tom. Sugar it; you should always have a sweet drink after a shock, and a little hot water. Now, Miss Mayfield, if you'll just swallow these and wash it down with . . . that's right. You should sleep after that. And now can you face the stairs, or shall Tom carry you?'

Remembering that she had been carried once that evening, Miss Mayfield elected to walk. In the bed, just before its warmth and softness engulfed her, she thought, the camera! But she was too far away to make her voice heard.

When she woke, it was bright daylight and the sun was shining on the gypsy geraniums and fuchsias on the wide window sill which Mrs Maverick used as a greenhouse through the winter. Ethel sat in a chair between the foot of the bed and the window; pale and red-eyed from lack of sleep, she looked more like a white rabbit than ever.

Miss Mayfield said 'Ethel', and was surprised to hear her voice come out so firm and clear.

'Hullo, Miss. I thought you'd never wake up. Thass gone ten. But we didn't get to bed till nearly six. Mr Maverick went straight off to see to the milking, and Mrs Maverick said it weren't worth her coming back to bed. I went in her bed, but I never closed my eyes. Thass the first time in all my life I gone through a night without sleeping.'

'Ethel, have you the camera?'

'Right here, where you towd me to keep it,' Ethel said, striking her chest. 'Mrs Maverick did give me a nightie, but I felt a bit cowd, so I put it on over my things and the camera stayed right where it was.'

'I shall need it presently.'

'What are you going to do with it, Miss, exactly?'

'If Mr Maverick has a safe, I shall ask him to put it in until tomorrow. Then I shall take it to the Bank and ask them to lock it up. Then I shall write letters to several trustworthy people, telling them where it is, and what is in it, and saying that if anything happens to you or to me, they're to get it out and have the film developed. When I have done that, I shall be in a position to deal with your granny and with the Canon and with Miss Thorby.'

'Not Miss Thorby, you 'on't. She's dead.'

Miss Mayfield raised herself a little, and the room went into a spin. She lay down again.

'How do you know? What happened?'

'How I know is, I seen her. Back of her head all bashed in and her neck lolling. Like this . . .' Ethel gave a horribly lifelike imitation. 'What happened I didn't stop to ask. I was more took up with keeping out of my gran's clutches, *and* out of the Rectory. We was nearly done for when Mr Maverick came roaring up and I screeched at him to take you to the doctor. He showed sense, I'll say that for him. I reckon myself he smelt a rat.' She drew breath. 'What next, thass what I wonder. The one thing I do know, I'll never go back to my gran; not after what she done to my rabbits.'

'You certainly shan't. You can come and live with me, Ethel. Unless there's anywhere you'd rather be.'

'What I'd like above all is to go and live with Miss Bedfellow, at Yarmouth. Oh, she is nice.'

'I could arrange that easily.'

'Just by *saying* you'd show some snaps? Without showing them, I mean.'

'It's rather more than snaps; it's a film, like you see at the cinema.'

'With everything on it that went on last night?'

'Yes. You see, now I have that, I can put a stop to it all. There's nothing they dread more than exposure.'

'Thass right,' Ethel said thoughtfully. Then she added, 'But if they never see you've got it . . . I mean, all along, couldn't you hev *said* you had it. Where's the difference?'

'Because now I have it. And if they don't give up the whole business, or if you and I have any "accidents", then it is there for all to see.'

'Yes,' Ethel said. 'I can see that.' She rose from the chair. 'Mrs Maverick said I was to tell her when you woke up. And what would you like for your breakfast?'

'Some tea, please, Ethel, and a slice of bread and butter, perhaps.'

Halfway along the landing, there was a bathroom. Ethel turned in to it and locked the door. Pulling up her cardigan, she took the camera from the pouch in which it had lain. She had never handled one before, so what she had to do took a little time. And she pulled the plug twice, just to make quite certain. She had no qualms over what she was doing. She had confidence in Miss Mayfield, and if she said she could do what she wanted with the camera locked up in a Bank, what did it matter whether there was a film in it or not? Why should she leave, for someone one day to see, a cinema film of herself, stark naked, with a wreath of flowers on her head? Wasn't that what she had objected to all along?